I0817685

Beyond & Within

THEN THERE WERE MORE

Short Stories of Vintage Crime

Edited by Martin Edwards

Beyond & Within
THEN THERE WERE MORE
Short Stories of Vintage Crime
Edited by Martin Edwards
FLAME TREE PUBLISHING
CWA

Publisher & Creative Director: Nick Wells
Senior Project Editor: Gillian Whitaker

FLAME TREE PUBLISHING
6 Melbray Mews, Fulham,
London SW6 3NS, United Kingdom
www.flametreepublishing.com

First published 2025

25 27 29 28 26
1 3 5 7 9 10 8 6 4 2

Hardback ISBN: 978-1-80417-728-0
ebook ISBN: 978-1-80417-729-7

Publisher's Note: This is a work of fiction. Names, characters, places, and incidents are a product of the authors' imaginations. Locales and public names are sometimes used for atmospheric purposes. Any resemblance to actual people, living or dead, or to businesses, companies, events, institutions, or locales is completely coincidental.

The cover image is created by Flame Tree Studio. Frontispiece illustration is based on *4321* © Oliver Hurst 2025.

A copy of the CIP data for this book is available from the British Library.

Printed and bound in China

Table of Contents

Introduction

Martin Edwards

WELCOME TO the latest anthology of stories to be published under the auspices of the Crime Writers' Association. This is the fourth CWA anthology to be published by Flame Tree (hence the title), but in fact the series dates back almost seventy years. During that time, rather more than one thousand stories have been included in the books. When one looks back over the years, the range of contributions is extraordinary, and the calibre impressive. So we thought it high time to indulge in a retrospective before producing another collection of brand new mysteries. As with *Vintage Crime*, the connecting theme is simply that this is a collection of stories by CWA members past and present, and all of them have previously appeared in CWA anthologies.

A glance at the list of contents will, I hope, give any reader confidence that there will be stories in this collection that are richly entertaining. There are some very well-known contributors, and no fewer than *seven* of the authors represented here have won the CWA Diamond Dagger, UK crime writing's highest honour. There are also stories that have won major awards. Anne Perry's 'Heroes' received an Edgar for Best Short Story from the Mystery Writers of America, while John Harvey's 'Fedora' won the CWA's Short Story Dagger and Kate Ellis's 'Les Inconnus' was shortlisted for the same Dagger.

In the course of editing more than fifty anthologies of short fiction, I've always striven to ensure that the contents of each book are diverse enough to appeal to a wide readership. One way to achieve this is to include stories with varied settings, styles, and plot-lines. Consider Peter Lovesey's 'Arabella's Answer', for instance. It's a terrific mystery – and written in the form of an agony column.

Another way to ensure variety is to mix some of the famous names with those who are perhaps not quite as high-profile but whose talents are considerable. An example is the late Bill Knox, a prolific writer in his day, who has happily been rediscovered in recent years and described as 'the god-father of Tartan Noir'.

One of the joys of editing the CWA anthology is that I have first sight of new stories by gifted authors, and it's been a recurring pleasure to see a good many writers whose early work appeared in this series become international stars. Examples include Ian Rankin, Val McDermid, Mick Herron, and Ann Cleeves. Ann's story in this book, 'Owl Wars', for instance, was written some years before she became a household name, but I think that in terms of quality much of her early fiction bears comparison with her more recent global bestsellers.

I would like to thank all the people who have made the publication of this book possible. Flame Tree have a well-deserved reputation for producing gorgeous books and it is a pleasure to work with their team. The CWA officers have been consistently supportive of my work as an anthologist over the years. Special thanks go to the authors, their agents, and in some cases their estates, for permitting republication of these stories.

Most of all, I'm grateful to you for reading this book. I hope you enjoy these stories as much as I did.

Martin Edwards
martinedwardsbooks.com

Heroes

Anne Perry

NIGHTS WERE ALWAYS the worst, and in winter they lasted from dusk at about four o'clock, until dawn again towards eight the following morning. Sometimes star shells lit the sky, showing the black zigzags of the trenches stretching as far as the eye could see to left and right. Apparently now they went right across France and Belgium all the way from the Alps to the Channel. But Joseph was only concerned with this short stretch of the Ypres Salient.

In the gloom near him someone coughed, a deep, hacking sound coming from down in the chest. They were in the support line, farthest from the front, the most complex of the three rows of trenches. Here were the kitchens, the latrines and the stores and mortar positions. Fifteen-foot shafts led to caves which were about five paces wide, and high enough for most men to stand upright. Joseph made his way in the half dark now, the wood slippery under his boots and his hands feeling the mud walls, held up by timber and wire. There was an awful lot of water. One of the sumps must be blocked.

There was a glow of light ahead and a moment later he was in the comparative warmth of the dugout. There were two candles burning and the brazier gave off heat, and a sharp smell of soot. The air was blue with tobacco smoke and a pile of boots and greatcoats steamed a little. Two officers sat on canvas chairs talking together. One of them recited a joke – gallows humour – and they both laughed. A gramophone sat silent on a camp table, and a small pile of records of the latest music hall songs was carefully protected in a tin box.

"Hello, Chaplain," one of them said cheerfully. "How's God these days?"

"Gone home on sick leave," the other answered quickly, before Joseph could reply. There was disgust in his voice, but no intended irreverence. Death was too close here for men to mock faith.

"Have a seat," the first offered, waving towards a third chair. "Morris got it today. Killed outright. That bloody sniper again."

"He's somewhere out there, just about opposite us," the second said grimly. "One of those blighters the other day claimed he'd got forty-three for sure."

"I can believe it," Joseph answered, accepting the seat. He knew better than most what the casualties were. It was his job to comfort the terrified, the dying, to carry stretchers, often to write letters to the bereaved. Sometimes he thought it was harder than actually fighting, but he refused to stay back in the comparative safety of the field hospitals and depots. This was where he was most needed.

"Thought about setting up a trench raid," the major said slowly, weighing his words and looking at Joseph. "Good for morale. Make it seem as if we were actually doing something. But our chances of getting the blighter are pretty small. Only lose a lot of men for nothing. Feel even worse afterwards."

The captain did not add anything. They all knew morale was sinking. Losses were high, the news bad. Word of terrible slaughter seeped through from the Somme and Verdun and all along the line right to the sea. Physical hardship took its toll, the dirt, the cold and the alternation between boredom and terror. The winter of 1916 lay ahead.

"Cigarette?" The major held out his pack to Joseph.

"No, thanks," Joseph declined with a smile. "Got any tea going?"

They poured him a mugful, strong and bitter, but hot. He drank it, and half an hour later made his way forward to the open air again and the travel trench. A star shell exploded high and bright. Automatically he ducked, keeping his head below the rim. They were about four feet deep, and in order not to provide a target, a man had to move in a half crouch. There was a rattle of machine-gun fire out ahead, and closer to, a thud as a rat was dislodged and fell into the mud beside the duckboards.

Other men were moving about close to him. The normal order of things was reversed here. Nothing much happened during the day. Trench repair work was done, munitions shifted, weapons cleaned, a little rest taken. Most of the activity was at night, most of the death.

"'Lo, Chaplain," a voice whispered in the dark. "Say a prayer we get that bloody sniper, will you?"

"Maybe God's a Jerry?" someone suggested in the dark.

"Don't be stupid!" a third retorted derisively. "Everyone knows God's an Englishman! Didn't they teach you nothing at school?"

There was a burst of laughter. Joseph joined in. He promised to offer up the appropriate prayers and moved on forward. He had known many of the men all his life. They came from the same Northumbrian town as he did, or the surrounding villages. They had gone to school together, scrumped apples from the same trees, fished in the same rivers and walked the same lanes.

It was a little after six when he reached the firing trench beyond whose sandbag parapet lay no man's land, with its four or five hundred yards of mud, barbed wire and shell holes. Half a dozen burnt tree stumps looked in the sudden flares like men. Those grey wraiths could be fog, or gas.

Funny that in summer this blood- and horror-soaked soil could still bloom with honeysuckle, forget-me-nots and wild larkspur, and most of all with poppies. You would think nothing would ever grow there again.

More star shells went up, lighting the ground, the jagged scars of the trenches black, the men on the fire steps with rifles on their shoulders illuminated for a few, blinding moments. Sniper shots rang out.

Joseph stood still. He knew the terror of the night-watch out beyond the parapet, crawling around in the mud. Some of them would be at the head of saps out from the trench, most would be in shell holes, surrounded by heavy barricades of wire. Their purpose was to check enemy patrols for unusual movement, any signs of increased activity, as if there might be an attack planned.

More star shells lit the sky. It was beginning to rain. A crackle of machine-gun fire, and heavier artillery somewhere over to the left. Then the sharp whine of sniper fire, again and again.

Joseph shuddered. He thought of the men out there, beyond his vision, and prayed for strength to endure with them in their pain, not to try to deaden himself to it.

There were shouts somewhere ahead, heavy shells now, shrapnel bursting. There was a flurry of movement, flares, and a man came sliding over the parapet, shouting for help.

Joseph plunged forward, slipping in the mud, grabbing for the wooden props to hold himself up. Another flare of light. He saw quite clearly Captain Holt lurching towards him, another man over his shoulder, dead weight.

"He's hurt!" Holt gasped. "Pretty badly. One of the night patrol. Panicked. Just about got us all killed." He eased the man down into Joseph's arms and let his rifle fall forward, bayonet covered in an old sock to hide its gleam. His face was grotesque in the lanternlight, smeared with mud and a wide streak of blood over the burnt cork which blackened it, as all night patrol had.

Others were coming to help. There was still a terrible noise of fire going on and the occasional flare.

The man in Joseph's arms did not stir. His body was limp and it was difficult to support him. Joseph felt the wetness and the smell of blood. Wordlessly others materialised out of the gloom and took the weight.

"Is he alive?" Holt said urgently. "There was a hell of a lot of shot up there." His voice was shaking, almost on the edge of control.

"Don't know," Joseph answered. "We'll get him back to the bunker and see. You've done all you can." He knew how desperate men felt when they risked their lives to save another man, and did not succeed. A kind of despair set in, a sense of very personal failure, almost a guilt for having survived themselves. "Are you hurt?"

"Not much," Holt answered. "Couple of grazes."

"Better have them dressed, before they get poisoned," Joseph advised, his feet slipping on the wet boards and banging his shoulder against a jutting post. The whole trench wall was crooked, giving way under the weight of mud. The foundations had eroded.

The man helping him swore.

Awkwardly carrying the wounded man, they staggered back through the travel line to the support trench and into the light and shelter of a bunker.

Holt looked dreadful. Beneath the cork and blood his face was ashen. He was soaked with rain and mud and there were dark patches of blood across his back and shoulders.

Someone gave him a cigarette. Back here it was safe to strike a match. He drew in smoke deeply. “Thanks,” he murmured, still staring at the wounded man.

Joseph looked down at him now. It was young Ashton. He knew him quite well. He had been at school with his older brother.

The soldier who had helped carry him in let out a cry of dismay, strangled in his throat. It was Mordaff, Ashton’s closest friend, and he could see what Joseph now could also. Ashton was dead, his chest torn open, the blood no longer pumping, and a bullet hole through his head.

“I’m sorry,” Holt said quietly. “I did what I could. I can’t have got to him in time. He panicked.”

Mordaff jerked his head up. “He never would!” The cry was desperate, a shout of denial against a shame too great to be borne. “Not Will!”

Holt stiffened. "I'm sorry," he said hoarsely. "It happens."

"Not with Will Ashton, it don't!" Mordaff retorted, his eyes blazing, pupils circled with white in the candlelight, his face grey. He had been in the front line two weeks now, a long stretch without a break from the ceaseless tension, filth, cold and intermittent silence and noise. He was nineteen.

"You'd better go and get that arm dressed, and your side," Joseph said to Holt. He made his voice firm, as to a child.

Holt glanced again at the body of Ashton, then up at Joseph.

"Don't stand there bleeding," Joseph ordered. "You did all you could. There's nothing else. I'll look after Mordaff."

"I tried!" Holt repeated. "There's nothing but mud and darkness and wire, and bullets coming in all directions." There was a sharp thread of terror under his shell-thin veneer of control. He had seen too many men die. "It's enough to make any man lose his nerve."

"Not Will!" Mordaff said again, his voice choking off in a sob.

Holt looked at Joseph again, then staggered out.

Joseph turned to Mordaff. He had done this before, too many times, tried to comfort men who had just seen childhood friends blown to pieces, or killed by a sniper's bullet, looking as if they should still be alive, perfect except for the small, blue hole through the brain. There was little to say. Most men found talk of God meaningless at that moment. They were shocked, fighting against belief and yet seeing all the terrible waste and loss of the truth in front of them. Usually it was best just to stay with them, let them speak about the past, what the friend had been like, times they had shared, as if he were only wounded and would be back, at the end of the war, in some world one could only imagine, in England, perhaps in a summer day with sunlight on the grass, birds singing, a quiet riverbank somewhere, the sound of laughter, and women's voices.

Mordaff refused to be comforted. He accepted Ashton's death, the physical reality of that was too clear to deny and he had seen too many other men he knew killed in the year and a half he had been in Belgium. But he could not, would not accept that Ashton had panicked. He knew what panic out there cost, how many other lives it jeopardised. It was the ultimate failure.

"How am I going to tell his mam?" he begged Joseph. "It'll be all I can do to tell her he's dead! His pa'll never get over it. That proud of him, they were. He's the only boy. Three sisters he had, Mary, Lizzie and Alice. Thought he was the greatest lad in the world. I can't tell 'em he panicked! He couldn't have, Chaplain! He just wouldn't!"

Joseph did not know what to say. How could people at home in England even begin to imagine what it was like in the mud and noise out here? But he knew how deep shame burned. A lifetime could be consumed by it.

"Maybe he just lost sense of direction," he said gently. "He wouldn't be the first." War changed men. People did panic. Mordaff knew that, and half his horror was because it could be true. But Joseph did not say so. "I'll write to his family," he went on. "There's a lot of good to say about him. I could send pages. I'll not need to tell them much about tonight."

"Will you?" Mordaff was eager. "Thanks… thanks, Chaplain. Can I stay with him… until they come for him?"

"Yes, of course," Joseph agreed. "I'm going forward anyway. Get yourself a hot cup of tea. See you in an hour or so."

He left Mordaff squatting on the earth floor beside Ashton's body, and fumbled his way back over the slimy duckboards towards the travel line, then forward again to the front and the crack of gunfire and the occasional high flare of a star shell.

He did not see Mordaff again, but he thought nothing of it. He could have passed twenty men he knew and not recognised them, muffled in greatcoats, heads bent as they moved, rattling along the duckboards, or stood on the firesteps, rifles to shoulder, trying to see in the gloom for something to aim at.

Now and again he heard a cough, or the scamper of rats' feet and the splash of rain and mud. He spent a little time with two men swapping jokes, joining in their laughter. It was black humour, self-mocking, but he did not miss the courage in it, or the fellowship, the need to release emotion in some sane and human way.

About midnight the rain stopped.

A little after five the night patrol came scrambling through the wire, whispered passwords to the sentries, then came tumbling over the parapet of sandbags down into the trench, shivering with cold, and relief. One of them had caught a shot in the arm.

Joseph went back with them to the support line. In one of the dugouts a gramophone was playing a music hall song. A couple of men sang along with it, one of them had a beautiful voice, a soft, lyric tenor. It was a silly song, trivial, but it sounded almost like a hymn out here, a praise of life.

A couple of hours and the day would begin, endless, methodical duties of housekeeping, mindless routine, but it was better than doing nothing.

There was still a sporadic crackle of machine-gun fire, and whine of sniper bullets.

An hour till dawn.

Joseph was sitting on an upturned ration case when Sergeant Renshaw came into the bunker, pulling the gas curtain aside to peer in.

"Chaplain?"

Joseph looked up. He could see bad news in the man's face.

"I'm afraid Mordaff got it tonight," he said, coming in and letting the curtain fall again. "Sorry. Don't really know what happened. Ashton's death seems to have… well, he lost his nerve. More or less went over the top all by himself. Suppose he was determined to go and give Fritz a bloody nose, on Ashton's account. Stupid bastard! Sorry, Chaplain."

He did not need to explain himself, or to apologise. Joseph knew exactly the fury and the grief he felt at such a futile waste. To this was added a sense of guilt that he had not stopped it. He should have realised Mordaff was so close to breaking. He should have seen it. That was his job.

He stood up slowly. "Thanks for telling me, Sergeant. Where is he?"

"He's gone, Chaplain." Renshaw remained near the doorway. "You can't help 'im now."

"I know that. I just want to... I don't know... apologise to him. I let him down. I didn't understand he was... so..."

"You can't be everybody's keeper," Renshaw said gently. "Too many of us. It's not been a bad night otherwise. Got a trench raid coming off soon. Just wish we could get that damn sniper across the way there." He scraped a match and lit his cigarette. "But morale's good. That was a brave thing Captain Holt did out there. Pity about Ashton, but that doesn't alter Holt's courage. Could see him, you know, by the star shells. Right out there beyond the last wire, bent double, carrying Ashton on his back. Poor devil went crazy. Running around like a fool. Could have got the whole patrol killed if Holt hadn't gone after him. Hell of a job getting him back. Fell a couple of times. Reckon that's worth a mention in dispatches, at least. Heartens the men, knowing our officers have got that kind of spirit."

"Yes… I'm sure," Joseph agreed. He could only think of Ashton's white face, and Mordaff's desperate denial, and how Ashton's mother would feel, and the rest of his family. "I think I'll go and see Mordaff just the same."

"Right you are," Renshaw conceded reluctantly, standing aside for Joseph to pass.

* * *

Mordaff lay in the support trench just outside the bunker two hundred yards to the west. He looked even younger than he had in life, as if he were asleep. His face was oddly calm, even though it was smeared with mud. Someone had tried to clean most of it off in a kind of dignity, so that at least he was recognisable. There was a large wound in the left side of his forehead. It was bigger than most sniper wounds. He must have been a lot closer.

Joseph stood in the first paling of the darkness and looked at him by candlelight from the open bunker curtain. He had been so alive only a few hours ago, so full of anger and loyalty and dismay. What had made him throw his life away in a useless gesture? Joseph racked his mind for some sign that should have warned him Mordaff was so close to breaking, but he could not see it even now.

There was a cough a few feet away, and the tramp of boots on duckboards. The men were stood down, just one sentry per platoon left. They had returned for breakfast. He realised he could smell cooking.

Now would be the time to ask around and find out what had happened to Mordaff.

He made his way to the field kitchen. It was packed with men, some standing to be close to the stoves and catch a bit of their warmth, others choosing to sit, albeit further away. They had survived the night. They were laughing and telling stories, most of them unfit for delicate ears, but Joseph was too used to it to take any offence. Now and then someone new would apologise for such language in front of a chaplain, but most knew he understood too well.

"Yeah," one answered his question through a mouthful of bread and jam. "He came and asked me if I saw what happened to Ashton. Very cut up, he was."

"And what did you tell him?" Joseph asked.

The man swallowed. "Told him Ashton seemed fine to me when he went over. Just like anyone else, nervous... but then only a fool isn't scared to go over the top!"

Joseph thanked him and moved on. He needed to know who else was on the patrol.

"Captain Holt," the next man told him, a ring of pride in his voice. Word had got around about Holt's courage. Everyone stood a little taller because of it, felt a little braver, more confident. "We'll pay Fritz back for that," he added. "Next raid – you'll see."

There was a chorus of agreement.

"Who else?" Joseph pressed.

"Seagrove, Noakes, Willis," a thin man replied, standing up. "Want some breakfast, Chaplain? Anything you like, on the house – as long as it's bread and jam and half a cup of tea. But you're not particular, are you? Not one of those fussy eaters who'll only take kippers and toast?"

"What I wouldn't give for a fresh Craster kipper," another sighed, a faraway look in his eyes. "I can smell them in my dreams."

Someone told him good-naturedly to shut up.

"Went over the top beside me," Willis said when Joseph found him quarter of an hour later. "All blacked up like the rest of us. Seemed OK to me then. Lost him in no man's land. Had a hell of a job with the wire. As bloody usual, it wasn't where we'd been told. Got through all right, then Fritz opened up on us. Star shells all over the sky." He sniffed and then coughed violently. When he had control of himself again he continued. "Then I saw someone outlined against the flares, arms high, like a wild man, running around. He was going towards the German lines, shouting something. Couldn't hear what in the noise."

Joseph did not interrupt. It was now broad daylight and beginning to drizzle again. Around them men were starting the duties of the day: digging, filling sandbags, carrying ammunition, strengthening the wire, resetting duckboards. Men took an hour's work, an hour's sentry duty, and an hour's rest.

Near them somebody was expending his entire vocabulary of curses against lice. Two more were planning elaborate schemes to hold the water at bay.

"Of course that lit us up like a target, didn't it!" Willis went on. "Sniper fire and machine guns all over the place. Even a couple of shells. How none of us got hit I'll never know. Perhaps the row woke God up, and he came back on duty!" He laughed hollowly. "Sorry, Chaplain. Didn't mean it. I'm just so damn sorry poor Ashton got it. Holt just came out of nowhere and ran after him, floundering through the mud. If Ashton hadn't got caught in the wire he'd never have got him."

"Caught in the wire?" Joseph asked, memory pricking at him.

"Yeah. Ashton must have ran right into the wire, because he stopped sudden, teetering, like, and fell over. Probably saved his life, because there was a hell of a barrage came over just after that. We all threw ourselves down."

"What happened then?" Joseph said urgently, a slow, sick thought taking shape in his mind.

"When it died down I looked up again, and there was Holt staggering back with poor Ashton across his shoulders. Hell of a job he had carrying him, even though he's bigger than Ashton... well, taller, anyway. Up to his knees in mud, he was, shot and shell all over, sky lit up like a Christmas tree. Of course we gave him what covering fire we could. Maybe it helped." He coughed again. "Reckon he'll be mentioned in dispatches, Chaplain? He deserves it." There was admiration in his voice, a lift of hope.

Joseph forced himself to answer. "I should think so." The words were stiff.

"Well, if he isn't, the men'll want to know why!" Willis said fiercely. "Bloody hero, he is."

Joseph thanked him and went to find Seagrove and Noakes. They told him pretty much the same story.

"You going to have him recommended?" Noakes asked. "Mordaff came and we said just the same to him. Reckon he wanted the captain given a medal. He made us say it over and over again, exactly what happened."

"That's right," Seagrove nodded, leaning on a sandbag.

"You told him the same?" Joseph asked. "About the wire, and Ashton getting caught in it?"

"Yes, of course. If he hadn't got caught by the legs he'd have gone straight on and landed up in Fritz's lap, poor devil."

"Thank you."

"Welcome, Chaplain. You going to write up Captain Holt?"

Joseph did not answer, but turned away, sick at heart. He did not need to look again, but he trudged all the way back to the field hospital anyway. It would be his job to say the services for both Ashton and Mordaff. The graves would be already dug.

He looked at Ashton's body again, looked carefully at his trousers. They were stained with mud, but there were no tears in them, no marks of wire. The fabric was perfect.

He straightened up.

"I'm sorry," he said quietly to the dead man. "Rest in peace." And he turned and walked away.

He went back to where he had left Mordaff's body, but it had been removed. Half an hour more took him to where it also was laid out. He touched the cold hand, and looked at the brow. He would ask. He would be sure. But in his mind he already was. He needed time to know what he must do about it. The men would be going over the top on another trench raid soon. Today morale was high. They had a hero in their number, a man who would risk his own life to bring back a soldier who had lost his nerve and panicked. Led by someone like that, they were equal to Fritz any day. Was one pistol bullet, one family's shame, worth all that?

What were they fighting for anyway? The issues were so very big, and at the same time so very small and immediate.

* * *

He found Captain Holt alone just after dusk, standing on the duckboards below the parapet, near one of the firing steps.

"Oh, it's you, Chaplain. Ready for another night?"

"It'll come, whether I am or not," Joseph replied.

Holt gave a short bark of laughter. "That doesn't sound like you. Tired of the firing line, are you? You've been up here a couple of weeks, you should be in turn for a step back any day. Me too, thank God."

Joseph faced forward, peering through the gloom towards no man's land and the German lines beyond. He was shaking. He must control himself. This must be done in the silence, before the shooting started up again. Then he might not get away with it.

"Pity about that sniper over there," he remarked. "He's taken out a lot of our men."

"Damnable," Holt agreed. "Can't get a line on him, though; keeps his own head well down."

"Oh, yes," Joseph nodded. "We'd never get him from here. It needs a man to go over in the dark and find him."

"Not a good idea, Chaplain. He'd not come back. Not advocating suicide, are you?"

Joseph chose his words very carefully and kept his voice as unemotional as he could.

"I wouldn't have put it like that," he answered. "But he has cost us a lot of men. Mordaff today, you know?"

"Yes... I heard. Pity."

"Except that wasn't the sniper, of course. But the men think it was, so it comes to the same thing, as far as morale is concerned."

"Don't know what you mean, Chaplain." There was a slight hesitation in Holt's voice in the darkness.

"Wasn't a rifle wound, it was a pistol," Joseph replied. "You can tell the difference, if you're actually looking for it."

"Then he was a fool to be that close to German lines," Holt said, facing forward over the parapet and the mud. "Lost his nerve, I'm afraid."

"Like Ashton," Joseph said. "Can understand that, up there in no man's land, mud everywhere, wire catching hold of you, tearing at you, stopping you from moving. Terrible thing to be caught in the wire with the star shells lighting up the night. Makes you a sitting target. Takes an exceptional man not to panic, in those circumstances... a hero."

Holt did not answer.

There was silence ahead of them, only the dull thump of feet and a squelch of duckboards in mud behind, and the trickle of water along the bottom of the trench.

"I expect you know what it feels like," Joseph went on. "I notice you have some pretty bad tears in your trousers, even one in your blouse. Haven't had time to mend them yet."

"I dare say I got caught in a bit of wire out there last night," Holt said stiffly. He shifted his weight from one foot to the other.

"I'm sure you did," Joseph agreed with him. "Ashton didn't. His clothes were muddy, but no wire tears."

There were several minutes of silence. A group of men passed by behind them, muttering words of greeting. When they were gone the darkness closed in again. Someone threw up a star shell and there was a crackle of machine-gun fire.

"I wouldn't repeat that, if I were you, Chaplain," Holt said at last. "You might make people think unpleasant things, doubts. And right at the moment morale is high. We need that. We've had a hard time recently. We're going over the top in a trench raid soon. Morale is important… trust. I'm sure you know that, maybe even better than I do. That's your job, isn't it? Morale, spiritual welfare of the men?"

"Yes… spiritual welfare is a good way of putting it. Remember what it is we are fighting for, and that it is worth all that it costs... even this." Joseph gestured in the dark to all that surrounded them.

More star shells went up, illuminating the night for a few garish moments, then a greater darkness closed in.

"We need our heroes," Holt said very clearly. "Any man who would tear them down would be very unpopular, even if he said he was doing it in the name of truth, or justice, or whatever it was he believed in. He would do a lot of harm, Chaplain. I expect you can see that..."

"Oh yes," Joseph agreed. "To have their hero shown to be a coward who laid the blame for his panic on another man, and let him be buried in shame, and then committed murder to hide that, would devastate men who are already wretched and exhausted by war."

"You are perfectly right." Holt sounded as if he were smiling. "A very wise man, Chaplain. Good of the regiment first. The right sort of loyalty."

"I could prove it," Joseph said very carefully.

"But you won't. Think what it would do to the men."

Joseph turned a little to face the parapet. He stood up onto the firestep and looked forward over the dark expanse of mud and wire.

"We should take that sniper out. That would be a very heroic thing to do. Good thing to try, even if you didn't succeed. You'd deserve a mention in dispatches for that, possibly a medal."

"It would be posthumous!" Holt said bitterly.

"Possibly. But you might succeed, and come back. It would be so daring, Fritz would never expect it," Joseph pointed out.

"Then you do it, Chaplain!" Holt said sarcastically.

"It wouldn't help you, Captain. Even if I die, I have written a full account of what I have learned today, to be opened should anything happen to me. On the other hand, if you were to mount such a raid, whether you returned or not, I should destroy it."

There was silence again, except for the distant crack of sniper fire a thousand yards away, and the drip of mud.

"Do you understand me, Captain Holt?"

Holt turned slowly. A star shell lit his face for an instant. His voice was hoarse.

"You're sending me to my death!"

"I'm letting you be the hero you're pretending to be, and Ashton really was," Joseph answered. "The hero the men need. Thousands of us have died out here, no one knows how many more there will be. Others will be maimed or blinded. It isn't whether you die or not, it's how well."

A shell exploded a dozen yards from them. Both men ducked, crouching automatically.

Silence again.

Slowly Joseph unbent.

Holt lifted his head. "You're a hard man, Chaplain. I misjudged you."

"Spiritual care, Captain," Joseph said quietly. "You wanted the men to think you a hero. Now you're going to justify that, and become one."

Holt stood still, looking towards him in the gloom, then slowly he turned and began to walk away, his feet sliding on the wet duckboards. Then he climbed up the next firestep, and up over the parapet.

Joseph stood still and prayed.

A Cabinet of Curiosities

Christine Poulson

A HARE STARTS UP in front of them and crouches there, quivering in the grass. Rufus is afraid that it will be trampled under the hooves of his horse. It is too young and frightened to understand that it can escape by dashing off to one side. At the last moment it shoots off and its white scut vanishes into the undergrowth.

Rufus glances at Simon. He hasn't noticed. No doubt he is preoccupied with the work ahead. They ride on in silence. It was scarcely light when they left Rufus's house. It is now six o'clock on a fine June morning and mist is rising from the fields.

Simon arrived at Rufus's house late the previous evening to request his services and a bed for the night. The two had not met since they were undergraduates together at Jesus College nearly twenty years ago. True,

Rufus is a magistrate as well as a priest – and for a search like this it is necessary that a magistrate be present – but Simon could surely have found someone closer to the house in question. Rufus suspects him of engineering an opportunity to bring home the way in which their paths in life have diverged. At Cambridge Simon was a raw-boned country boy, his father a yeoman in a small way. Rufus was of far superior birth, but somehow Simon always had the upper hand. Since then he has grown rich on confiscated estates and has married above his station, while Rufus has progressed no further than his first living – and it is not a large or a prosperous parish.

Rufus looks sideways at his old friend. The diamond ring, the boots of supple Spanish leather, the fantastical high-crowned hat tilted sideways: such finery sits strangely with the thick nose, broken more than once, and the jutting jaw. Simon has the vanity of an ugly man. That is not a thought that would have occurred to Rufus in the old days. He glances down at his own sombre costume, kept decent by Sarah's deft needle. Sarah's family, if truth be told, is scarcely even of the middling sort, but she is a good housekeeper and an excellent mother to their children. Rufus reminds himself that Simon has only one daughter surviving, but of the eight children Sarah has borne Rufus, six remain, four of them sons, and every one of the brood healthy. God has indeed blessed him. Those are *his* jewels—

Simon breaks into his thoughts. "Women, children, servants, they are the weakest links and today we will find the mistress of the house alone. Her husband is a barrister who has been detained on business in London."

"That is fortunate."

"Indeed," Simon says dryly.

Rufus understands that Simon has arranged this. He had been naïve to suppose that anything would be left to chance.

To cover his embarrassment, he says, "How will you go about the search?"

"I have my methods, my *modus operandi*. I begin with those parts of the house where there is a solid mass of masonry: chimney breasts, turrets, in which a hollow space could have been fashioned. Where one part of the house is newer than another, we look for discrepancy in floor levels, any space, however narrow, into which a man might crawl. In one house – that was in Lancashire – we searched for days before I noticed a chimney that had no smoke blackening at the top. It was a shaft to allow air to a hide at the side of the fireplace. It had been concealed by bricks and mortar fastened to planks and then painted and blackened to look like part of the flue."

"It took days?"

"Six days." He laughs at the expression on Rufus's face. "It won't take that long today. I'll wager this diamond ring against – against what, let me see, one of your wife's excellent cream cheeses – that I'll flush the fellow out by sunset. Such men are evil. Purveyors of death and sin, corruptors of the state, they must be hunted down like the vermin they are."

Rufus hesitates. A diamond ring against a cream cheese: it's an insult.

"Come on, man! Between old friends! It'll lend some zest to the game. If it goes against the grain for a man of the cloth, you can sell the ring and feed the poor in your parish."

Against his better judgement, Rufus finds himself agreeing.

* * *

They breast a rise in the rolling Warwickshire countryside and there the house lies before them, nestling in the hollow of a park. They rein in their horses. The sun gleams on the water in the moat and bathes the honey-coloured stone in a golden light. Deer graze in the park, there are fish-ponds close to the house, gardens too, bright with flowers. In the hazy morning light, it seems unreal, dreamlike. In a few moments, Rufus thinks, they will shatter this idyll. There will be rich pickings if all this is confiscated. He feels something he can't name. Excitement? Dread?

There is a rustling nearby and two men on horseback emerge from a clump of birches.

"Has anyone left the house?" Simon asks them.

They shake their heads.

"I have two more men waiting at the back," Simon tells Rufus.

"Are you sure he is there?" Rufus half hopes that he will not be, and not just because of the wager. He thinks of the fate that awaits the hunted man – it is necessary, no doubt about that, the security of the state must be preserved – but it is best not to dwell on the details.

"I believe he is. I have intelligence that he was seen heading for the house early yesterday morning."

Simon nods to his henchmen and they fall into line behind him. He digs his heels into his horse's flanks and it breaks into a canter, and then a gallop. It's a high-spirited bay, a world away from Rufus's stolid cob, which struggles to keep pace. As they thunder down the slope, Rufus's heart thumps in time to the thud of the horse's hooves. He too is used to a more sedentary life. They clatter across the bridge over the moat. Entering the quiet courtyard, they come to a halt and for a moment or two the only sound is the breathing of their horses. The silence is broken by a dog barking.

Simon nods to his men. They dismount and hammer at the door. It is opened sooner than Rufus expects and the men rush in. Simon dismounts at leisure, tethers all four horses, and follows the men into the house. Rufus goes with him. Looking around the hall, he sees a gleaming oak floor and staircase, a credenza elaborately carved and gilded, paintings on the wall.

He becomes aware of a girl in a white night-smock standing at the top of the staircase. His first thought is that she is a daughter of the house. Then he sees the swell of her belly: she is five or six months gone. This must be the mistress, though it seems to him that she is scarcely older than Jenny, his eldest daughter.

"You are Elinor Hardcastle?" Simon asks.

She nods.

Simon bows. "I bear papers that give me the authority to search your house and I am accompanied by a justice of the peace."

She says nothing. A woman appears behind her, a servant, a nurse, Rufus guesses, carrying a well-grown child in her arms. The women don't so much as glance at one another, yet it seems to Rufus that some communication passes between them.

One of Simon's men appears in the hall and shakes his head.

This seems to give Elinor courage and at last the words come, though it's little more than a whisper.

"You will find no priest here."

* * *

Sunlight reflected from the moat throws watery green shadows on the walls and ceiling of the parlour. The scent of roses drifts in through an open window and for Rufus will ever afterwards be associated with that time and that place. He takes in every detail of the charming apartment: the table bearing an embroidery frame and a half-finished sampler, the ample hearth piled with logs, a harp, a child's cart full of toy bricks. Sarah will be curious when he gets home.

Elinor Hardcastle stands by the door watching as Simon opens a linen chest and rifles through the contents. Rufus feels rather than sees her suppress a wince. She is fully dressed now and her farthingale conceals her pregnancy. She is perhaps nineteen or twenty. With her brown hair smoothed back and her pale complexion she has the kind of beauty that Rufus admires. He thinks again of his own daughter, who by this hour will already be helping Sarah in the dairy. He feels like an intruder here. Elinor's face is impassive, but Rufus knows as well as if she had spoken that she hates to see Simon's thick fingers handling her fine sheets.

At the far side of room there is a large cabinet veneered in walnut and mounted on barley sugar legs. Simon opens the two doors that front it and Rufus can tell that he is surprised. He shifts so that he sees what Simon sees.

There are numerous small drawers, inlaid with delicate marquetry, and in the centre a mirrored recess. Rufus moves closer. The recess has been decorated to resemble an elegant little room with gilded colonnades on either side and a black and white diaper floor. It holds a silver gilt inkpot, too large in the little room and strangely out of keeping. There is something fascinating about this world in miniature and Rufus sees that Simon is attracted by it, too. Elinor has come closer and Rufus is conscious of her standing by his side.

Simon opens a drawer, puts in a hand and takes out a handful of coins.

"Roman," he says, and tips the coins back into the drawer, leaving one in the palm of his hand. He seems about to pocket it. Then he shrugs, replaces the coin and shuts the drawer. Why bother? When the estate is confiscated, he'll take this as part of his share. He opens drawer after drawer, revealing wonder after wonder: shells, coral, ivory, semi-precious stones, cameos and intaglios, more coins and medallions, birds' eggs, flint arrows.

"A cabinet of curiosities. I have heard of them," Simon says, "but I have never seen one before. It must be worth a great deal," he adds in an undertone.

"It's very precious," Elinor says. There is something in her voice that makes Rufus glance at her. She looks back at him, but he cannot read her expression.

Simon is frowning and Rufus knows he is disappointed not to have found evidence of Catholic sympathies. Certain books, a rosary – a makeshift shrine, even – these are illegal and would have allowed him to threaten and intimidate her. But he has looked everywhere in the house and there is nothing. Her child – a lusty fellow of around two years – is too young to be interrogated and there's no joy to be had of the servants either. They are a brazen, tight-lipped lot. No doubt they have been carefully chosen and are themselves adherents of what they dub 'the Old Faith'.

"Well," Simon says. He brushes one hand against the other to indicate that it is time to get down to business. "I'll get the men – and the measuring chains."

It is time for the search proper to begin.

* * *

The men measure the thickness of the walls, the window embrasures, and the chimney breasts. Simon is occupied with more skilled employment.

"The greatest difficulty is in disguising the entrance," he explains to Rufus. "We look for places where ornamental mounding might conceal an opening, we look for gaps between floorboards, we look for false panelling, particularly in wardrobes or cupboards."

The sun climbs the sky. The heat and the humidity rise. The men wipe the sweat from their brows. Simon seems unaffected and works on methodically, tapping panels, running his hands over floorboards, feeling inside cupboards. If there is indeed a man hidden in some cramped compartment, how he must be suffering, Rufus thinks.

Elinor too is feeling the heat or maybe it is simply apprehension. She remains in the parlour, coming from time to time to watch their progress. And it is on one of these occasions that it happens. Simon is on his knees in a small first-floor room, running his hands over the floor boards. Rufus sees Elinor come in and stop by the door. There is something in her posture that alerts him, a kind of stillness. She recovers instantly, but Simon has seen it too. He gets to his feet and fixes his eyes on her. She tries to leave the room, but he shakes his head and she remains where she is. Her face is as pale as whey.

Simon starts to move about the room, his eyes fixed on Elinor, judging her response, following the movement of her eyes. Rufus understands with a thrill of – what? anticipation? no, apprehension – that Simon is guided by what she is *not* looking at. From what is she so anxious to avert her eyes? It is a sinister parody of the searching game that Rufus's children play: "Am I getting warm?" "Yes, yes, no, no, you're getting cold, yes, warm again."

Simon moves towards the window, where a seat is set into the embrasure. Elinor has schooled herself not to react, but it is hard, so hard when a man's life is at stake. Her eyelids flicker. That's it. Simon's face relaxes. He has seen it now. He squats before the window seat. And now Rufus sees it, too: a scrap of rough material, sacking perhaps, hardly more than half a dozen threads, caught in the joint where the seat is attached to the base. Very gently Simon feels around, pressing, gently manipulating, and he finds the trick of it. The seat slides forwards. Simon climbs into the space. He slides forward, feet first, only his hands remain clasping the edge of the seat, and then they vanish too.

Rufus runs over and looks down. A narrow chute set at a diagonal angle has delivered Simon to a space which must be over the kitchen. Simon's face appears a few feet away. He shakes his head. Moments later, with a helping hand from Rufus, he is back in the room. Rufus expects him to be angry at finding the hide empty, but on the contrary, he appears stimulated by this turn of events. Elinor on the other hand looks so ill that Rufus fears for her unborn child. Perhaps she does too, for she presses a hand to her side. Rufus helps her to a seat.

Simon is examining the interior of the window seat. "The workmanship – wonderful, is it not? To me, it bears the mark of one man and one man only. Master Nicholas Owen."

He beckons Rufus over. Together they gaze down at the stone floor of window-seat.

Simon pauses, leans right in and crooks his fingers round the edge of the stone where it meets the shaft to the hide. He sets his face and exerts his strength. There is a grinding of stone against stone. Simon lets the stone fall back into place.

"It is a peculiarity of his work that so often one hiding place conceals another," he remarks. "This stone is too heavy for one man to shift, so I will ask you, Rufus, to fetch the men."

* * *

The stench when they remove the stone slab is unbelievable.

"This was a garde-robe," Simon explains. "The shaft goes down to a sewer that discharges into the moat."

He does not go down himself. Two of his men lower a third – a surly-looking rogue – on a rope, candle in hand. He makes no objection – he will be well rewarded.

Elinor remains in her chair in the corner of the room, looking on. Rufus wants to tell her that she should not be here – it is no place for a pregnant woman – but he senses that he would be ill-advised to betray his sympathy for her. The heat of the day, the smell, the tension that fills the room: Rufus wishes with all his heart that he had not agreed to come with Simon. He finds he has no appetite for hunting a man down like a rat in a sewer. And terrifying this young woman perhaps to the point of miscarriage, how can this be right? She is no doubt obeying her husband's orders and that is but her bounden duty.

Simon is pacing up and down. He returns to the window-seat and shouts down the shaft. "What can you see?"

"Nothing yet, master," comes faintly echoing from somewhere down below.

Simon stands waiting, a hand on either side of the window-seat, seemly impervious to the smell.

A minute or two later, there is a cry and Simon leans eagerly forward, "What is it?"

"A dead cat. I put my foot on it."

Simon shakes his head, He begins to unbutton his doublet. "I'm going down myself."

Moments later, he too disappears down the shaft.

Rufus persuades Elinor to leave the room. She will not lie down, but allows him to settle her by an open window in the parlour. Rufus stays with her. He cannot help putting himself in the place of the hunted man for whom these are the last moments of freedom. And he cannot help remembering what Simon told him last night: the last priest he captured was taken from the gallows too soon and dragged conscious to the quartering block. He feels queasy.

It is some time before Simon comes to find them. He is wearing a fresh suit of clothes. Nevertheless he brings with him a faint whiff of ordure.

"I found the hide," he said.

Rufus's heart is in his mouth. What must Elinor be feeling?

"It was empty," says Simon. "Except for this."

He dangles a necklace in front of Elinor's face and allows the beads to run through his fingers.

"Well, Madam?" he says.

And now Rufus catches sight of a little cross. It is not a necklace, but a rosary.

"Paris is worth a Mass, so they say. Are all your husband's estates and riches worth this bit of Catholic trumpery?"

He drops it on the table beside her.

Elinor's eyes are fixed on it. She seems scarcely able to breathe, let alone speak. Simon towers over her. Rufus remembers the hare, quivering with fear, that was nearly trampled beneath their hooves that morning.

"In God's name, Simon, she's little more than a child!" he bursts out.

Simon seems at first not to hear him. He is staring at the table, not at the rosary. Then he turns to Rufus. "What did you say?"

"She's very young," Rufus says half-apologetically.

Simon turns to Elinor and searches her face. "How young, would you say? Eighteen, nineteen? And her child is two years old, and a son at that." No reply is necessary and she makes none. "And yet here on this table is a half-finished sampler." He strikes the side of his head with his open palm. "Dolt that I am. She is the second wife. And there is a child of the first marriage."

He turns to Rufus. "Don't you see? Fearful that she will betray them, they have sent this older child away, along with her clothes and toys – leaving only that sampler behind."

He says to Elinor, "She must be brought back at once."

* * *

They wait in the parlour in silence, while the child returns from a neighbouring farm, where she has been lodged.

By the time the little girl arrives the air is tinged with the blue of a late summer dusk. She stands in the doorway with her nurse behind her. Rarely has Rufus seen a child as beautiful as this, a veritable angel. No more than seven, she is as fair as her stepmother is dark.

Elinor puts out a hand. The child goes directly to her. Elinor leans forward to smooth back a lock of flaxen hair that has escaped from a plait.

"Come here, my little wench," Simon says, beckoning to her. His voice is unexpectedly gentle.

The child looks up into Elinor's face for permission. Elinor nods and the child steps forward.

Simon squats down so that he can look into her face. "What is your name?" he asks her.

"Hannah."

"Hannah. It means 'favoured by God' and judging by your pretty face it seems that He has indeed favoured you."

The child smiles.

"That's right," says Simon. "We are friends, are we not? Now, tell me, has there been a strange man here?"

The child looks at her stepmother. Elinor seems to have recovered from her earlier apprehension. Her face is as calm and relaxed as if the question were of no moment.

The child looks back at Simon. "Yes," she says.

Elinor turns her face away.

"Ah. And where is he now?" says Simon.

Rufus holds his breath.

"Oh, he went away. Mama told him to go away, and he did."

"When was this?" Simon asks.

"Yesterday," the child says. "And then I went away myself," she adds with a simplicity that nearly breaks Rufus's heart.

"Did you see him leave?"

She nods.

"Which way did he go?"

Simon lifts the child up to the window and she points to the south. When he puts her down, she goes to Elinor and buries her face in the stuff of her gown. Elinor presses her close.

"Why didn't you tell me this?" Simon speaks sternly to Elinor. "It was your duty."

"I was afraid."

"Did he tell you where he was going?"

"He did not." She looks piteously into Simon's face. "He said it was better that I should not know."

* * *

"You were right to exact no punishment," says Rufus, as they ride away from the house.

The evening sky has deepened to a rich, soft blue dusk. A single star has appeared.

Simon shrugs. "These Jesuits are sophistical, deceitful. Her husband was away and she had no one to guide her. Women are easily swayed."

"The weaker vessel."

"Indeed." Nevertheless he speaks as someone who has himself been detected in a weakness.

He slips the diamond ring off his finger. "Here." He tosses it to Rufus, who puts out a hand and catches it in mid-air. "I did not find my quarry, so I have lost the wager."

As they ride on, Rufus takes a sideways look at Simon. He is not as clever or as observant as he thinks – or as Rufus thought him. A fig for the *modus operandi*! Simon looked everywhere and he saw nothing, except what he was meant to see. It was intended that he should discover the first hiding place and then the second. What foresight! What cunning! It was as good as a play.

The return of the child – was that intended? He thinks not. That was their one mistake as they rushed to hide the priest and set the scene. Elinor's heart must have been in her mouth. But the daughter was worthy of the mother. When she said that the priest had gone, Rufus saw Elinor's face reflected for a moment in the mirrored interior of the cabinet. She had managed to hide her fear, but she could not hide her relief. Simon missed that, as he missed so much else.

In his mind's eye Rufus sees the fireplace in the parlour. Did it not occur to Simon to wonder why logs should be piled high on the hearth at the height of summer?

Rufus smiles to himself and pockets the ring.

A huge moon is rising through the trees. It will light their long ride home.

* * *

"Is it safe yet?" Hannah asks.

The priest hears this, just as he has heard every conversation in the parlour during this interminable day.

"What do you think, Father?" It is Elinor's voice, close at hand. She must be kneeling in the hearth. "I sent James to follow them and he has just returned. The poursuivants are miles away."

"It is time," he says, his voice sounding strange in his ears after such a long silence. He hears them removing the logs one by one. The flags are lifted up and there is the glint of candlelight. He struggles towards it, pulling himself up with one hand, while with the other he holds a jewelled casket to his breast. Brawny arms reach down and haul him out.

A servant is waiting with a bowl of water so that he can wash. Elinor has brought bread and meat and wine with her own hands.

The priest looks at her bright eyes and laughing face, and he too begins to laugh.

"That Nicholas Owen is a craftsman *sans pareil*. With food and water and my piss-pot I could have held out for days. I am a little stiff, it is true, and a trifle more air would have been welcome – but what is wrong, my little one?" he asks Hannah.

There are tears in her eyes.

"She was afraid for you," says Elinor. "And she is sorry that she had to tell a lie. But I tell her that she is a good girl and it would have been a worse sin to betray you. You can absolve her, Father, can you not?"

"I can."

"And, Father, you will not think of leaving tonight? You must rest."

He shakes his head. "I have rested enough – and you have risked enough, my gallant girl. I will head north tonight."

"But before you go?"

"Yes, we must give thanks."

While he washes his hands and consecrates the wine, she removes the silver gilt inkpot from the mirrored recess of the cabinet of curiosities. She presses one of the black and white squares near the back and a panel slides open. She takes out two little paintings of Saint Jude and Saint Luke and a third of the Virgin Mary, all in gilded frames. She fits them into place over the mirrors and stands back.

The priest steps forwards with the jewelled casket that contains the Host and places it in the recess.

Behind him he is aware of his little congregation: the servants, the mistress of the house, and her resourceful little stepdaughter. It all seems to drop away – the loyal friends, the warmth and the scent of the summer night.

A cold wind blows. He sees a ruined house, its occupants in exile. He sees himself with a noose around his neck. In that moment it comes to him that his escape today has been merely a reprieve. Somewhere ahead of him lies that terrible fate. But for the time that remains, whether it be long or short, he thanks God. There is work to be done.

He makes the Sign of the Cross. He speaks the familiar words, so full of comfort.

"*In Nomine Patris et Filii et Spiritus Sancti*..."

The Mass begins.

The Cost of Living

Andrew Taylor

EVERYTHING takes twice as long when you're in a hurry. Add panic to haste and time becomes more elastic still, a noose around eternity.

In the end William Dougal despaired of finding a gap in the traffic. He pushed the Honda into the endless stream of cars travelling south down Kew Road. A Mercedes braked sharply, its horn blaring like an angry trumpet.

Thank God the traffic was moving. It was mid morning so the worst of the Monday rush hour was over. The long high wall of Kew Gardens slipped by on the right. A few minutes later, the cars ahead slowed for the Richmond roundabout.

Can't you bloody hurry?

The world through the windscreen belonged elsewhere: shops on either side of the street; smears of dirty snow on gutters and roofs; pedestrians and cyclists weaving through the traffic; parked cars and a delivery van partly blocking the road. Dougal glanced at the phone and wondered yet again whether he should call the police.

If only this hadn't been his day off. If only he had got up earlier. If only he had stayed in London last weekend. He shivered violently. The car hadn't warmed up yet.

This is my fault. I should have phoned Alan on Saturday.

At last he was on the Twickenham Road. The traffic was beginning to move faster, slipping past the railway on the left and the recreation ground on the right. The Honda rolled over Twickenham Bridge, over the dull, seagull-haunted waters of the Thames.

The Twickenham Road hit a series of roundabouts and at length became the Chertsey Road instead. It was dual carriageway here. Dougal moved into the outside lane and pushed the car well over the speed limit. There was the possibility – probability? – that he was too late, far too late. Better not to think of that.

And then the question of blame. It was all very well saying that a private investigator was merely an agent acting within certain ethical constraints on behalf of a client. It wasn't Dougal's fault that Alan hadn't liked the information Dougal had brought him. Truth wasn't always desirable: facts could be awkward, clumsy things with sharp corners; small wonder, then, that many people preferred the rounded edges and streamlined shapes of convenient fictions. Not Alan, though.

It wasn't Dougal's fault, either, that he liked Alan. It happened that way sometimes, and with the most unlikely people: a spark of shared humanity leapt from one to the other, connecting if only for an instant what age and background usually divided.

There were roadworks near the junction with Hounslow Road, complete with temporary traffic lights and long queues. Dougal hammered the steering wheel in frustration. Once more he glanced at the phone. As he reached out his left hand for it, the lights changed and the cars ahead of him began to inch forwards. No point in calling the police – with any luck he'd be there before them.

Besides, what if this were a false alarm? Alan would never forgive him for making a fuss. Alan hated looking ridiculous. That was part of the problem. That was why he'd hired Dougal in the first place.

By now the traffic was moving with some speed. The start of the M3 loomed up ahead. At Sunbury

Cross roundabout, however, Dougal swung right and accelerated hard into the Staines Road. Half a mile later he made the sharp left-hand turn into Roth Road.

Roth had neither beginning nor end. Once upon a time it had been a village. Few traces were left. Sandwiched between reservoirs and the motorway, Roth was a state of mind as much as a place: a miniature suburb within a suburb, clinging to the tenuous remnants of its old identity. Alan lived in one of the older houses beyond the church.

Dougal drove over the bridge that crossed the river, a tiny tributary of the Thames. Alan's house was set back from the road and sheltered from the eyes of strangers by a privet hedge in need of trimming. Dougal turned into the drive. The house, which stood sideways to the road, was late-Victorian with more recent extensions sprouting in several directions. Alan had bought the place just after his retirement and spent thousands doing it up. He had installed three bathrooms, each with a bidet. ("Don't use them, mind, but Susie likes them.") There were double-glazed windows and solar heating panels. He had built a garage block, the newest of the extensions, with room for two large cars and a workshop at the side.

"It's funny," he had said to Dougal on Friday evening, when Dougal told him the news. "I did a lot of carpentry before I retired. Any brains I got are in my hands. Used to make beds, chests of drawers even. And when I retired, I thought I'd have all the time in the world for it. But it didn't work out that way." He poured himself some more brandy, slopping a few drops on a table he had made himself. "Nothing ever turns out how you think it's going to, does it? There's always a price to pay." He stared at Dougal over the rim of his glass. "Still, it's the same for everyone, I suppose. No sense in grumbling."

Dougal braked sharply and the car skidded on the gravel. He got out, leaving the keys in the ignition. The house loomed, a dream turned sour, against the blank winter sky: the windows were dirty; the rendering, once painted a brilliant white, was smudged with green; the flowerbeds on either side of the front door were thick with weeds. It was a cold day, and Dougal wished he had brought his coat.

"You have to take consequences," Alan had said on Friday evening. "No point in whingeing about it. I'll pay your bill before you go, all right?"

"There's no hurry. The company will send you an invoice. That's what they usually do."

"It's up to you." Alan had swallowed another mouthful of brandy. "'Permanent Peace of Mind,'" he said, quoting the motto of Custodemus, the company Dougal worked for. "That's a laugh."

Dougal hadn't laughed then and he wasn't laughing now. He pressed the doorbell which chimed somewhere in the house. He tried the door, which was locked. He rang the bell again, stepped back from the door and looked up at the windows of the house. No sign of movement. The curtains were drawn back. There was a burglar alarm, not a Custodemus model, under the eaves.

He walked quickly along the side of the house, peering into the two windows he passed. The first gave him a view of the little room where he had sat with Alan on Friday. Alan called it his den. The bottle of brandy still stood on the filing cabinet. Above the desk were framed photographs of the two shops he had once owned, one in Staines, the other in Shepperton High Street.

"Hardware – DIY: that's what they call them nowadays," Alan had said. "But I was an ironmonger – that's the real word. That's what my old dad was. The Staines shop was his." The eyes behind the glasses were bright and moist.

Dougal pushed aside the memory. The next window belonged to the kitchen: a long thin room, expensively gloomy with fumed oak, wrought iron and panels of leaded glass. The sinks and the draining boards were piled with dirty crockery. Open tins and frozen-food wrappings littered the work surfaces.

He reached the garage. The wide up-and-over door was closed. Without much hope, he twisted the handle. It turned. The door slid back into the roof space with a metallic rumble.

"Shit," said Dougal.

Alan's Rover was still there. The space beside it was empty. Dougal felt the bonnet of the car as he passed: it was cold.

There were two doors at the back of the garage. Dougal tried the one which led to the house. It was locked. But the other door was slightly ajar.

The workshop, Dougal guessed. He gave the door a sharp push. It swung back, but stopped abruptly halfway through its arc. Dougal stepped into the doorway.

Oh Christ. No.

Alan Rushwick was hanging by a thin blue nylon rope from one of the tie beams that held the roof together. Except that it wasn't Alan any more. It was no more him than an empty house is a home.

Unwelcome details flooded into Dougal's mind and lodged in his memory. Alan was wearing the same clothes as on Friday: brown corduroy trousers, a baggy cardigan and a checked shirt; and his scuffed maroon-leather slippers lay untidily on the concrete floor, one on its side. The body bulged against the clothes as potatoes bulge against the sack containing them. Alan's lank grey hair had fallen forward over his face. The lips and the tips of the ears were a bluish purple. There were streaks of dried blood at the base of the nostrils. The tongue had been forced out, poking in the direction of Dougal, and the hands were clenched. It looked as if the noose had been made not with a knot but with an old-fashioned brass ring which had lodged under the angle of the left jaw.

Primitive, Dougal thought, and very efficient. And at that precise instant he noticed something else, something which did not belong in Alan's workshop: the strong, fresh smell of a woman's perfume.

Dougal pushed the door as hard as he could. There was a gasp, high and sharp, on the edge of a scream. He grabbed the handle, stepped into the room and pulled the door back.

"Good morning, Mrs. Rushwick."

"Who the hell are you?" Susie Rushwick was breathing fast, one hand raised to fend him off, the other touching her white throat as if showing on her own neck the precise spot where the brass ring was pressing into her husband's. "What are you doing here?"

"I'm doing a job for Mr. Rushwick."

She lowered her hands. Susie Rushwick was a tall woman, much the same size as Dougal, with dark hair and very long legs. She was dressed for business in jeans and an open navy-blue cashmere overcoat. "I've only just got here. God, what a thing to come home to."

"Where's your car?"

"None of your business." She glanced sideways through long lashes at him. "A friend dropped me off. Do you think it – he – do you think it was an accident?"

"Do you?"

"You read these stories about middle-aged men." She moistened her lips. "You know, they say it increases the pleasure if a man half strangles himself when..."

"Does he look as if he was on the verge of having an orgasm when he died?" Dougal asked.

"I don't know, do I?"

Dougal moved into the workshop and looked around. The woman watched. She seemed not to have recognised him. She hadn't asked about the nature of the job he was doing for her husband; perhaps she already knew.

The body did not move. Now Dougal was nearer to it, he noticed a smell of excrement mingling with Susie Rushwick's perfume.

"I – I need to make a phone call," she said.

"The police?"

She shrugged. "I suppose so. It seems so pointless."

"They usually like to be notified in cases of suspected murder."

"What? Are you out of your tiny mind? If it wasn't an accident, he topped himself. It's obvious."

"It would only be obvious if he'd left a note. Have you found one?"

Susie Rushwick hugged the overcoat around her body. "As it happens, no." She stared vaguely around the room. "But lots of suicides don't leave notes."

"But I don't think many suicides practise levitation."

"What are you on about now?"

Dougal nodded towards the body. Alan had been a small man. His feet dangled nearly three feet above the ground. There was a hole in one of his socks.

"How did he get up there, fix the rope, put the noose round his neck and hang himself at that height? If it was suicide, there'd be something he'd kicked aside, something he'd stood on. But there isn't." Dougal nerved himself and touched the right hand balled into a tight little fist: it felt very cold. "So if it was suicide, it must have been levitation." He swung round to look at her. "Don't you agree?"

The aggression seeped away from Susie's face. She wore bright red lipstick, applied in a way to make the lips look more generous than they really were. The colour served to emphasise the underlying pallor of the skin.

"Listen, I've been away for ten days." Her voice had become soft and low, almost seductive. "I only got here a few minutes before you did. He wasn't in the house so I thought he must be in here." She hesitated, choosing her words with care. "The door to the workshop was shut. When I opened it, it hit something – that stool, see?" She pointed at a tall, paint-stained wooden stool that stood beside the workbench several yards from the body. "I picked it up, I had to, didn't I, or I couldn't have got into the room. And it wasn't until I'd moved it that I realised—"

She broke off with a little sob. Her eyes flickered towards Dougal. Then she turned away, her shoulders heaving, and extracted a wad of tissues from a duffel bag made of soft black leather which was standing on the workbench. She dabbed carefully at her eyes.

Dougal stared at her. "Was Paul Newland with you?"

Susie Rushwick whirled round. "Have you been sticking your nose into my affairs? Who the fuck are you?"

Dougal dug a card out of the top pocket of his jacket. He handed it to her and watched her lips moving very slightly as she read: *Custodemus – Permanent Peace of Mind – William Dougal – Private Investigation Division*.

"Are you telling me Alan hired you to *spy* on me?"

Dougal nodded.

"What did you tell him?"

"I'm sorry," Dougal said untruthfully. "I can't tell you that. Client confidentiality."

Susie Rushwick moved slowly towards him. For a moment he wondered whether she might intend to attack him. He tensed himself, ready for fight or preferably flight.

"So he knew. The bastard knew."

"Only since Friday. He didn't know for sure until then."

"I know what you're thinking but you're quite wrong. It's—"

"It doesn't matter what I think," interrupted Dougal. "But I have to warn you that it's company policy to cooperate fully with the police."

"And what's that supposed to mean?"

"I'll have to tell them exactly how I discovered the body. I'll have to tell them that you were here. I'll have to tell them that I couldn't understand how Mr. Rushwick could have hanged himself. Not until you explained about the stool, that is." He glanced from the congested face of his former client to the cosmetically disguised face of his former client's wife. "They'll ask me why I'm here. And of course I'll have to tell them Mr. Rushwick hired me, and why. The simplest thing would be to give them a copy of my report."

"What's in it?"

"The usual stuff. Photographs of you and Paul Newland. A detailed breakdown of your movements in the seven days up to last Friday."

"It meant nothing – it was just a fling. Alan must have known it wasn't serious."

"It wasn't just a fling. The weekend before last you were at an antiques fair. You and Newland stayed there as man and wife. The chambermaid remembered the pair of you staying twice before over the last twelve months. I've got photocopies of the hotel register to prove it."

Her face twisted in disgust. "I hope it gave you a thrill."

"You spent three extra nights at the hotel and did a bit of business at a country house sale while you were there. On the Wednesday of last week you both came back to London. During the day you went to your shop in Staines, and at night you drove back to Newland's flat in Ealing. On Thursday evening you went out to dinner at an Italian restaurant called La Ventura. The waiter said you had three bottles of wine between you. By the end of the evening, you were talking rather loudly about how you wanted to get a divorce as quickly as possible so you could marry Mr. Newland. The only problems seemed to be financial ones, didn't they? Mr. Rushwick owned everything including the lease of your shop."

"You'll tell the police all that? You bastard."

"Company policy, I'm afraid."

There was a moment's silence. Unspoken words hung in the cold air between them. Susie was probably in her late thirties, and she was still very good-looking. Her good looks had won her a doting husband, a comfortable home, her own subsidised business and a handsome boyfriend who looked younger than she did.

"Do you know," Alan had said just before Dougal left him on Friday evening. "Me and Susie, we haven't made love for nearly two years." He was in his fifties but he looked like an old man. "I don't think she ever really enjoyed it, not with me at any rate. Now she's always too tired, or it's her time of the month, or she's got a headache. You know. So I've stopped asking." He'd looked at Dougal, his face stern. "You don't want to hear all this, do you? And what's the point in talking about it? I've made my bed and now I must lie on it."

Susie stirred. The smell of her perfume grew stronger. She moved slowly nearer to Dougal and touched his arm in a gesture that was almost a caress.

"Listen – he killed himself. It's as plain as the nose on your face. You didn't know Alan like I did. He'd cut off his nose to spite his face. If he hasn't left a note it's just so he could cause more problems when he's gone. Problems for me." She glanced at the corpse and quickly looked away. "Couldn't we talk somewhere else?"

"Maybe I should phone the police now."

"No – wait a moment. Can we come to an arrangement? There's no need to say you've seen me here. It'd be much simpler, wouldn't it?" She looked at her watch. "Paul will be outside in a few minutes."

She was taller than Alan had been, younger and fitter. According to Alan, she took care to keep herself fit. She even went to karate classes. Physically she would have been perfectly capable of stringing up her husband and trying to make it look like suicide.

And morally?

"I bet Alan didn't remember to pay you," Susie said brightly. "Still, no harm done." She stretched out her arm and dug a red-tipped hand into the leather duffel bag, which was still standing open on the workbench. She produced a roll of notes and fanned them out like playing cards: tens and twenties and fifties. "There's fifteen hundred pounds there. Would that do for starters? Cash is easier than cheques, I often think. I do a lot of my business in cash. Of course if it's not enough your company can always invoice for whatever's owed." She tried the effect of a smile. "Take it – no need for a receipt."

Dougal wasn't looking at the smile or the money but at Alan's face.

The talons dipped back into the handbag. "Actually, I've got another thousand here. Twenty-five hundred: can't say fairer than that, can I?"

Dougal held out his hand. "I don't know. I just don't know."

With indecent haste she put the money into the palm of his hand and folded his fingers over it. Her hands were warm and sticky with sweat. "There'll be more, I promise. Look – the important thing is the stool. I'll put it back where – where I found it. OK?"

Dougal shrugged. "I'd better ring the police." He went out into the garage, saying over his shoulder, "I'll use my mobile: it's in the car."

"Just a minute." Though still low, the voice now held an unmistakable note of command. It was surprising what a little bit of money could buy. Dougal heard the scrape of the stool's legs as Susie moved it across the room and the clatter of wood on concrete as she pushed it over. A moment later she joined him in the garage.

"There's one or two things I need to get from the house," she told Dougal. "It won't matter if you don't phone right away, will it? I shan't be a moment."

Dougal felt the rolls of notes in his trouser pocket and nodded.

Susie let herself into the house by the door from the garage. On the threshold she turned and bestowed another smile on Dougal. When the door closed behind her he walked through the garage and on to the gravel. It was even colder outside than in the workshop.

She needed to repair her make-up, he thought; the crocodile tears had caused several small blemishes to its perfection. More importantly, she would want to lay her hands on Dougal's report, assuming Alan had left it somewhere easily accessible. Forewarned was forearmed. And almost certainly there would be other things – passbooks to joint accounts, perhaps; portable valuables which she would prefer not to be included in the valuation of Alan's estate; or items which might interest the police if they searched the house. With luck she would be at least five or ten minutes.

Dougal opened the door of the Honda. He slipped the phone into his pocket and took the Polaroid camera from the bag on the back seat. Shielding it from the windows of the house, he returned to the workshop, where he photographed the body and its surroundings. He pushed the Polaroid into the pocket of his trousers, the same pocket which held the notes, to finish developing.

He was lucky in his timing. As he was putting the camera in the Honda, he heard a car pulling up in the road. Fragments of red glowed through the green of the privet. Dougal strolled down the drive.

Paul Newland was sitting in his Mazda, a red soft top, drumming his fingers on the steering wheel. Dougal tapped on the passenger-side window. The window slid down. Newland switched off Bruce Springsteen and stared at Dougal.

"I wonder if I could have a word." Dougal passed one of his business cards into the car.

"What about?"

"Your relationship with Mrs. Rushwick. And the sudden death of her late husband."

Newland blinked. Then he opened his door, extracted himself from the car and marched round to Dougal. He was a big man with sleek fair hair, a small skull and very blue eyes. Dougal knew that he worked as a salesman for a garage in Shepherd's Bush which did a brisk and possibly suspicious trade in second-hand cars. He was wearing the suede jacket which Susie had bought him last week.

"Now what is this? And where's Susie?"

"You'd better see Mr. Rushwick."

"See him dead?"

Dougal took out the Polaroid and showed it to him.

"Oh my God." Newland studied the photograph for a moment. "How – how did it happen?"

"That's the question. See that stool on the floor? When I got here a few minutes ago, it wasn't there. I actually saw Mrs. Rushwick putting it underneath the body."

"But why would she do that?"

"Otherwise there would be nothing Mr. Rushwick could have climbed on to reach the noose."

"He must have had something."

Dougal ignored him. "So the police will want to speak to Mrs. Rushwick."

At last Newland understood. "They won't think she killed him, surely?"

"Why not? She had the opportunity, she certainly had the means, and as for the motive, well, I imagine she's Mr. Rushwick's sole beneficiary: and of course, now he's dead, she can marry you. I think that's her general idea."

"Now look—"

"I'll have to tell the police about her moving the stool. They'll draw their own conclusions."

"This is nothing to do with me." Newland backed away as if Dougal had suddenly become infectious. "Nothing at all."

"I don't blame you." Dougal stared thoughtfully at the Polaroid. "Still, it's up to you, really. I'm going to phone the police."

He nodded pleasantly to Newland and walked up the drive. Before he reached the Honda, he heard the virile roar of the Mazda's starter motor. He glanced over his shoulder in time to see the red car streaking across the mouth of the drive. At that moment the front door opened.

"Was that Paul?" demanded Susie. "What's he think he's playing at?"

"I don't know."

"But I need him to drive me. I can't take Alan's car. I can't exactly phone for a taxi. Perhaps you—"

"I need to phone the police. Anyway, we shouldn't be seen together."

Susie frowned at him. "I suppose you're right." She came outside, her body lopsided because of the large black bag slung over her right shoulder.

"I think I saw a bus stop near the church."

"Oh for heaven's sake." She flounced down the drive.

"Susie," Dougal said.

She stopped and turned round. "What?"

"Do be careful."

She twitched her shoulders and scurried towards the road. Dougal walked back to the garage and through to the workshop. Alan's cardigan had deep pockets. Holding his nose, Dougal gingerly investigated the pocket on the right and found a small brown envelope. It was addressed to the coroner. He left it in the pocket.

Dead bodies made Dougal uncomfortable for all sorts of reasons so he went back outside. He patted his trouser pocket and felt the comfortable shape of £2,500. In the other trouser pocket was a letter he had received that morning. He took it out and read it once more.

Dear William Dougal,
It was nice of you to listen to me. You didn't say much, either, which I appreciated, because there was nothing much to say. I've thought it through and I think the best thing for all concerned is if I take the easy way out. I never much fancied growing old anyway.

You should get this on Monday morning. If no one's found me before then, you can tell the police there's a letter for the coroner in the pocket of my cardigan. The cardigan I'll be wearing. Sorry to be such a nuisance.

Susie can have the money and live happily ever after with her fancy man. Except that she won't and he won't. But that's their affair. Nothing's for free in this world, is it?

All the best,

Alan Rushwick.

Dougal folded the letter and put it carefully away. Time to call the police: delay wouldn't make Alan any less dead. Dougal took out his phone. It was a cold day, so cold it brought tears to his eyes.

Who Killed Adonis?

Amy Myers

"BY THE WAY, Aphrodite—" My darling Adonis lounged back against the grassy knoll preening himself in the afterglow of our yearly tryst. Though he is officially dead, the Underworld grudgingly allows him to return to earth for a few measly months of summer, in accordance with the terms of the Zeus–Hades custody order. "—it wasn't you who murdered me, was it?"

"*What?*" I screeched, sitting bolt upright, partly in shock, and partly because flowery bowers tend to have by-products of uncomfortable thorns and thistles. (This one is allotted for our use alone, but since Adonis is – or was – mortal, I have to put up with such inconveniences.) Handsome he might be, but my darling Adonis is none too bright at times, and his memory is not what it used to be. Murdered indeed! And I, the goddess of love, the chief suspect. I was extremely annoyed, but not wishing to mar the celebration of our reunion at least twice more I spoke to him gently. "You were killed by a wild boar, darling. Everyone knows that."

Certainly I was only too well aware of the fact. On that fateful day four years earlier I had driven down from Mount Olympus for a delightful rendezvous with the handsomest man on earth only to find him full of holes and blood, and the undergrowth heavily trampled by some wild animal. In the midst of my grief, however, it had occurred to me that I, as the laughter-loving queen of delight, should consider my reputation. I had instantly summoned Iris, the gods' messenger, to get a divine order signed for any tears I shed to be turned into anemones when they hit the ground, and sweet Adonis' red blood into red roses. In a trice our bower was sprouting flowers everywhere, and all traces of nasty blood had disappeared. Only the merest speck on one wrist remained as a delicate reminder of the kiss of death. Tenderly I wiped it off as one last service to my love.

Having prettied up the scene, I had then departed back to Olympus to plead with my father, Mighty Zeus, that I needed Adonis more than King Hades of the Underworld. (I'd long suspected Proserpina, his queen, had her eye on nabbing Adonis as soon as she could.) Even Father couldn't completely sway Hades on this occasion, however, and a time-share arrangement had been worked out.

Now, enjoying its fruits on our third tryst since that terrible day, I suddenly found myself accused of murder. How could he be so horrid? He'd never mentioned murder before. How did this horrible idea come to plant itself in his head, which is adorable despite his limitations in the brain department? And why, oh why, accuse *me*? Tears filled my eyes, and the thick mass of anemones all round me prepared to squeeze up to allow a few more in. (Father, Dread Son of Cronos, had never rescinded the order for flowers.)

"No." Adonis' long curls shook vigorously. "I've travelled across the Styx and drunk from the River Lethe of Forgetfulness so many times, I've forgotten who did kill me now, but I know it wasn't a boar. The murderer set it on me to hide the traces of the poisoned arrow."

"But even if you're right, whatever gave you the idea it was me?" I wailed. "If it hadn't been for me, you wouldn't be here now. I pleaded for your life. Remember?"

He blushed. "It's just that one of our sex games is Me Little Deer You Mighty Huntress. I thought your foreplay might have gone wrong – by accident, of course," he added hastily.

"No," I replied coldly.

"Then find who did it. Then I can sue in the Low Court of Hades."

This was most unpleasant. My reputation now was in severe danger, and so – as I looked longingly at that handsome body – was my love life. No one wants to expose their most tender organs to someone suspected of having a penchant for poisoned darts. My tears began to fall, and a fresh crop of anemones sprang up. It was time for firmness. "You have a lot of lady friends. Naturally they are jealous of me."

"Then why kill *me*?" he muttered.

"Because I'm immortal, so they couldn't murder me." I told you he was none too bright.

Adonis sulked. "King Zeus was threatening to expel you from Olympus to Hades. That would make you mortal."

"Threatened, perhaps." I was highly indignant. "But of course he never would." He'd wipe out not only his own love life, but that of all the gods and goddesses with any *ichor* in their veins on Olympus. Try telling them their love lives were at an end because Aphrodite had been sent packing to Hades, and taken her magic girdle with her. It suddenly occurred to me to wonder *how* Adonis had discovered such Top Secret Information, for I would never confide in a mere mortal. Department OI6, the Olympus Intelligence service, makes us all sign the Immortal Secrets Act, and as the proceedings to which Adonis referred were held *in camera* it had to be someone present at my so-called 'trial'.

Unwillingly I was forced to think back to the terrible day of Adonis' death. Only the day before it took place I had been in a very good mood indeed. That charming young man Paris, prince of Troy, during his apprenticeship year as a shepherd on Mount Ida, had awarded me the Golden Apple for being the fairest goddess of all. I admit that considering the competition this was no great surprise: this consisted of Ox-eyed Hera, Mighty Queen of Zeus's Humping Bed, wallowing in transparent gauzes in the belief they make her look thinner, and six-foot Pallas Athene clomping along in a full suit of armour. How could they compare with *me*, clad with the help of the Three Graces, in a blue silk *chiton* girdled with my magic *cestus*, and a cunning little arrangement of blue forget-me-nots and love-in-a-mist in my hair?

When Paris naughtily suggested we all strip off so that he could judge us better, I knew he had already made his decision. Hera, built like an ox, couldn't wait to get her clothes off, and six-foot Athene blushed virginally as she struggled to whip off breastplates and helmet provocatively. She couldn't provoke a Centaur who'd been deprived of nymphs for a year. (She'd tried hard not to remove a single item, on the grounds that Paris had used the words 'strip to your birthday suits', and armour *was* her birthday suit. She had sprung fully armed from Father's head instead of taking the more usual roundabout route via a mother.)

Paris made a thorough job of looking us up and down, but just to be on the safe side I took the precaution of whispering in his ear: "Choose me and you shall have the fairest woman on earth for your own."

"Oh."

He had been momentarily distracted from eyeing parts of goddesses rarely seen by mortal men, and pressed the Golden Apple warmly into my hand. (On the way back to Olympus, I decided I'd give him Helen of Greece. Unfortunately I didn't realise this would begin the ten-year Trojan War when Paris changed her surname to 'of Troy' but omitted to inform her husband first. It's Father

Zeus's fault; he's supposed to be the all-knowing one with the direct line to Destiny.)

My two mountainous naked rivals have sharp ears and had overheard my private remark to Paris. When they saw the Apple in my hand, all Hades was let loose.

"You've cheated," Hera roared.

"You're perfectly horrid." Athene burst into tears. So much for the goddess of wisdom and mighty warriors. "I'll tell Father of you."

She did too. The very next day, just as I was stepping out of my shell-bath in pleasant anticipation of the afternoon ahead with Adonis, Hermes flew in to summon me to an extraordinary session of the Olympus Assizes. This is called whenever Father gets bored with Olympus; he orders an ambrosia picnic and takes the court down to his temple on Mount Ida on the pretext that a mortal witness has been called. Paris had been superpoenaed to give evidence and Father said he wasn't going to have any clod-hopping shepherds trampling sheep's muck over the Hall of the Golden Floor, and expecting to stay on for a nectar lunch.

So poor Paris (*almost* as good-looking as Adonis), peacefully snoozing on Ida while his dog did all the work, had woken up to find himself surrounded by all the senior gods of Olympus, perching on rocks to avoid all the animal dung. Ox-eyed Hera had landed on a sheep just as she was materialising and Aesculapius, the gods' doctor, had to do some hasty work to prevent its being shipped down to adorn Hades' lunch table.

"I accuse Aphrodite of cheating," shrilled darling Athene to the jury. Everyone not personally involved in the case was on the jury, but Father never listens to a word they say, on the grounds that he is All-Seeing and All-Knowing, and they aren't. You might think therefore that he would know whether I'd cheated, and incidentally who killed my poor Adonis. The trouble with Father is that he never does. He always has some excuse, usually that he was 'asleep' (in other words, either preparing for, indulging in or recovering from his multitudinous erotic entanglements). The only time he's wide awake is when he's trying to avoid his legal wife.

"She always cheats," piped up an 'impartial' juryman, my darling sister Artemis, goddess of the chase.

"That's right. She wouldn't let me catch up with Daphne," whined Apollo. Not that he'd have known what to do if he had snared her, in my opinion. To be changed into a laurel tree was a merciful release for the poor girl.

"What say you, O Queen?" enquired Zeus cautiously.

Hera's broad hips wobbled indignantly. "She *must* have cheated, O Mighty Son of Cronos. I revealed myself in all my wondrous naked beauty and Paris still chose her."

"Hum." Father studiously avoided looking at me. *Hum* meant he was trying to get out of that one. Being Father, he did.

"I call Paris," he thundered, so loudly that several desert tribes cheered up and rushed buckets to their nearest oasis. "And if he bears out this accusation, Aphrodite, you can get your fare ready for Charon. It will be Hades for you."

Paris, I decided, even as I trembled with fear, had his points. At any other time I might have... I dragged my libido away and reminded myself that I'd allotted Helen to him. Anyway, his head was getting far too big for his calf boots. He winked at me, and then humbly fell on his knees before Father – always a good ploy. Mighty Zeus swelled with power and pride.

"Did Aphrodite cheat to win this Golden Apple?"

"No, Mighty Son of Cronos. I was blinded by the beauty of all three goddesses – who would not be? I, a mere mortal, was offered Power, Wisdom or Love – and what man would not choose love?"

Quite a few in my experience, but it was prettily spoken, and Paris won a round of applause led by me. Zeus, no doubt bearing in mind he needed my magic *cestus* that afternoon, brought in a not-guilty verdict. “What do you say, Aphrodite?” He beamed graciously.

Meekness was the best policy. “Thank you, Father. Love does indeed rule all. This afternoon, my beloved Adonis is restored to my arms thanks to your mighty victory over Hades, and I therefore declare in his honour that my *cestus* is available to anyone who requires it.”

There was a sharp intake of breath from someone. I’d forgotten my husband (Hephaestus, god of the forge) and my lover Ares (god of war) were present, and I briefly wondered whether I had been entirely wise to mention Adonis. The very thought of him and our forthcoming reunion made my legs tremble, not to mention their effect on other parts of my body, and I forgot all about Hephaestus and Ares, as I swept out triumphantly, singing a little ditty I had just composed:

“Goddesses three to Ida went…” For some reason this seemed to upset my two mighty rivals in the Golden Apple contest, and they snarled their resentment of me. “You wait, Aphrodite, I’ll get you,” Athene shouted, brandishing a mailed fist, and Hera glowered.

I had won. I dressed carefully, then danced into luncheon to build up stamina for the afternoon ahead with Adonis. The *chiton* was exceptionally pretty, Doric style with one of these fashionable new metal pins to hold it up. Not that that would be necessary for long. Adonis might be My Little Deer, but he was a Tiger when it came to ripping off silk *chitons.*

Thus it was that I had set off to our bower full of the happiest expectations, only to find not the amorous lover I had so confidently expected, but my beloved's dead and bloody body.

Now, three yearly trysts later, he was accusing me of *murdering* him. Having delivered his Parthian shot, Adonis dozed off, looking more handsome than ever. Hades had made a good job of patching up the holes, I'll say that for him. I pondered whether to wake my beloved up immediately for another round of lovemaking, but reluctantly decided it would be prudent to clear myself of suspicion and deduce who this murderer could be.

Hera and Athene had to be top of the scroll. But which? Perhaps I needed Adonis' help. I shook him rather abruptly, and with a sigh he reached out his hand.

"Not yet," I said uncharacteristically. "Do any of these names jog your memory as having murdered you? Hera, Athene."

He gaped. "No."

I produced a trump card. "Artemis." My darling sister is very jealous of me, for all she stomps around proclaiming what fun it is to be virgin.

"She'd tackle you, not me. She can wound you, even if she can't kill you." We gods can certainly be wounded and *ichor* running from your veins, believe me, is every bit as painful as blood. However, I was quite sure he was wrong.

"Artemis," I informed him, "has a record of killing young men with arrows. It makes a change from chasing animals. She'd have shot you just for your temerity in preferring me to her."

Once such a remark would instantly have called forth tender assurances that there was indeed no comparison between us. Now, all Adonis replied was:

"Who else knew you were coming to see me?"

Typical male. They always want to take the whole show over. It was I who was supposed to be asking the questions.

"Father, everyone on Olympus, Paris of Troy."

"What about him?" Adonis asked eagerly.

None too bright, as I said. "I gave Paris Helen. He's got nothing to complain about."

"Your husband?"

I gave a short laugh. "Plenty to complain about, but impotent to do so." To do anything in fact.

"Apollo?"

"Possible. He was very annoyed with me over that nymph, and he does like playing with bows and arrows."

"Ares?"

"No." You've heard of a bull in a glazed pottery emporium? That's Ares. Thunders around as if he's Father. No fiddly arrows for him.

"It has to be one of you lot, if it's not you."

You lot? Hardly respectful. Keeping company with Queen Proserpina of the Underworld was giving Adonis ideas above his station, and he still had a distinctly suspicious note in his voice. I briefly considered whether Proserpina could have emerged to kill Adonis, but dismissed the idea. A breath of fresh air and she'd faint.

Then I had a bright idea. I'd look at the Olympus Meal Register, for whoever did it must have missed lunch on that day in order to arrive at the bower before me. The Register had been one of father's worst ideas, but suddenly I saw its advantages. Father had got it into his head we were all one big happy family, and therefore ought to eat family meals round the table, and not grab a bite on the way to our next temple, or curled up in front of Earthvision, a hole specially cut in the clouds to give us a running peepshow onto earth. (*Such* fun at times, a real situation comedy.) We have to sign out if we are going to miss a meal, and state our reason. Even Mighty Queen Flat-Feet Hera has to toe the line.

"Wait, darling," I commanded, dematerialising rapidly, and leaping into my carriage. Swans are far too slow for emergencies, I'll hire the communal horses next time, I vowed, as I dashed into the Hall of the Golden Floor to study the register. It was an immortal register luckily, so the records were still there. I quickly swept through the book to the fated day and saw that my four suspects, Hera, Athene, Artemis and Apollo, had all been 'out to lunch' that day. Sulking over my acquittal, I expect. The excuses made fine reading.

Hera: gone to see Mother Rhea. The oldest excuse under the sun and only she could get away with it. Her Titan mother-in-law hasn't had a visit in years. Athene: chasing a rainbow – my foot. She might have been chasing her chum Iris, goddess of the rainbow. If you could find the end of a rainbow, there'd be no crock of gold, merely Athene, flat out after her love exertions. Apollo: bringing sunshine to Norway. Funny name for a nymph! Artemis: chasing wild boar. She always comes striding back with a bloody carcase over her shoulder – so unpleasant.

My mouth fell open. People say that without meaning it, but mine really did. I must have looked momentarily quite ugly, but I didn't care. I *knew* who had murdered Adonis, and I performed a little dance of victory. Then, highly pleased with myself, I debated my next move...

* * *

I tracked Paris down in Troy where he was in bed making love to Helen while all his brothers fought the Greeks. He didn't even notice me when I materialised, although I coughed politely.

There was a shriek from Helen, clearly thinking she was about to incur immortal wrath. "We were only playing knuckle-bones."

"Get out, Helen," I ordered, a little unfairly.

She vanished, her peerless white body swathed in a sheet, as if I cared. Even Paris temporarily lost interest.

"I'm glad you're pleased with my choice," I said to him furiously.

"Your choice?" Paris looked startled, but gathered his wits instantly. "Of course, Great Goddess. You promised me the fairest woman on earth."

"Yes, and you assumed, you miserable mortal, I meant myself. Naturally," I added more gently. "I didn't tell you on Mount Ida whom I would allot to you, and as I was standing on earth at the time, you had every right to think it was me. So when next morning I said I was off to see Adonis, you were jealous."

He looked down at his feet, remembered his nakedness and, rather to my regret, popped on his tunic. "Yes," he admitted sulkily.

"So you *murdered* him," I shrieked. He cowered in a corner.

"For you, Great Goddess," he gabbled. "Helen is but second best."

"She's not bad-looking." I decided to be gracious. It was, after all, very flattering. I just couldn't be too cross, as I gently removed the tunic again.

Later I had to explain to Father why I had done nothing to punish naughty Paris. I could manage Adonis, but Father was more tricky. I decided to show I was his daughter in wisdom.

"I applied logic, Father, like you always do."

He looked interested.

"After your gracious order to turn Adonis' blood into red roses," I continued, "there was a single speck of blood left. As it was still there, I knew it must be the murderer's blood. Perhaps he pricked himself on a thorn when checking the pulse to see his victim was indeed dead."

"And how did you know the murderer was Paris?"

I smiled. "It was *blood,* Father, not *ichor*, and Paris was the only mortal who could have known where Adonis was."

"Very clever. But," Father wasn't letting me off lightly, "you realise what you've done by not slaying him, especially as you were so careless in letting him have Helen?"

"Please, Father, don't kill him. He's such a *handsome* young man." Paris would make a most interesting mortal lover.

He sighed. "I'll have a word with Destiny."

Father came back from the Room of the Future downcast. "I'm afraid the Trojan War is still going to have to last its full term, and Paris is doomed to die. However, for your sake, Aphrodite, I won't kill Paris till right near the end."

"Oh *good*." I was so pleased. "I can have Paris till then? It's not a lot to ask, during all those winter months when Adonis is away."

Father looked cunning. "Yes, but I want that girdle of yours. Those Greeks are fine-looking women."

It was a small favour to grant, and I did so, for I was in Seventh Olympus. I had my Troy-boy.

Stranger in Paradise

Judith Cutler

THE GATES SWUNG to and fro, to and fro, on their handsome gateposts. I closed them firmly. That was it, then. I turned and left.

* * *

There's nothing like redundancy and an unexpected bequest to make you change your ways, even when as a middle-aged widow you might be expected to be somewhat set in them. I would abandon London and go and live in my new country property. But when I looked at the cottage I'd been left, down in Withycombe Magna, where Exmoor confronts Dartmoor, I wondered if I'd made the right decision.

I'd have liked the cottage to be olde-worlde, with one of those enigmatic names that tantalise you about their origins. In fact, it was called Moor View, and wasn't at all the sort you'd expect to nestle between two national parks. It had neither thatch nor thick cob walls, having been built in the nineteen-fifties, when English domestic architecture was not especially memorable. There were no close neighbours to make me feel welcome.

Withycombe Magna itself was no picture-postcard tourist-trap. There was no romantic cluster of cottages about the village green, the church one side and the pub the other, with the flannelled fools of cricketers starting their Sundays in one, and progressing at last to the other. The rather squat church was at one end of the straggle of buildings sprawling along an unlit, unpavemented road, the pub at the other, with no green in between. There was a service just once a month: not much opportunity for socialising there. The pub was simply a drinking place for old men, with no hope of the enticing ploughman's lunches I'd hoped to enjoy after a long morning's tramping on the moors. There was a village school, but that was in the process of conversion to a bijou home for another incomer like me. At least there was a village shop-cum-post office, but that wasn't picture book either, with enticing boxes of fresh local vegetables tumbling onto the pavement. No, it proudly proclaimed itself to be a Spar. A chain! I would have little compunction in heading for Taunton to find a proper supermarket.

One thing the village did have was a huge pair of gate-posts. Not the sort of turreted affairs you associate with a stately home – though they would have been wide enough to drive a coach and four through – and not part of the village itself. They were supported by a most elegant pair of curved matching walls, beautifully graduated from about four feet at the outside edges to about six feet at the hinge face. In the cleanly pointed modern brick, each pier carried a granite oblong, incised with gold-blocked italic letters declaring the gates to belong to Paradise Mews. They and the wrought-iron gates hanging from them would have been perfect in well-heeled suburbia: in Withycombe Magna they looked plain odd. Since I knew no one to ask, I simply smiled at their absurdity every time I walked past them.

Moor View Cottage needed a lot of work doing to it, especially in the garden. It would have been easy to turn tail. But I don't like giving up. In any case, it would be a good entrée into the village to ask a local builder – if I could find one – to sort out matters of rotting window frames and drooping gutters.

Meanwhile I took advantage of the remaining summer weather to tackle the profusion of greenery that shut out the light from the kitchen and dining room. The garden might resemble at a casual glance the hotch-potch cottage garden immortalised on a thousand jigsaws: in fact, any surviving perennials were tangled with couch grass and harboured a surprisingly vicious strain of stinging nettle.

I was filling my fifth sack when I realised I was being watched.

Smiling, I glanced up to see a cyclist, a rosy-cheeked woman somewhat older than myself, watching me closely. "What are you planning to do with all that stuff?" she asked without preamble, her approach at odds with her appearance.

"In an ideal world I'd compost it," I said, glad to straighten myself and hoping for a prolonged chat. "But—"

"Oh, no. Not with all that squitch grass," she said. "Burn it or get it disposed of. You want to ask Mr. Taylor at the bungalow by the phone box to take it away."

"Thanks—" But I was talking to thin air.

At least if I spoke to Mr. Taylor it would mean I had another acquaintance in the village. Total, two –

Rosy-Cheeks and Mr. Taylor, who turned out to be as cadaverous as she was rounded.

"Ah, I'll take those two leylandii too, while I'm at it," he said. "No room for them in a garden that size."

"I'll have to see if I can afford—" I began.

"I'll be round first thing on Saturday," he said.

And was.

"The garden feels very empty," I ventured, meaning that I felt surprisingly vulnerable without the trees.

"Sometimes," he said earnestly, hands on hips, "everyone needs a good clear out. Shift all the rubbish. Be ruthless. Start again afresh."

I nodded.

"You'll have an extra couple of hours' daylight, and when you've dug in some decent horse muck you'll really start growing things. You mark my words."

Was I surprised when four sacks of manure arrived overnight? Or when a bandy-legged old geezer, eyes mere blue slits in the crumpled face, turned up with a tape measure just as I was sitting down to my pasta supper on Monday? He stared at it disparagingly as I covered it against the flies that plagued me – they were on visiting terms with the cows in the adjoining field.

"It's no good you thinking you can have they uPVC frames," he declared, "because this here's a conservation area, see, and they planning folk won't allow them. So you've got to have proper wood frames, painted properly, like, none of your dark stain."

"But the cost—" I protested.

"You can't leave them like that," he pointed out, digging a horning thumbnail into the hollow mess of my kitchen window frame. "I'll order everything now and start third week in September."

"Thank you – er—?"

"Henry," he said enigmatically, pocketing his tape and notepad, and turning on his heel.

I could afford it, whatever I'd said to Mr. Taylor. My redundancy payment still lurked, easily accessible, in my building society account.

The following morning I found a freshly-cut lettuce and a paper bag of late peas on my doorstep. Well, they were scarcely a Trojan Horse. The worst the lettuce harboured was a pale green caterpillar, arguably more scared of me than I was of it. All the same, it would have been nice to know whom my benefactor might be. Rosy-Cheeks or Mr. Taylor or Henry? I would make a pilgrimage to Spar to see if I could get any clues.

Perhaps I'd been prejudiced before. Of course, the prices were higher and the range much more limited than in a supermarket. But what I spent there, I'd save in petrol. Did I need ready-made dishes when I'd got all the time in the world to cook? I peered tentatively into the freezer chest.

"You don't want none of that frozen rubbish," a voice hissed in my ear. "You want to ask Mrs. Gaye at the counter about proper meat."

There were a couple of women peering at shelves and queuing at the post office counter – I didn't know which had spoken. Nonetheless, I acted on orders. It seemed it was possible to order local meat, delivered to the shop fresh by the farmer down the road. And chickens. Organic!

"Eggs?" I asked.

Mrs. Gaye looked shocked. "I can't compete—" she began.

I almost switched off. She was going to talk about supermarkets and bulk-buying, wasn't she?"

"—with the eggs sold at the roadsides," she finished. "Mrs. Collarcott's are best."

"Where would I find them?"

She roared with laughter. "You might find them in your garden! Her hens are the ones in the field behind your house, you see, and hens have a habit of laying where they shouldn't. Her house is along your lane – thatched, with pink-washed walls. You can't miss it, Helen."

I didn't ask how she knew my name. I had more interesting enquiries to make. "That'll be near those gates—" I fished.

"Now, were you wanting me to save you a paper every day?" she asked briskly. "*The Times*, is it? Or *The Telegraph*?"

I ordered *The Guardian*. Shaking her head, she gave a sad smile and wrote in her book. I might have been back with my grandmother, when she wrote in an identical ledger. I'd be very surprised if I got the paper of my choice.

"And what fish would you like for Friday? A nice bit of cod?"

"Salmon?"

To my amazement, she raised her eyebrows, and touched the side of her nose. "From the river."

I knew better than to comment. "Tell me," I said, as I popped all the change into the Air Ambulance tin, "who would have been kind enough to have left some wonderful fresh vegetables on my doorstep?"

"Could have been anyone," she smiled.

So now I had regular provisions and a daily paper, but I was none the wiser about my gifts. Or about those gates.

Another inch and I'd have cared about neither – ever again. I was ambling gently home – on the correct side of the road, facing oncoming traffic – when a car approached me from behind so fast that I was literally swept off my feet. Staggering, I just avoided the ditch. The car was a top-of-the-range BMW – plenty around in the London suburbs, but a tad out of place round here, where if you went expensive, you went four-wheel drive. It didn't take long to establish that Mr. Beamer and Paradise Mews were intimately linked, largely because whoever I questioned would drop their eyes and fidget, like five-year-olds caught picking their noses.

A trip for autumn clothes took me to Taunton, and curiosity took me into County Hall for a look at recent applications for planning permission in the vicinity of my house. I came up with some story – largely true – about how I'd been left my new home and had no idea how I might extend it. Or sell it. Something like that. It must have been convincing. Despite mutterings about written notice, the clerk produced various plans, none of which seemed particularly relevant – replacement farm buildings, a new telecoms mast, that sort of thing.

At last I asked point blank about Paradise Mews.

"Drawings submitted by Mr. Crompton Gledstone?"

"Yes. Those, please." Now was not the moment to comment on his name, preposterous as his proposals. Were the plans really for a stable? Well, horses and mews had a long and no doubt honourable association, though, like the BMW, were surely more what you'd expect in an urban setting. Mews were where posh people used to keep their carriages, horses and grooms. Well, any groom tending his equine friends in these mews would have thought he'd died and gone, yes, to Paradise. As would the horses.

I had this naïve belief that horses were outside creatures. I'd seen them, even in the dead of winter, covered by those big waterproof capes, munching away in fields. Some, without capes, seemed simply to have become remarkably hairy at that time of year – presumably they did as other animals did, growing a thick, insulated coat of their own. Any horses over-wintering in Paradise Mews would positively need shaving. Unless they were Arab thoroughbreds used to much warmer climes, I couldn't see how they would cope with underfloor heating and double-glazing, or even the sauna, rather larger than my kitchen. I'd heard that swimming was good for horses – but to build them a swimming pool, heated, of course? How silly of me – that would be for the use of whoever resided in what was labelled 'Staff Quarters'. These were found in a suite of first-floor rooms running the entire length of the block: four double bedrooms, all with en suite bathrooms, naturally, a staff kitchen and a staff sitting room, the floor-to-ceiling windows of which offered – on three sides – views of the surrounding countryside. Mr. Crompton Bledstone clearly valued his staff as highly as he valued his horses. How touching.

No, the clerk assured me: planning permission hadn't yet been granted. In fact, the plans had been rejected once and were to be resubmitted soon. As someone living in the vicinity, I should submit, the clerk told me, my responses to the plans in writing before the next planning committee meeting. He even wrote down the correct reference for me. Thanking him, I headed briskly out.

Crompton Gledstone. A name like that would have rung bells had I ever come across it before. Forgetting the thick tweeds, cosy sweaters and waterproofs, I headed instead for the library and its reliable Internet. I wanted information now!

If I hadn't heard of the man, the financial press certainly had. Crompton turned out to be part of his surname, his given name being Giles. I'd always thought that a nice, reassuring name – maybe a Victorian novel's hero – but it was clearly deceptive in his case. Mr. Giles Crompton Gledstone, proud owner of the latest Beamer and of Paradise Mews and of a property empire I'd never heard of, was not a nice man to know. He went round the whole of the country snapping up rural properties, raising the sitting tenants' rent to enormous heights or persuading them to leave (somehow this never took long) and leasing their homes out to incomers at prices that no native villager could afford. He bought up shops to convert into more bijou homes, and snaffled up pubs to convert them into exclusive restaurants. What an asset to the village he and his house – correction, mews! – would be.

I must put pen to paper – and do some serious thinking.

Fortunately, the thinking fitted in well with taming the back garden. Soon a dozen or so bags awaited Mr. Taylor.

As he loaded the last one, he pointed out that my apple trees were diseased. I knew they were in poor condition – the few apples the birds had spared me were bitter and tough – but I didn't realise that cutting them down and burning them was the only solution. I spread my hands – there wasn't enough room for a decent bonfire.

"You want to saw up the trunks and best branches for your winter fires," he said. "Can't always rely on the electric, you know, not if it snows hard."

I swallowed. I didn't know if I could use logs in that grim little fireplace, and I wasn't at all sure about the chimney. But I wouldn't panic – if I knew my villagers, he'd have a perfect solution. "And the rest?"

"November's not all that long away – you want to get on to the Scouts," he said, hefting the last sack of assorted nettles and convolvulus. "Over Prestcombe way."

"Isn't there a troop in the village?"

"No hut."

At last I could come into my own – all those years of planning and guiding projects would not go to waste after all. "Shouldn't we get together and build one? Not just a Scout hut, but a proper village hall? We could raise some of the money ourselves with craft and produce sales and get sponsorship for events. I know about Lottery Fund applications and—"

To my amazement, he spat. "There's one as wants to build us one all by hisself. At least, throw some cash around for others to do the work. The bas— sorry, but I get worked up, see."

Clearly any expressions of delight would be inappropriate to say the least. He was talking about Mr. Paradise Mews, wasn't he? Mr. Crompton Gledstone.

"Like as if his cash would buy us! Mind you, it might make a difference to them as matter, they say." He gestured back-handers and spat again.

"This person – the one trying to bribe us – does he live in the village?"

"Live here? No! But that doesn't stop him buying folk out. And then selling their houses. Well, you must have seen the asking prices. People born and bred here afford their own place? Not a chance. But he'll never be one of us, never call this place home, not if I have anything to do with it." One more spit and he was in his pick-up cab, pulling away. "And I'll send Fred Babcombe over at the end of next week to sweep that chimney of yours. Don't light a fire till he's been, mind."

The following morning I found runner beans and a bag of just-ripening tomatoes on my step. Rosy-Cheeks – whom I now knew was Carol – was cycling slowly past as I picked them up.

"I've got a fairy godmother," I said, as she stopped by the gate. "Hey, what's wrong?"

"Oh, I'm all right," she said, wincing as she put her foot to the ground.

As she staggered I hurried towards her. "No wonder you're in pain! Look at you!" Her right ankle was tightly strapped, and purple bruises stretched up her leg. There were deep grazes on her knees – the sort kids get in playgrounds, but not respectable women in their sixties. "And your hands?"

She spread her fingers gingerly.

"An accident?"

"If you can call it that!"

"A black BMW?"

She stared, not quite blankly.

"A big, posh car? Maybe the one that nearly had me in a ditch the other day?"

"Maybe." But she was already back on her bike and pedalling away.

Leaning on the gate, I watched her on her way. And thought a great deal.

* * *

Next time I went to the shop, I managed to catch Mrs. Gaye on her own. I talked about standing up and being counted and not taking injustice lying down. OK, we'd been discussing a court case in all the newspapers, but she knew what I meant. Afraid of pushing too hard, I paid for my cabbage and, with a final word of regret that the village had never yet managed to raise funds for a hall without outside interference, I left the yeast to work.

* * *

I'd thought, as a townie, that I'd find the countryside quiet. Not a bit of it. Screeching barn owls woke me sweating in terror each night; other owls merely called a polite "to-wit, to-woo". Dogs barked at whatever gave them doggy nightmares – and please don't mention mating foxes, and their human screams. And there were shots – dawn or dusk. Perhaps someone was as incensed by the inane coo-cooing of the wood pigeons as I was, or furious with lettuce-munching rabbits. Or perhaps, Mrs. Gaye said, as I picked up my inevitable *Times*, they were shooting pheasants.

"I hope they remember there's an aitch in the word," I laughed, "and don't start shooting us peasants."

The shop went very quiet. I'd obviously committed a dreadful solecism. Or had I? I'll swear someone winked at me, albeit fleetingly, before they ducked down to pick up some bleach.

Another source of noise was farm machinery. Even I hadn't been naïve enough to expect scythes and horse-drawn ploughs – why, back in the nineteenth century Hardy had written about mechanised threshers – but I was amazed by the sheer size of the vehicles and their trailers and other attachments. Apparently these days farmers didn't own such heavy plant themselves; they hired it, farm by farm, in rotation. If you came on one of the behemoths on the move, you might have to reverse a mile or so up a narrow line to get out of the way. So, out of consideration to other road-users, many contractors moved them round in the late dusk or early dawn: huge diggers, enormous combine harvesters, mammoth ploughs.

It was time to write to the County Council about Paradise Mews, outlining my objections. I made up my log fire – no hint of smoke, thanks to Fred Babcombe, just the wonderful smell of applewood. In keeping with the ambience, perhaps I should employ pen and ink, but after all my years hurling words on to a computer, the only way I could produce a well-organised letter was on my laptop. In brief, I said that any fool could see that the council was being conned, A horse might – *might* – occupy the ground floor of the Mews for half an hour but it'd soon be in a field, their accommodation seized by the humans who'd intended to live there all along. I wanted to add a purple PS: *If the property is built and we suddenly find our councillors swanning round in new cars, we shall know what to think.*

How fortunate I had been writing extremely rude letters in the most measured and polite language most of my working life.

* * *

The date for the Planning Committee meeting was announced. I put up a notice or two in the shop, just to encourage everyone. And I typed up and printed leaflets which I distributed to every house in the parish – even those well off the beaten track. On the appointed evening, villagers arrived in Taunton in force, those of us with cars ferrying those without. Some of us made it into the council chamber; those who didn't waited outside, their chanting and jeering audible inside. When Mr. Crompton Gledstone was late, a rumour burgeoned that he was demanding a police escort. Perhaps he was refused one. At any rate, he never appeared.

The Planning Committee conceded outline permission, but demanded major changes to the interior. It would still, however, look like an extremely des res with a pretentious entrance. What would the horses make of it?

And how would the villagers react?

After all that passion, I was expecting people to chain themselves to railings or organise a lynch mob. To my surprise, however, many were philosophical. We drove home soberly, but as if by instinct gathered in the bar of the George and Dragon. To accommodate us all they had to clear out all the tables and prop open the doors to the snug. Fresh sandwiches appeared by magic. Locally-brewed cider flowed freely. In any other circumstances I'd have said we were celebrating something.

Or holding a wake.

* * *

During the winter, my garden subdued if not yet conquered, my pantry shelves full of preserves and pickles bought at the now regular fundraising events, my diary bulging with the details of sponsors, I could pause a little and look around. My house was freshly painted, inside and out. I'd bought paintings from a talented young artist, now off studying in Birmingham. Someone's aunt had run up new curtains. The wiring was safe. Yes, it was time to resume my walks – just as soon as I had completed all the documentation need to apply for a Heritage Fund grant for a barn that would make a wonderful village centre.

Sometimes I'd tramp a whole day, sometimes seeing no one, occasionally greeted by a friendly wave. Or I'd be invited into an isolated farm kitchen for a cup of tea and a slice – "Oh, have another, do!" – of home-made cake. Then one day, on a field five or six miles from even a single-track road, I came across a field that interested me. Something seemed to have disturbed the surface – though if we hadn't had such a dry autumn the turf and gorse would have covered it again completely.

As I looked, a man strolled over, stiff-legged, as if spoiling for a fight. Then, recognising me as one of the new village finance committee, he nodded politely.

"Afternoon, Mr. Doone. How are things?" It didn't do to rush in with questions. He'd know what I'd been looking at.

"Middling," he said, "pretty middling." He bent to scratch his dog. "One of my old horses died. Big, strong old lad. No, he'd not pulled a plough in years, but he was part of the family, like. Couldn't find it in me to send him to the knacker's."

"So you buried him here?"

"Ah. Sentimental old fool, I am."

I sighed in sympathy. If you had to bury a cart horse, of course you'd need a grave at least that big. Of course. I shivered.

"I'd best be turning for home," I said. "It'll be dark soon."

"You want to take care – those narrow lanes."

I touched my bright-wear waistcoat and flourished my torch. "But they seem to have been a bit quieter lately."

"Ah. Trippers have left for the year."

"And that black BMW and its crazy driver seem to have left too."

"Damned Jehu," he agreed. "City type." He spat like Mr. Taylor. "Couldn't adapt to country ways, that's what. He'll be back where he belongs." He touched his cap, called his dog, and melted into the twilight.

As I too turned for home, I tried not to look again at that patch.

* * *

My route took me past Paradise Mews. The handsome gateposts looked almost forlorn in the half-light, couple of brambles already snaking over them. The gates swung to and fro, to and fro. I closed them firmly. That was it, then. I went on my way. There was a village hall fund-raising meeting in a couple of hours, and as Treasurer I mustn't be late.

I should be having one last glance over the accounts, not speculating on the fate of Crompton Gledstone.

Gunshots. Odd looks. The righteous hatred felt by tenants bled dry and families left homeless. Young people who could never hope to live in the place of their birth. And I had fanned the flames, urging the downtrodden to fight for justice. His failure to appear at the council meeting.

A burial site big enough for a BMW, especially if it was torched first.

I told myself I was being too fanciful. No, he must be harassing innocent people in other parts of his kingdom.

These days people didn't just disappear – road-side cameras sprouted everywhere. Phone records and mast triangulation – though there was a shortage of phone masts and hardly any cameras in the entire area. Even so, there'd be credit card records. When his friends alerted the police, we'd all have been questioned.

But perhaps men like that didn't have any friends, just dodgy associates only too glad to see the back of him. A cowed wife, brow-beaten servants – now they might be relishing freedom.

I gathered up all my papers, but hesitated, looking round my territory with a satisfied smile. What was it Mr. Taylor had said? "Sometimes everyone needs a good clear out. Shift all the rubbish. Be ruthless. Start again afresh."

Original Sin

Gillian Linscott

Pensarn, Betws-y-Coed.
23 July 1866. 6.55 a.m.

I have been wrestling in prayer all night, kneeling at the window that looks onto the woods, beseeching Him to let me see clearly His will. Just now as the morning mist rose from the hillside, my prayer was granted. He has shown me that it is my clear duty as a Christian to kill Edward Bowman.

CALM as a sheep grazing, Joshua Green blotted the little blackbound diary given to him by his mother, stowed it away in his case and pushed the case back under his narrow and undisturbed bed. Moving stiffly because the warm and comfortable feeling that was in his mind hadn't yet spread to his knees, he walked across to the toilet table with its china basin and ewer, unbuttoned his shirt and hesitated for a moment before pulling it down from his shoulders. He had never in his life before worn a shirt, an ordinary day shirt, from one sunrise to the next. He had never in his life before stayed awake the whole night. The strangeness of that twisted at his stomach, although the decision itself hadn't troubled it at all. Then, resolute, he stripped off the shirt, sponged his face, arms and chest in the cold and moss-smelling water that he'd watched the girl carrying in a pail from the stream behind the cottage, dressed and went down to breakfast.

Even that early, there was somebody before him in the cramped little room, standing by the window and looking out on the road and the other side of the valley. He was dressed for walking in breeches and thick woollen stockings, and even from the back view there was a holiday air about him, practically on tiptoe to rush out of the house and up the hills, the sun catching his yellow hair and side whiskers. He turned, beaming, as he heard the other man coming in.

"Morning, Green. Did you sleep well? Isn't this grand? Do you think there's something special they put into the air in Wales?"

"Good morning, Bowman."

Not answering his questions, hardly looking at him after the first glance, Joshua moved over to the table with its snowy white cloth. There was a loaf of white bread, a bowl of brown boiled eggs, a pitcher of milk and a slab of golden butter. No teapot though. A night wrestling in prayer had left Joshua thirsty for hot, strong tea. He'd have remarked on the absence of it if there'd been anybody to hear him but Bowman. As it was he moved over to the door, intending to remind their landlady Mrs. Pritchard of her duties, and had to step back quickly when the door opened and Mrs. Pritchard herself sailed in bearing the big brown teapot. Her daughter Myfanwy came in her wake, carrying a tray of china and cutlery and Edward Bowman was at the door in a moment, holding it wide open for the girl. She smiled at him, blushed and looked away. In twenty years perhaps she'd be as rounded and comfortable as her mother, but now, at sixteen or so, any artist needing a model for a milkmaid or wood nymph could have set his easel down in the little back yard of Pensarn.

Mrs. Prichard said, "If the other gentleman wants more eggs when he comes down, tell him to knock on the kitchen door. The hens are laying enough to feed a regiment."

Then she said something in Welsh to the girl, who was arranging cups and plates very precisely in a row, with the occasional sideways glance at Bowman.

"I'm telling Myfanwy not to forget to bring in your lunch. Made some of those little cakes you like specially, she has."

"The raisin cakes? That was kind of you, Myfanwy."

She gave a little shiver of the shoulders when she heard him say her name. Joshua lunged past her for a teacup, spoiling the neat row, filled his cup too full, spilled tea on the white cloth. At another word from her mother the girl left the room and came back with a dish rag in one hand, a small canvas satchel in the other.

"Is that my lunch? Thank you."

The girl handed it to Bowman like a precious thing.

Her mother said: "There's some of the ham you liked last night in a piece of bread, a bit of cheese and lemonade in a bottle."

Bowman opened the satchel and rummaged like a child in a bran tub.

"And Myfanwy's raisin cakes."

He drew out a crumpled brown paper bag with exaggerated care, undid a corner and peeped inside. The eyes of both the women were on him. Green drank tea and stared intently at an engraving of a ruined abbey on the wall above the sideboard.

"Four, five, six of them, all for me."

He closed the bag and stood with it in his hand, smiling.

"The question is… the great question is…"

Myfanwy giggled like a child and her mother smiled, accepting the game.

"…can I wait until lunchtime? The spirit may be willing but in the matter of raisin cakes the flesh is all too weak."

Green screwed his eyes up and wished he could do the same with his ears. How could a man seeking to be ordained into the Church of England use the holy writ to banter over cakes? But then, Bowman was so deep in the mire that this was a small thing to him. The bag rustled again. He could tell from the pitch of the girl's giggling that Bowman had fished out one of the little cakes.

"The raisin toward my mouth. Come, let me bite thee."

At least not the Bible this time, but Shakespeare too deserved respect. Bowman had no respect for anything. In spite of himself, Green turned. Bowman had taken an actor's stance, feet apart, holding the little cake at arm's length, a golden puff with a plump, tea-soaked raisin sticking out from the top like a… like a raisin on a cake. He advanced it towards his mouth, eyes shining.

His shirtsleeve slid back and the sun glinted on the fair hairs on his arm.

Green thought: He's probably hairy all over. That's why he can believe what he does.

Bowman bit, closed his eyes in mock ecstasy, munched. Green turned away, the tea rising back up his throat in disgust.

* * *

The two women left the room and there was silence until, ten minutes later, a third man came in. He was in his fifties, a little stooped, in black jacket and clerical collar. The two young men, who had been sitting at opposite ends of the table, stood up respectfully and hoped he'd slept well.

"Tolerably, tolerably. I see Mrs. Pritchard's hens have favoured us as usual. No thank you, Green. There are more than enough for my appetite." Several weeks ago, back in Oxford, the Reverend Peter Crediton had suggested to six of his more attentive theological students that they might make up a reading party in the long vacation, to enjoy the beauties of nature, take a little healthy exercise and read the New Testament together in Greek. The village of Betws-y-Coed with its woods and healthy air from the mountains of Snowdonia a few miles away had proved ideal for all three purposes, with Crediton, Green and Bowman lodging with Mrs. Pritchard and the other four men in the house next door. As Revd Crediton pointed out, they had a chance to know each other's minds and characters in these peaceful surroundings in a way that was not possible in the bustle of an Oxford term. In most cases those minds and characters had proved as compatible among the woods and rocks as in the cloisters and lecture halls. Bowman was known for his odd views, but liked for his good humour and sporting nature. But Green, although orthodox in his views, was regarded as an odd fish at Oxford, studious to excess and fond of his own company. When they found themselves lodging together at Pensarn, Bowman had made an effort to be friendly but was far from inconsolable when it was rebuffed. Bowman had other interests – too many, some said. Geology was a passion, also botany and archaeology and insects. He'd go wandering in the woods or even up the mountains from sunrise to sunset, equipped with his packed lunch, his collecting tins and his pocket edition of the Greek Testament. Crediton, noticing Bowman's walking clothes and lunch satchel, said he supposed he was planning one of his expeditions.

"Yes, sir. There are some old lead mines the Romans used in the woods. I thought I might root around and see what I could find. I'll be back for our teatime reading."

"Very well."

Revd Crediton glanced towards Green, who was apparently intent on buttering a piece of bread at the far end of the table. Bowman obligingly picked up the message.

"You'd be very welcome to come along too, Green. There's plenty of lunch for both of us."

Green said no thank you without looking up. Bowman shrugged, asked them to excuse him and picked up his satchel. They heard the door open and close and the clatter on the step as he got into his nailed boots, then the dog barking and rattling its chain as he strode across the yard.

Crediton said: "You should have gone with him. A little recreation does no harm."

"Shall a man touch pitch and not be defiled?"

"I'd hardly call Bowman pitch. As you know, I deplore the views that he's fallen into as much as anyone. Still, a young man's opinions are feathers in the wind. It's our duty to reason with him and pray for him and bring him back to a true frame of mind."

"He's beyond that."

"Nobody's beyond God's grace."

Green stared at his plate and said nothing. Revd Crediton sighed and wiped his mouth with a napkin. On the way out of the room he put a hand on Green's shoulder.

"You're reading too much. You'll harm your eyes. Get out into God's good air, like Bowman."

* * *

As promised, Bowman was back for their teatime reading and discussion. At the end of it, under Revd Crediton's eye, Green went up to him.

"Thank you for inviting me to come with you this morning. I think I should like to see the lead mines after all."

Bowman tried to look delighted.

"Good. We can't get all the way up there and back before supper, but there's a bit of a crag we could climb just outside the village for a view of where they are. Get your boots and I'll meet you outside."

Crediton beamed on both of them. Green was silent walking up the woodland path but Bowman chattered on happily, about the trees, the view, the quite possibly Roman buckle he'd found on a pile of stones by one of the mines. The path sloped steeply up to an outcrop of rock and he helped Green to scramble up it, showing him footholds on ledges and handholds on scrubby bushes. At the top Bowman put a hand on Green's shoulder and turned him towards the waves of forest rising into the distance.

"You see that pile of stones up there? That's the spoil heap from the nearest mine. The old Romans must have had a road up to it, but it's no more than a fox track now."

He pointed towards other mines further into the forest, invisible to them. Green looked where he was pointing, but his shoulder stayed tense under Bowman's hand. After a while he pulled away and walked to the other side of the outcrop, overlooking the slate roofs of the village.

Bowman warned: "Be careful there. It's a sheer drop."

"May I ask you something? Something personal?"

Green was still facing away from him. The voice was tense, high.

"Ask away, old chap."

"About what we were discussing."

"I don't know that there's any more to discuss. You and Crediton and the others take one line, I take another."

"Not the main question. I know you're mistaken on that as surely as I live and breathe." Bowman grimaced, but didn't rise to the bait. "No, it's what you might call a contingent question."

"Well, ask it."

"What you believe, mistakenly believe, would you preach it from your pulpit?"

"It would be my duty as a rational man and a Christian."

"Would you teach it to the children in your Sunday school?"

Bowman started to laugh but stopped himself, realising how seriously the other man was taking it.

"Yes. Adapting it, of course, to their childish understanding. But I think I'd owe it to them to show the wonder of how God works and the ingenuity of man in understanding part of His design."

"'Whoso shall offend one of these little ones which believe in me, it were better for him that a millstone were hanged about his neck, and that he were drowned in the depths of the sea.'"

There was something in the voice and the stiffness of Green's figure against the evening sky that took away Bowman's urge to laugh.

"I think we should be getting back down, old man. It gets darks quite soon under the trees."

Without replying or turning, Green sat on the edge of the rock and began to slide down.

"Not that way, for goodness' sake! Round there, the way we came up."

But Green continued to slide until only the back of his head and his shoulders were visible from where Bowman was standing.

"No, don't move. You'll break your neck."

Bowman rushed across and tried to hook his hands under Green's armpits to haul him up. Green twisted suddenly sideways and locked both his arms round one of Bowman's. The surprise of it almost tipped Bowman over the edge of the rock.

"What are you doing? Let go. You'll have us both over."

Roosting birds, alarmed, flew up screeching from the treetops below them. The clutch of Green's fingers on Bowman's arm tightened. "Let go!"

With a grunting effort, Bowman threw his weight back and tore his arm from Green's grip. Green, without a word or cry, had slid almost out of sight by the time Bowman recovered and caught him by the collar of his jacket. It was good fabric, from the best ecclesiastical tailor in Oxford. It held and Bowman landed Green like a fish on the top of the rock. For a long minute they stayed there, not saying anything, Green kneeling, his head sunk on his chest, Bowman sitting with his knees drawn up, sucking the deep scratches Green's fingernails had gouged on the back of his hand. After a while Bowman spoke.

"Do you think you can make it down now? I'll help you."

He guided Green down the side of the rock, going slowly. When they were back on the path through the woods he spoke again.

"We don't need to say anything to them about this back at the house. Not everyone's got a head for heights."

Green, trudging along, head down, didn't answer.

* * *

As soon as they opened the front door of Pensarn and walked into the lamplight, Mrs. Pritchard and her daughter came hurrying up the passage in a flurry of Welsh and English, Revd Crediton not far behind them.

"Worried, so worried we've been, with you out so late and what's happened."

Myfanwy was actually in tears. Bowman and Green drew back, both believing that the events on the crag had somehow got home before them.

"A big desperate man, and no further away than Capel Curig. Nothing to lose now he knows they'll hang him anyway and hungry as a beast of the wild."

Mrs. Pitchard went running on, until Revd Crediton caught his pupils' questioning looks and managed to get past her to explain.

"It seems there's a murderer loose. A quarryman from Llanberis. He killed one of his fellow workers in a drunken brawl last week. Yesterday he attacked a farmer at Capel Curig. Quite naturally with the two of you out late, Mrs. Pritchard was concerned."

"I'm sorry we worried you, Mrs. Pritchard. I can promise you we didn't meet a murderer."

Myfanwy glanced up at him and said something to her mother in Welsh.

"Is that blood on your hand there?"

Bowman moved smartly away from the lamplight.

"Nothing serious. Are we too late for supper? After that walk, I'm as hungry as a beast of the wild myself."

Green said he wasn't hungry and went straight up to his room, leaving Revd Crediton and Bowman to their supper together. Afterwards they read a little. As Crediton collected his candle to go upstairs for the night he raised something that had clearly been on his mind all evening.

"You know, Bowman, I think you should be careful in your wanderings. Without sharing all the fears of the womenfolk, it is a fact that there's a desperate man at large."

"I should hope, sir, that I'd be a match for some brute of a quarryman."

Crediton looked at him for a while over the candle flame. "It's right for a young man like you to glory in the strength of his body and mind. Nevertheless, I should urge on you a proper diffidence. You might, with advantage, pay a little more respect to the opinions of your elders."

They both knew that he was talking less about the quarryman than the other matter that loomed over their holiday – Bowman's stubbornness in his young man's belief.

"I'll try to remember, sir."

"Do. Try – and pray. But it was charitable of you to walk with Green. We must try to stop him overtaxing his brain."

"Yes, sir. I hope you sleep well."

Pensarn. Betws-y-Coed.
23 July 1866. 11 p.m.

O God, who hast shown me my duty, now show me the way to do it. When he led me up to the high place I thought it was Thy chosen way, but his animal strength overcame me. O Lord, strengthen the arm of Thy servant against the ungodly.

24 July. 5 a.m.

I have had the most terrible dream. I think it is from the influence of Bowman. The very presence of the man sucks evil into the house through every crevice. I dreamed I was awake and that the girl came in with her hair down over her shoulders and her front. When she saw me she smiled and parted her hair back with her hands from the front of her and there were two of those cakes with raisins. "Eat," she said. She said it in Welsh, but I understood all the same. I won't sleep again tonight. I won't sleep again until it's done and over. The light is coming up over the trees. I shall go and walk and pray in the clean air outside where his filth can't touch me.

The road through the village was white with dust in the early light. Green walked along it in the direction of the mountains, taking quivering lungfuls of the morning air. A noise on the road behind him had him spinning round, but it was only the carrier with his pony and trap. They overtook him at a fast walk and the carrier wished him good morning in Welsh then, taking a closer look, in English.

"Are you one of the young gentlemen staying with Mrs. Pritchard?"

Green, not wishing for conversation, said shortly that he was.

"Would you give her this for me? I was going to leave it for her on the way back, look, but seeing I met you she might as well have it early."

He rummaged under his seat and passed down a small, blue, paper parcel into Green's reluctant hands.

"Don't drop it, now. Tell her, the chemist says it will only need a drop in his mouth and it will see him off as clean as anything, no mess or pain."

Green, fingers not yet closing on the parcel, asked what it was.

"For that old dog of hers that's taken to biting people. Cheaper than wasting a cartridge, cleaner too, but only a drop, mind."

Green asked the question again, more urgently.

"Cyanide, that is. Tell her I'll bring those knitting needles she wanted when I come back down. Good morning."

He raised his whip and clattered away. Green stood there for a long time in the open road holding the parcel, then went under a tree, took his hat off and fell down on his knees.

* * *

At breakfast, Bowman was determined on another day at the lead mines. If the spoil heap had yielded a buckle, why not a Roman sword and helmet? Revd Crediton advised caution on grounds both of archaeology and safety but didn't forbid the expedition. The quarryman, they thought, would stick closer to the farms where food was to be had and the village people probably overrated the danger. Neither of them paid much attention to Green, beyond observing that he was paler than ever. They hardly noticed his absence when he left the room. He shut the door behind him and went down the narrow passageway towards the kitchen. The door was half open. He hesitated a moment, then flung it back.

"Oh!"

Myfanwy was alone in the room. Bowman's lunch satchel was open on the dresser and she was about to tuck a paper bag into it.

Green said: "I'll take that to him." His voice was harsh. She stared at him, alarmed, as if she didn't understand. "I'll take his lunch to him."

Without answering she put the bag into the satchel and buckled the straps. As she came towards Green he put out his hand for it but she kept walking towards him, clutching it to her chest. If he'd been prepared to stand his ground he might have got it from her, but the memory of his dream came back to him and the thought of any contact with her, even of his jacket against her apron, was horrible. He shrank back against the door frame. She walked past him as if he weren't there and into the breakfast room. He heard Bowman's voice raised in hearty thanks and felt his whole body shrivelling with contamination and failure. He was watching from his window as Bowman went across the yard and into the trees, lunch satchel on his shoulder.

* * *

The sun rose high over the valley. Flies buzzed around the chicken yard at the back of the cottage and were yapped at by the old dog. From the kitchen, Mrs. Pritchard shouted at it to be quiet and cursed the carrier. High up on the hillside, where the woods gave way to spoil heaps of an old mine, Bowman felt the sun hot on his shirted back. So far he'd found a piece of rock that might have been a Stone Age axe but probably wasn't, and a second buckle that somehow looked less Roman than the first. His lunch satchel was a long way below him, out of sight behind a slab of rock. The noise of his nailed boots clattering over the rocks seemed to him to fill the valley but once, in the silence when he paused to look at something, he thought he heard a sound of stones clinking below him.

He called, "Hello. Hello down there."

No answer. He waited for a while, called again, but there was no other sound. He worked on until, at the top of the tumble of loose rocks, he came to a little plateau and a cavern behind it that he thought might be the mouth of the old mine. Heather and bilberries grew round the plateau and the view out over the woods made him catch his breath. It was already past lunchtime and he decided he'd eat there, with the woods spread out under his feet and the heather round him. It took him only a few minutes to get down to his satchel, rather longer to bring it back up to his rock perch. By the time he was sitting down and starting to ease the cork out of the lemonade bottle, his legs were aching and his thirst was heroic.

A grunt behind him from the cavern mouth. Such a grunt that, before he turned, he thought that wild boars might have survived in the land. As he turned he saw and remembered at the same time. The man looked as solid as the rock pile itself. Almost endlessly large he seemed to Bowman from his sitting position, shoulders as broad as the dark gape in the rock behind him. He came forward in a lumbering walk, round face jutting forward with a stubble of black beard. His smell came surging in front of him, like an earth closet in the heat. Bowman's mind told him, *The quarryman. The murderer*. But the muscles of his stomach leapt with the excitement of a stranger discovery. He'd come looking for Romans, but here was something older. Caveman himself from the very dawn of humanity, living, breathing, smelling. He felt no fear – or only fear so smothered by excitement that it didn't matter. But part of his mind must have warned Bowman that if the quarryman continued on his present course he'd be knocked off his perch and down on the rocks. His hand went up in a gesture half of warning, half of greeting. He'd forgotten that it was still holding the lemonade bottle. Then the bottle wasn't in his hand any more. It was up above him, in the paw of the quarryman, glinting in the sun. Dazzled, Bowman heard a clink of tooth against glass, a gulp, then a tinkle of glass to rock. When he managed to see against the glare of the sun there was blood round the bristled lips and the neck of the lemonade bottle was jagged. In his need to drink the quarryman had broken it and was pouring the liquid down his throat, careless of glass fragments. When the last drop had gone he flung the bottle down the spoil heap, shook his head and seemed to notice Bowman for the first time.

"I'm afraid there's no more lemonade," Bowman said, "but there's plenty of food. We could share it."

A missionary surrounded by a cannibal tribe might have spoken as reasonably, and with as little effect. The quarryman stared down at him, as if he didn't understand the language, then scooped up the satchel and tucked it under his arm.

"You want it all? Well, I suppose that's understandable. And I, as you see, am not strong enough to prevent you."

Bowman was a tolerable athlete in rowing and boxing but in a struggle with that mass of desperation wouldn't have lasted a moment. He marvelled at his own coolness.

"You're the stronger, after all. You eat and I go hungry."

Another uncomprehending stare, then the quarryman pushed past him and was away down the rock pile, jumping from slab to slab, as sure as any animal in its native habitat. Bowman waited until he was out of sight and the slap of his boots on the rocks had died away, then stood up, feeling as charged with life as after a swim in a cold river. He found a way down from his plateau without following the route the quarryman had taken and was soon on a path in the woods. He walked at random, his mind racing. A question of adaptation. He is stronger therefore he eats. How many generations of him before the moral man comes in? What little quirk or fluke of nature, magnified age after age, makes from a brute who knows nothing but his own appetites a man who can see and understand and exult in the grand design that uses both of us? And, above all, how privileged I am to see, telescoped into a few hours, the whole story of our development from when an ape first walked upright to rational man. From the quarryman… to me. A thought came to him and he laughed.

"He may be fitter for survival here, but after all I don't suppose he'd do very well at Balliol."

* * *

The quarryman got to the bottom of the spoil heap, glanced round then chose a seat on a slab of rock. The bread and ham went in seconds, scarcely chewed. He munched the hard boiled eggs with fragments of brown shell sticking to the blood on his lips. Then, searching in the bottom of the satchel, he came to the paper bag and opened it.

"Don't eat those."

The quarryman blinked. The voice, shrill with tension, was coming from behind a rock opposite where he was sitting. Automatically his hand went on foraging in the bag and came out holding a yellow raisin cake, as insubstantial as a dandelion in his fingers.

"Don't eat it. It will kill you."

The quarryman couldn't see anything to fear in the thin, dark-suited figure that came out from behind the rock. He stared at Green as if he were no more than a new variety of insect and didn't pause in what he was doing. The hand with the raisin cake went up to his mouth.

"No. It's not for you. No."

Green, as he shouted, flung himself across the few yards that separated him from the quarryman, grabbed at the raised forearm with both his hands and tried to cling to it. Without any apparent effort, still with the puzzled expression on his face, the quarryman pulled his arm away, dropped the cake, picked up a piece of rock and hammered it down with all his force into Green's forehead. Green fell backwards without a word or a groan and blood spread round his head. The quarryman put down the rock, picked up the raisin cake before the blood could get to it and stuffed it whole into his mouth.

* * *

Bowman's walk took him a long way from the spoil heap, so far into the woods that he didn't know where he was. The exultation of the meeting stayed with him through the long afternoon and it was only when the sun began to dip that he started looking for the way back to his lodgings. Once his feet were on the familiar path down to the village he began to think what a story it would make for Crediton and Green over their supper. Further down still, when the roofs of the village were visible in the last of the light, he had another thought. "I suppose I'm going to have to inform a magistrate."

That thought took away some of his pleasure in the day. The last of it went when he came out above Pensarn and saw that something serious was happening. The lamps were lit in every window of the cottage and a cart and a gig standing in the road outside. He could hear urgent voices rising up, sense the panic and bustle. It occurred to him that they must be so worried about his absence that they were forming a search party and that his day would end after all in embarrassment. He hurried down, heavy-footed, to be met by Revd Crediton with a lantern at the back door.

"Bowman. Oh, God be thanked. We thought the brute had killed you as well."

His heart plunged.

"As well, sir? Who else?"

"Poor Green." Then, as Bowman staggered from the shock of it, "You'd better come inside and sit down."

* * *

They sat on either side of the dining table with its red cover, the lamp between them. Bowman stripped his adventure to its nakedness.

"The quarryman stole my lunch."

"Yes."

"Did he kill poor Green before that?"

"No. Afterwards."

"How do you know that, sir?"

Revd Crediton was silent for a while, hands locked together in the lamplight, then: "The murderer is dead too. They found him fallen across Green's body. There were the remains of a cake in his mouth."

"One of Myfanwy's raisin cakes?"

"I'm afraid so. There were some more of them in your satchel."

Bowman tried to stop his mind from somersaulting, to make sense of this.

"What are you telling me, sir? That the brute murdered Green and instantly ate a cake and choked on it?"

He couldn't fathom the expression in his tutor's eyes, as if the thing were somehow Bowman's fault.

"He murdered Green and he ate the cake, but it wasn't simply choking on it that killed him."

"I don't understand, sir."

"Cyanide. It was in the cake. The first bite would have been fatal. We think it was in the other cakes in the satchel as well, but they're on their way to the coroner."

Bowman bent his head into his hands.

"But why should Myfanwy put cyanide in my cakes? I thought she liked me."

"Not the girl. Green did it. We found the empty bottle in his pocket."

"Green? Why?"

"To kill you. He must have followed you. Did you leave that satchel out of sight?"

"Yes, for a long time. But why did Green want to kill me?"

Revd Crediton's hand went into his pocket and came out holding a small black book.

"After we found the bottle we looked in Green's room. This is his diary. We shall have to show it to the coroner, but I believe you should see it first."

Bowman took it reluctantly. "Does it say why?"

"He believed that your opinions on a certain matter were so damaging to the faith of others that it was his duty as a Christian. Of course, I can't agree with him on that—"

"Of course not. He must have been quite mad."

"—on the other hand, I believe you should read it and understand that a man's unorthodox beliefs, however sincerely held, may have consequences far beyond his own life. I advise you to read and prayerfully and humbly reflect on what has happened today."

He went out, leaving the book on the table.

* * *

Alone in his room, Bowman read and reflected far into the night. At daylight the mists of guilt and shock were still round him, but something stubborn in his mind was beginning to demand its due.

"After all," he said to himself, "the poor fellow was mad."

Which disposed of Green, but left him with the problem of the quarryman. If the brute had been less strong, less admirably adapted to his rocky life, then the struggle for lunch would not have gone so easily his way. And if the struggle had gone the other way, then it would have been his own white teeth meeting in the poisoned cake. Being the weaker, he had survived. His faith was not exactly shaken, but he had to acknowledge it had hit a knotty point. He pondered for a while then remembered something his tutor had said about young men needing guidance from their elders. It was, he admitted to himself, good advice. He found an envelope, went over to the table by the window and addressed it in a firm hand: *c/o Mr. John Murray, Publisher, Albemarle Street, London*. Then he took a sheet of notepaper and began his letter. *Dear Mr. Darwin...*

War Rations

Martin Edwards

ONE OF THE CHILDREN was screaming. Amy Jessop scanned the crowd of youngsters, but she could guess who was making all the fuss. For many of the others, this was the most exciting day of their lives. It was seven o'clock on a bright September morning and they were being evacuated from their homes in Leeds, heading for safety before war broke out. They were laughing, giggling, pulling faces and playing games outside the school gates. But Tom Harker always had to be different. Today he wasn't the centre of attention and he did not like that one little bit.

She hurried along the pavement to comfort the boy, only to find that a couple of the older girls already had their arms around the skinny six-year-old. With his blonde curls and blue eyes, he never seemed to be short of people to cuddle him. Rather like his mother, Amy said to herself.

"He's heartbroken, Miss Jessop," one of the girls said.

"Come on, Tom. The trams will be here any minute. No one else is crying. Your mother would expect you to be brave."

The tear-stained face turned towards her. "I want my mummy!"

"You'll see her soon. I promise." Amy crossed her fingers behind her back. Elsie Harker had, so far as she could tell, always resented the burdens of motherhood. Now Elsie would have the chance to spend even more time with that fancy man of hers. What on earth had John Harker ever seen in her? He was a decent respectable man who kept one of the shops on the little parade. Elsie came from the vast estate behind the parade which housed people who had once lived in the endless rows of back-to-backs in the centre of Leeds. She was the youngest of a family of ten; none of her brothers and sisters had ever done a hand's turn in their lives, so far as Amy could tell.

Tom muffled a sob. Amy gazed at the blonde curls and eyes that, although puffy, still were beautiful. On second thoughts, it was all too easy to understand why

John Harker had been smitten. Elsie Cornforth had, so Amy understood from Mary Brough, who also taught the infants, found herself a job behind John's counter when he was short-staffed. Within a short time, she'd also found herself pregnant and of course John had done the decent thing. That sort of man did. Amy sighed. More fool him, for walking into the trap.

A cheer went up. "Miss! The tram's coming!" the girl said, letting go of Tom.

Although close on a thousand children and staff were waiting to travel to their unknown destination, they all crammed into a dozen of the double-decker trams. At City Square, everyone had to get out at the station and pile into the waiting trains. It was a complicated journey, with innumerable stops and, when they had reached the North Riding, another transfer, this time to a fleet of buses. Amy did not have a moment to herself; the children kept plying her with innumerable questions. She had few answers for them and concentrated on vague words of reassurance. At least the endless distractions saved her from having to speculate about what the future might hold.

At about midday they arrived in Helmsley. Amy knew it as a pretty market town with a large square and the ruins of an old castle. She and her parents had come here for days out in her own schooldays in the early thirties. Today, though, it had lost its charm. By now the children were tired of travelling and Tom Harker was not the only one who could not stop snivelling. But they had to march to the local school, along streets lined with onlookers.

"Poor mites!" she heard a woman say. "They'll never see their homes again!"

Everyone was fed with corned beef and given a brown paper carrier bag containing two days' rations: evaporated milk in a tin, cocoa, a few biscuits, more corned beef. Then it was time to assemble in the yard and divide into groups before the final stage of the journey. She and Mary were in charge of a couple of dozen small ones, including Tom.

Another bus took them out to a village called Coldkirby where once again they gathered in the playground, waiting to be told where they would spend the night. A worried-looking man told them that there seemed to have been some mistake. The villagers had been expecting to take no more than half a dozen evacuees. It was evening before all the children were found a bed. The two teachers slept the night on rough made-up beds in the school hall.

The next day, a Saturday, was spent getting organised. A farmer's wife offered Amy a poky room with a window which commanded a view of the pig sty. That afternoon she wrote a letter to her widowed mother, who lived in Wakefield, to explain where she had finished up. *This place is pretty enough,* she wrote, *but I bet in winter it's like the back of beyond. The sooner we are allowed home, the better. I could very easily get bored with corned beef! Perhaps even now it isn't too late. War may still not be inevitable.*

In less than twenty-four hours, she knew better. She was with the farmer and his family, clustering around the wireless when the Prime Minister announced that a state of war existed with Germany. There was a sick feeling in her stomach. So many people, she knew, would die senselessly. No one could tell what the future might hold. Amy resolved that she would return to Leeds as soon as she could. It might be less safe there, but she needed to be in a place where she felt she belonged. In a moment of self-awareness, she thought: *That's what I need, somewhere to belong. And, who knows, perhaps someone to belong to.*

Others felt much the same. Parents started to arrive to collect their children and take them back home. After three or four weeks she and Mary only had a handful of pupils to look after. It was agreed that Amy should return to the city. When she got back, the schools were closed, but she was given a series of jobs. Useful work to help the war effort. She checked census forms, and wrote out identity cards and ration books. Although some of the schools soon reopened, Amy's was being used as a temporary barracks for newly called-up soldiers and so she helped out elsewhere until it was ready again and she returned to her digs with Mrs. Garbutt in Ephraim Street.

One day, on her way home, she bumped into John Harker. He was just shutting up shop and in response to his greeting she asked how Tom was.

"All right, I think. I went up there a fortnight back. They seem to be looking after him, as far as I can judge. I miss him, of course, but he's in the safest place."

After that she often stopped and spoke to him. At first they would just pass the time of day for a few minutes, discussing the previous night's air raid and the people they knew who had been killed in the bombings. John was just too old for the call-up and she sensed that he felt it keenly that he was unable to fight for King and country. He was a pleasant man, muscular but kind and softly-spoken. Gradually their conversation began to range more widely. He told her a little about his business, of how he had grown up in the seaside resort of Scarborough before his parents had moved to Leeds twenty-five years earlier. She told him about her own past, school in Ossett and teacher-training here at Beckett Park. She'd always loved children; teaching was all she had ever wanted to do. Increasingly, though, she felt as if she were just marking time, that there must be more to life than this.

"What about boyfriends?" he asked. "I bet you're not short of admirers."

She blushed and shook her head. She'd never considered herself pretty: she had a nice enough face, she thought, but her appearance was compromised by a tendency to put on weight if she so much as looked at a good meal. She liked her food too much, that was the trouble. The young men who had taken her out on dates had been amusing enough for a short time but soon the attractions of their company had palled. They seemed somehow callow, immature, embarrassingly incapable of taking their eyes away from her ample bosom. Of course, the war had taken them away from home and although the city was full of soldiers, Amy had resisted their wolf whistles and cheery invitations to the pub.

When John Harker pressed her, she said something of this. His response startled her.

"You know, Amy, if I were a few years younger, I'd ask you out myself."

Again she felt herself colouring. "But... you..." she stammered.

"What, Amy?"

"I mean, you're married."

"She's left me, Amy. Run off with that chap of hers."

"Oh, I'm sorry. I didn't know."

She felt foolish, embarrassed, wholly unsure of herself. He bent his head closer to hers and she wondered whether he was about to kiss her. The thought alarmed her, but she realised that it excited her too. When he simply said, "I haven't gone around shouting it from the rooftops," she felt a rush of sympathy for him.

"No, no. Of course not."

"Look, would you like to have a drink with me this evening? We could walk over to Beeston, if you like. People won't know us there." He was sensitive enough to realise how much that mattered, she thought. If they turned up together at the local pub, tongues would soon start wagging.

"That would be lovely."

"Seven thirty, then?"

"I'll meet you here, if you like."

"All right, but I make it a condition that I walk you home afterwards. You don't want to be hanging round these streets on your own in the blackout."

The evening they spent together was the most enjoyable Amy had known since war broke out. John proved to be an agreeable companion, but when they said their farewells outside Mrs. Garbutt's, he became hesitant again. After a brief pause, he gave her a peck on the cheek and asked if she would mind seeing him the following day.

"Mind? Of course not. I'd love to."

His craggy features lightened. His surprise and gratification were flattering, for during the past few hours, Amy had been appraising him quietly and deciding that, despite the age gap between them, he was really rather a handsome man. No Flash Harry, far from it, but strong and possessing, she felt sure, hidden depths. The grey touches in his hair simply added to his distinction. She realised that she would be counting the hours before their next date.

As the days and weeks passed, their relationship – she soon began to think of it as a relationship – deepened, even though John always behaved like a perfect gentleman. He wasn't one for dancing, but then neither was she. Once or twice they went to see a film and sometimes to a pub. More often, she would go over to his house after he had shut up shop and they would spend the evening together, just talking. He always cooked the evening meal; he really was very domesticated and steaks were his speciality. Running a shop was hard work, but there were compensations: it was usually possible to supplement basic rations.

Neither he nor she had any time for the spivs who ran black market rackets, but making the most of the chance of something a bit special to eat was rather different.

She gladly allowed him to kiss her at the end of an evening, but she didn't want to rush things. For the first time in her life she had found someone whom she could, she told herself, depend upon in an uncertain and dangerous world. From odd things he let slip in conversation, she guessed that he bitterly regretted having let himself be swept off his feet by Elsie Cornforth. Much good had it done him, being dazzled by her brassy good looks.

He never talked at length about his wife, and Amy could understand why. She suspected that the marriage had been unhappy once the first infatuation had worn off. John must have realised the mistake he had made and Elsie would soon have become bored with such a sober, respectable husband. He had a certain dogged Yorkshireman's pride and must have felt humiliated by her desertion. Perhaps in the long run he would see it as a blessing in disguise. Yet Amy couldn't help being curious. He'd never mentioned the possibility of divorce. She wondered what he intended to do. Was it possible that he had lost all faith in the institution of marriage, that his motto was once bitten, twice shy? If so, did that matter?

Every now and then she asked after Tommy, but John's answers were monosyllabic.

She did not doubt that he cared for the boy, but his attitude seemed dutiful rather than devoted. He had made occasional visits to Coldkirby since the evacuation, but they were few and far between. Perhaps there were understandable reasons for that: the boy's physical appearance and wilful temperament must have been constant reminders of Elsie. All the same, it struck her as odd, for she was sure that John Harker was, beneath his surface reserve, a man of intense feeling.

One evening, on their way back to Mrs. Garbutt's, she was emboldened by an extra glass of port and lemon to ask if Elsie kept in touch with the boy. John paused in mid-stride.

It was as if he were trying to choose his words with special care, knowing that a few drinks had dulled his judgement.

"Well – no, she doesn't."

"It's so sad."

"She was no good," he said roughly.

"Do you ever hear from her?"

"No. I don't."

They were turning into Ephraim Street. Amy knew that he would like to change the subject, but she could not let it go. "And she walked out on you – just like that?"

"Aye."

"It must have been just after the evacuation."

"Day after you and the other teachers took the kids off," he said grudgingly.

"She seized her chance as soon as her child was off her hands," Amy said, half to herself. It wasn't unknown. At school she'd heard several tales of parents who had not seen their children since their evacuation. Some of them hadn't even bothered to keep in touch.

One couple had moved over the Pennines to somewhere in Lancashire and according to gossip their three youngsters, housed with a retired couple in Bawtry, did not have the faintest idea. The old woman at Coldkirby who had prophesied that the evacuees would not see their homes again might not have been so far off the mark after all.

"Don't worry about Elsie," he said. "She's not worth it."

"But it's so unfair! She's left you with all the responsibility for the child. But Tommy is hers as much as yours."

"More than that," he said grimly.

Now it was her turn to hesitate. "What do you mean?"

He sighed and faced her on the pavement. "You might as well know the truth. The evening she left, she told me that I wasn't Tommy's father."

"What?"

"It's the truth, I'm afraid. I'd suspected as much from the outset, but like an idiot I chose to believe what I wanted to believe. She owned up whilst she was telling me that she was off to make a new life with her fancy man, some travelling salesman who owned a car. Apparently she knew she was pregnant when she started giving me the glad eye. Needless to say, I fell for it. Then she broke the news that I'd got her pregnant and asked what I was going to do about it. The father was some lad off the estate who'd never have kept Elsie in the style she wanted to become accustomed to."

Amy gripped his arm. "You poor dear."

"I've treated the boy as my own for six years. I couldn't abandon him. I make sure he's all right, you can count on that."

"I know," she said. Shock was beginning to turn to anger, hatred almost, directed at the long-gone Elsie. "And that bloody woman never goes near him?"

He cleared his throat and said gruffly, "For a while after she'd gone, I was in a daze. Mortified. No, worse than that. It was a kind of madness, I reckon. When folk asked where she was, I said she'd gone to look after Tommy. A lot of mothers did, I knew that. But I suppose plenty of people started putting two and two together ages ago. The fact her fancy man disappeared at the same time made it easy for them to see through what I was saying. I don't encourage questions, but now when they do ask, I admit that she's run out on me. I've decided it's the best thing."

"And where is she now, have you any idea?"

He shrugged. "I don't think about that. It's over between her and me. I have to get on with my own life.

Let's face it, I'm no spring chicken. Moping's a waste of precious time."

She touched his hand. "You're very brave."

He coloured. "I don't see it like that. But you've helped, Amy. You've really helped with putting the past behind me."

"I'd like to keep on helping."

"I'd like that too."

They paused, not knowing what to say next. She looked into his eyes and realised that he was making up his mind about her. The next moment, she was in his arms.

Some time later they were interrupted by the sound of Mrs. Garbutt's front door opening.

"Are you going to be carrying on out there all night, Amy Jessop? Have you any idea what time it is?"

She pulled away from John. "Sorry, Mrs. G. I'll come in now."

The landlady stared. "And you, John Harker. A married man! You ought to be ashamed of yourself."

He stood his ground. "My wife's left me, Mrs. Garbutt. As far as I'm concerned, it's as if I'm divorced."

"And what if your Elsie turns up again, like a bad penny?"

"She won't. We'll not be seeing her or her boyfriend again, I'm sure of that."

Mrs. Garbutt sniffed. "A right carry-on!"

"Don't worry, we won't be embarrassing you again after tonight," he said. "Amy's coming to live with me. Aren't you, Amy?"

His sudden boldness stunned her. It was as much as she could do to gasp her agreement. Mrs. Garbutt tossed her head and went back inside.

He shook his head. "Sorry, love. I shouldn't have startled you like that. You don't have to move in, you know. I realise it might look bad, you being a teacher and all."

"I don't care!" she said. "As long as I can be with you..."

He considered her for a moment. She was acutely conscious of his eye settling on the ample curves of her figure, but somehow it did not displease her. "That's settled, then. How long will it take you to pack your things? Ten minutes, maybe? I'll wait out here, then we'll walk back to my place."

She went inside and raced up the stairs. Her mind was whirling. She was barely conscious of the sound of Mrs. Garbutt's footsteps, padding up the stairs, of the old woman's sceptical expression as she peered into the tiny back bedroom where Amy was flinging clothes into a suitcase.

"And what do you do if Elsie Harker does come running back to him? She may be a trollop, but she has a way with men. They can never resist a pretty face. He may change his mind if she begs him for a second chance."

"She won't," Amy said calmly.

"You can't be certain. Neither can he. At first he gave out she'd gone off with the rest of the evacuees. Until you came back, you who knew better because you'd been with the boy all that time. Then he changed his tune."

"If he says he's sure, he's sure," Amy replied. The jealousy of an old woman was not about to rattle her. Her life was on the point of being transformed. She did not yet know John Harker well, not as well as she yearned to – and would do. But he had said with unshakeable authority that his wife was gone forever and that assurance was good enough.

Mrs. Garbutt grunted. "He's been downright shifty over it, if you ask me. Makes you wonder what's happened to her and that other fellow."

"I couldn't care less," Amy said brusquely. "Now, if you'll let me finish my packing, I'll be away inside ten minutes. I'm more than up to date with my rent, I think."

Mrs. Garbutt allowed herself a parting shot. "And what a comedown! A young schoolteacher, gone to live under the brush with the local butcher! A fine way to behave."

"At least I'll eat better with John than I ever have done here," Amy said sharply.

And although it was nothing more than a small bonus to a woman in love, it was perfectly true. John said he still had a few choice cuts in his cold store. He reckoned it was the finest meat he'd ever eaten, a delicacy too good to fritter away on customers, so he kept it just for the two of them. Only last night he'd said he was afraid he had acquired a taste for it. When she'd asked why it was a worry, he'd explained that it was very hard to find. But perhaps he'd have the chance to get some more, one day. After all, these were strange times: there was a war on. And he'd gazed at her generous figure with an expression that had made her feel needed. She told herself happily that he had begun to hunger for her.

The Death of Spiders

Bernie Crosthwaite

I WAS PEERING down the microscope at the spinneret of the arrowhead spider, *Micrathena sagittata*, when the telephone rang. I picked it up reluctantly.

"Professor Hannah Staples," I said, feeling the strangeness of that title, conferred on me at the end of the last academic year. It still made me feel both powerful and terrified.

"My name's Detective Inspector Croft. I'm in need of your expertise, Professor."

"Concerning what?"

"Concerning a suspicious death."

"I don't see how I can help you."

"You're an expert on bugs, aren't you? There was that thing about you in the local paper recently."

I grimaced slightly, recalling the headline *Spider Woman Made Top Prof*.

"It depends what you mean by 'bugs'. If you mean insects, then no, I'm not an entomologist. I specialise in arachnids, with a particular interest in—"

"Apparently you're the go-to person, so I need you here straight away – before they remove the body."

I was silent. I glanced along the cluttered bench to the tower of wooden racks containing specimens of every type of arachnid. In the corner a sweep net stuck out of a rucksack that I hadn't had a chance to unpack after a recent field trip. The shelves above me were badly bowed with the weight of textbooks and files. The first semester, with its influx of new students and the creation of new courses, was always intensely busy. How could I possibly take time off? After all, I had lectures to write, a failing PhD student to deal with, not to mention my own research into the medical uses of spider silk that had reached a crucial stage.

"Time's passing, Professor. Every minute counts in a case like this."

"I understand that." I thought about it. I'd never been part of a police investigation before. It might be interesting. I took a deep breath and plunged in. "All right," I said. "I'll come."

* * *

Blue and white plastic tape had been strung across the alleyway behind the row of shops on Victoria Road. When I gave my name, the WPC on guard lifted the barrier and I ducked under it.

"Down the end," she said. "Back of the Turkish takeaway."

I picked my way around discarded packaging, overflowing refuse bins and piles of rotting rubbish, trying not to stain the hems of my trousers. A man in white paper overalls came towards me. He was squarely built, with unruly blonde hair. His forehead was furrowed into creases.

"Professor Staples?"

"Yes."

"I'm D.I. Croft. This way."

At the end of the alleyway there was more tape. This time it said *Crime Scene – Do Not Enter*. I was handed an anti-contamination suit, overshoes and gloves. I put them on and was allowed to pass through.

I could just see, sticking out from the space between a parked Vespa scooter and a crumbling stone wall, a pair of feet in trainers. As we drew level I saw the body of a man lying on the ground, his upper body in shadow. I thought fleetingly, inappropriately, that he had adopted the Pose of the Corpse, a yoga position I used for relaxation. Then I noticed the dark pool of congealed blood that had leaked from under him. A cigarette stub and a tiny pile of ash lay near his left hand.

"Looks like he came out here for a smoke," said Croft.

"Who is he?" I asked.

"Demir Kemal. He worked here. The last time the owner saw him was at the end of his shift last night, around midnight. He must have come out the back door to collect his scooter, stopped to light up a fag, and—"

"And then he was attacked."

"Looks like it. The owner arrived mid-morning, came out here with a bag of rubbish and there he was." Croft nodded towards a woman with a clipboard taking notes. "The M.O. reckons he was stabbed from behind. It's like someone was lying in wait for him. We'll know more when we do the post-mortem."

"Poor Demir."

"You knew him?"

"No, not at all. It's just that I use this takeaway occasionally – it's on my way home – I had a very good lamb souvlaki only the other night – but I never knew any of them by name." This was all very interesting but I was growing impatient. "Why did you ask me to…?"

"Take a closer look." He pointed to where the upper part of the body lay in shadow.

I edged my way around the scooter and squatted down. I recognised him. It had been a handsome face, olive skin, black hair. Late twenties, always ready with a flirtatious wink, a charming smile. But now his face was as pale as marble. Glancing down the body I saw that his heart was impaled by a thin spike like an old-fashioned hat-pin, and under the pin lay a spider.

"What is it?" asked Croft.

I peered closely, not touching. A hairy long-legged specimen, yellowish-brown in colour. It was in a sorry state. The cephalothorax and abdomen looked flat and misshapen. Two of its legs were missing. "It's *Phoneutria nigriventer*. Also known as the Brazilian wandering spider."

"Sounds exotic."

"They're not uncommon in this country. They arrive in container ships, usually in crates of bananas. Extremely venomous, actually."

"The way it's pinned to the body – what's the significance of that?"

"I'm not an anthropologist, I'm afraid. You could try the School of Social Sciences." I stood up, feeling dizzy.

"Unless there's anything else, I really must get back to work."

"That's it for now. At least we know the species."

"Glad to help."

"Thank you, Professor. I'll be in touch."

* * *

I've always loved spiders.

No, that's not quite true. As a small child I was terrified of them – the plump bodies with their oddly human waists, the many legs bent like prongs, their rapid scuttling movements.

One day, when I was six, I was lying on my bed reading. Somewhere in the house Simon, my older brother, was playing his guitar, loudly and tunelessly. I looked up from my book and saw a large black spider working its way around the skirting board. I started screaming and Simon burst in.

"What the hell's the matter?"

I pointed. He smiled, and bending down, deftly scooped the spider up in his bare hands and released it through the open window.

"You've saved my life!" I threw myself at him, clutching at his knees.

"Don't be so soft, Hannah." He prised my arms away. "It's stupid to be frightened of spiders. They spin webs to catch their favourite food – *flies*." He put on a monster face and chased me round the room. I remember the delicious terror of it, the relief when he stopped, picked me up and swung me round, my legs flying out. "Flies are the nasty ones, not spiders."

"But flies are harmless," I panted.

"What? They vomit on your food and give you diarrhoea."

"Yuk! Why did you have to tell me that?"

He plonked me on the bed, ruffled my hair, and went out grinning, back to his guitar. It was a shame he never made it as a musician. I regretted that we hardly ever saw each other these days, not since that last awkward occasion when he got drunk and asked me for money.

But I'll always be grateful for the precious gift he gave me when I was six. The next time I saw a spider I remembered what he'd said and my panic disappeared. I became fascinated by these crafty industrious creatures. At that stage I still couldn't touch a spider, but with the help of an empty yoghurt pot and a postcard I could remove them to safety, hating the thought of them being trodden on.

As I learnt more and more about them I became hooked. Who wouldn't be? There are over forty thousand different species and every one of them is extraordinary. The more bizarre they are, the better I like them. I have great affection for the bird dung crab spider that looks and smells like excrement to attract insects, and the Saharan rolling spider that cartwheels across the desert. I even admire the species where the young hatched spiderlings eat the mother – a practical and efficient use of resources. Perhaps my favourite is the Bolas spider that spins a line with a sticky ball at the end which it twirls to attract moths, then reels them in to enjoy them for dinner. Genius.

Then there's my own area of expertise – spider silk. It's a thin, tough polymer made up of the same three building blocks as human tissue. Already knee cartilage has been created from it and not rejected. We can't be far off the next target – replacing damaged spinal cord. Captivated when young, I've never faltered in my passion for spiders. What other creature is so useful or so amazing? A few years ago, in a museum, I saw a coat woven from the silk pulled from the abdomen of the golden orb-weaver spider, and stood for hours in front of the glass case, enraptured by its beauty. I heard a woman ask her husband why there wasn't a spider silk industry, and I interrupted to explain that these creatures weren't like silkworms: in captivity they eat each other – they're cannibals. The couple didn't stay long after that.

Early on in my studies I came across the idea that spiders cannot die. The theory is that they can be killed – crushed, drowned, starved. But if protected from outside dangers, they can, theoretically, live forever. Some say there are spiders in Chinese temples that are nearly three thousand years old. It's a myth of course. Most spiders live less than a year, others take a couple of years to mature then die soon after producing young. A few, such as tarantulas in the family *Theraphosidae,* can live for several decades in captivity, but that's it. It took me a long time and a lot of research before I finally accepted the truth. But there is still something in me that longs to believe that spiders are immortal.

* * *

When I got back to the lab after helping D.I. Croft, there was a student waiting for me. It was Jack Lomax, whose PhD thesis on spiders' fangs – *chelicerae* – I was extremely concerned about. It was already overdue and of poor quality, and I was convinced that even if he completed it he would fail to gain his doctorate. I'd warned him on several occasions that I was unhappy with his work. Now I had made the difficult decision to advise him to drop out, saving him – and the department – the embarrassment of failure.

"Professor Staples..." He stood up from where he was slumped at the bench. Long straight hair hung in an untidy curtain down both sides of his face, giving him a mournful look.

He took the news with an increasingly resentful expression on his face. "No, no..." he muttered when I'd finished. His red-rimmed eyes burned at me. "You can't do this."

"I can't force you to stop, it's true. But I've spoken to your second supervisor, and he agrees with me. Think about it, Jack – it's for your own good. At our last meeting I gave you a detailed list of changes you needed to make to bring your thesis up to standard and you've merely tinkered with it. In its present state it has no chance of passing."

"I've worked so hard," he whined.

"On the contrary, your research is derivative and lazy."

He banged his hand down on the wooden bench. I flinched at the sharp sound but stood firm.

"Don't try to intimidate me, Jack. It won't work. Now if you don't mind..."

The look in his wild eyes narrowed into a beam of hatred. "You'll be sorry, Professor." He kicked stools aside as he stormed out, making a clattering sound that nearly deafened me. I waited until I heard his footsteps recede along the corridor, righted the stools, made myself a cup of coffee and got back to work.

* * *

A few weeks later I had another call from Detective Inspector Croft.

This time it was a middle-aged woman, a dental receptionist, murdered in Jubilee Park. Could I come at once?

Once again I hesitated. On top of my normal workload I was staying up late every night writing articles for science journals, and when I finally put my head down I was plagued by thoughts of Jack Lomax, whose barrage of emails veered from pleading to vengeful. My sleep had been thin and broken for many days. I closed my eyes.

"Professor? Are you still there?"

I snapped to attention. "I'm sorry, I was distracted for a moment. Can I ask if you've made any headway with the Kemal case?"

"The investigation is ongoing. But now there's another one…" Croft's voice dropped, almost as if he was speaking to himself. "…God knows what we're dealing with."

How could I refuse?

Just as I was about to go my laptop bleeped. Another email from Jack. I skimmed it rapidly. The words 'cow' and 'dictator' leapt out. I shook my head. He seemed to be losing all self-control. I was about to delete it, as I'd done with all the others, then stopped. No. It was evidence. I might need it if this came to a bare-knuckle fight in front of the Dean of School. I shut my laptop and left the office, locking the door behind me.

* * *

She was lying behind the bandstand in the same supine position as the first. And just like the other one, a spider was impaled on a spike driven into the heart. Croft stared at the body intently as if willing it to give up its secrets.

"Carolyn James," he said. "Divorced, lived alone. Wasn't missed until she didn't show up for work this morning."

"At the dental practice on Queen Street."

He looked at me sharply. "Friend of yours?"

"No. I'm just a patient there. I had an emergency appointment recently – an abscess – and she was on the desk. She was very… chatty." I looked away, remembering how she told me she'd seen the article in the local paper.

"A professor – fancy that! Congratulations. What exactly do you study?" she'd asked. I'd explained that I specialised in arachnids, creatures with eight legs and two body parts, like scorpions, ticks and mites, but my chief area of expertise was spiders. "Creepy crawlies, you mean? Yeuch!"

She'd shuddered so violently I didn't go on. It was a reaction I was used to.

"I'm sorry," Croft said quietly.

"No, really… she wasn't… I didn't even know her name."

"And the spider?"

I knelt down on the cold flagstones and examined it. Dark brown body with pale brown lateral bands, squashed almost flat. Its once long slim legs had curled inwards: when spiders die it causes a drop in the pneumatic pressure in their leg joints, making them into shrivelled versions of their former selves. It was a sight that always filled me with sadness. "It's a common house spider – *Tengenaria domestica*."

"Nothing special, then?"

I stood up. "All spiders are special."

"If you say so." He glanced around the park, at the ironwork bandstand, the rolling stretch of grass, the pond in the distance. "I can't work out any connection between a man working in a Turkish takeaway and a dental receptionist. Why these two? It seems so random."

I shook my head. "I'm afraid I can't help you there. I only know about spiders."

* * *

When I accepted a Chair in the Faculty of Natural Sciences I hadn't quite realised how much my workload would increase. I was now responsible for making important departmental decisions, as well as the vital business of submitting grant proposals to funding bodies. A lot of time, thought and effort went into every aspect of my duties. It was hard work, but I was beginning to enjoy it. At the same time I was on the verge of an exciting breakthrough in my own research – the creation of artificial human nerves from spider silk.

The only downside was the constant stream of Jack Lomax's emails, growing steadily more offensive and menacing. Now he had lodged a complaint with the Dean of School about my behaviour and a date had been set for a preliminary hearing.

I was fully stretched. Perhaps that was why my heart sank when I heard D.I. Croft's voice on my office phone.

"There's been another one."

* * *

It felt odd to be driving along my own street in the early afternoon. Even odder to see police cars and crime scene officers in white overalls clustered round a dense copse of trees fifty metres from my house. Tape barriers had been erected, and when I'd covered up, Croft ushered me through.

"It's a bad one," he said, staring at the body lying on the ground, almost hidden in the undergrowth.

I reluctantly followed his gaze. A young boy. The Pose of the Corpse. A spider impaled on his heart. I leaned over to inspect it.

"Family *Lycosidae.* A wolf spider. Female." It was easy to identify from the egg case attached to its spinneret. It had lost all eight of its legs.

"You live on this street, don't you?"

I nodded.

"I expect you know the child?"

"By sight, yes. Not by name."

"He's called Scott. Aged ten. He was supposed to be sleeping over at a friend's house around the corner last night. The other boy says they argued and Scott came home before bedtime. But he never made it. His parents went off to work this morning, thinking the boys had gone to school together. Mum texted him at lunchtime, got no reply, spoke to the school. He'd been marked absent. She rushed home, started searching. Found him here."

"That's terrible."

"Have you ever met him, spoken to him?"

"Once or twice."

"Recently?"

"No. The last time was weeks ago. He wanted me to identify a spider he'd found. I thought he was taking a real interest but I don't think it was genuine. To be honest he was a bit wild, noisy. I avoided him."

Croft massaged his creased forehead. "Why are they doing this – this – spider thing?"

"I suppose it's a way of leaving a mark, a signature."

"But what does it mean?"

I shrugged.

He looked at me intently. "I'm beginning to see a link."

"What link?"

"You."

I almost laughed. "You think I—?"

"What I'm saying is that you knew all of them. They're all in some way associated with you."

"Very tenuously."

"Then how do you explain the spiders?"

"I can't."

Croft turned, walked a few paces away from me, strode back.

"You bought a takeaway from Demir a few days before he was murdered. You saw Carolyn at the dentist's, then shortly after that, she was killed. And now this poor little boy… OK you haven't spoken to him recently, but you have done in the past. And then there are the spiders…" He began pacing again. "I've checked the distances. Prestige Takeaway is about three-quarters of a mile from here. Jubilee Park no more than half a mile. And here we are on Langley Road – the street where you live."

"What are you implying?"

"These murders… it's almost as if they're closing in on something… or someone."

"On me?"

"I think that's the meaning of the spiders left at the scene. A warning."

"Of what?"

He looked at me thoughtfully. "I think you're next."

"That's ridiculous."

"Is there someone with a grudge against you? Someone who's out to get you?"

I felt a strange sense of calm, the way I always do when a scientific problem is solved.

"Actually, yes. There is someone."

* * *

We sat in my front room, drinking tea. Croft sat forward on his chair as though afraid of breaking it. He was trying to persuade me to accept twenty-four-hour protection. I refused.

"I spend most of my time at the university where I'm surrounded by students, colleagues, admin staff. If I stay late there are janitors and nightwatchmen. I'll be perfectly safe."

"All the same I'd like to put surveillance cameras in your lab and office."

"Absolutely not. I couldn't bear to be under scrutiny all the time. How would I get my work done? How would I think?"

Croft frowned, looking doubtful.

"I'll be fine. I've done many field trips in inhospitable places. I've learnt to look after myself."

He ran both hands through his thick fair hair. "At least let us put a watch on your home at night. I'd say that's when you're most vulnerable."

"All right, agreed." I offered the plate of biscuits but he shook his head. "Any news about Jack?"

"He's not at his flat and no one seems to know where he's got to. A bit of a loner, I take it?"

"I imagine so. He's certainly obsessive and unstable." I nodded towards the open laptop on the coffee table. "You can tell that from the emails I showed you."

Croft stood up and reached for his raincoat. "Be careful, Professor."

"Don't worry about me. I know what I'm up against now."

* * *

I followed the detective's advice, taking extra care locking doors and windows, not going out alone at night, getting my assistant to vet anyone who came to the office to speak to me.

Jack's emails stopped coming. He wasn't answering his mobile. The police kept an eye on his flat but he didn't reappear, and there was no sign of him at his parents' house. I didn't like it. Despite what I'd said, it unnerved me. I wanted to flush him out in the open where he could be dealt with. But there was nothing I could do. It was a waiting game.

One night, when I was working late in the lab, I heard noises – a door opening and closing, footsteps. I raised my head slowly from the microscope. The nightwatchman doing his rounds? But his tread was heavy and slow. These footsteps were rapid, and as they came nearer I heard laboured breathing.

I slid silently from my stool. Again I felt that sense of icy calm. I could deal with this. Through the glass panel in the door I saw a shadowy shape, then the door was flung open and Jack Lomax stood there, breathing in shallow gasps. He looked ill. His long hair was scraped back into a ragged ponytail, revealing sunken cheeks. His eyes had lost their wildness. They looked blank, like dead men's eyes.

"Good evening, Jack. Where have you been these past few weeks?"

"On my hols." He tried to smile. "Lying low – literally – in a tent by a lake, very remote, very quiet – I didn't see a soul." His face crumpled like a child's. "I had to get away – I tried to go home one day and there were policemen outside my flat. I ran." His expression switched in a moment from bewilderment to anger. "It was you who put them on to me, wasn't it? What did you accuse me of? Stalking? Harassment?"

"Hardly the worst of your crimes."

"What?"

"How long have you been back?"

"A few days. I've tried to see you, but there's a policeman outside your house all night. I've tried to get into the department several times but they've changed the security code. Every evening, if your light was on, I've tried the basement service door. No good. Then tonight, for the first time, it was unlocked."

"That was me. I thought you might come. Tomorrow is your big day after all."

"My meeting with the Dean, yes. I'll tell him how you've treated me."

"Up to now, Jack, I've treated you very fairly." My voice was calm but my palms were clammy with sweat.

"But I'm afraid that's about to change."

"What do you mean?"

"Three murders, Jack. You must be called to account. You must pay for your crimes."

His eyes narrowed. "Murders…?"

"Your campaign against me has been very useful." I reached into my pocket for the smooth familiar handle of the bowie knife I used on field trips. "The police believe the others were a warning, a premonition if you like, that I was your real target, your final victim."

"You… a victim?" He tried to laugh, but only managed a rattling cough.

I closed the short space between us, sliding the blade into his chest. It went in easily, between the ribs and into the heart.

As he staggered and folded to the floor I felt a pang of sorrow for Jack. After all, he had never killed a spider.

I'd seen people destroy spiders before and it had always made me angry. But that was nothing compared to the fury I felt when Demir, shouting absurdly with panic, picked up a huge sauce dispenser and crushed the beautiful Brazilian wandering spider that scuttled across the counter, then flung it out of the back door.

Something inside me splintered and a desire for justice overwhelmed me. As a newly-appointed professor I was growing used to making important decisions. Choosing to kill Demir was one of the most crucial. It was like crossing a boundary from one country into another, where the rules were different and I was the one who made them. Jack was right – I was a dictator.

Carolyn had stamped on the spider harmlessly traversing the grey carpet at the dentist's. As for Scott, I'd noticed him acting suspiciously from my window. I fetched my binoculars and saw what he was doing – plucking the legs from a live wolf spider before throwing it on the ground and hitting it with a stone. I knew the research – boys who perpetrate unspeakable acts of cruelty on animals eventually become serial killers. I was doing the world a favour.

Each time, I had rescued the corpse of the spider, planned my revenge and carried it out without a moment's regret. Impaling the dead spiders on their black hearts was a private gesture, of meaning to me alone. Now I saw that it forged a suspicious link between the killings, a link that would now end. In future there would be no connections. The deaths would appear random and inexplicable.

Jack's blood was seeping across the floor. I stepped around him and reached for my phone.

"Detective Inspector Croft," I said when he answered. "It's Professor Staples." I let my voice shake. "Something terrible has happened."

Home Is the Hunter

Catherine Aird

"EVER HAD ANYTHING to do with an Extradition Order, Sloan?" asked Police Superintendent Leeyes.

"No, sir," said Detective Inspector Sloan warily.

"Now's your chance then," said Leeyes.

"Sir?"

"It's never too late to learn," said Leeyes. "All the good books say so."

"Yes, sir," said Sloan, since this was very true.

The superintendent consulted a piece of paper on his desk. "It's from France."

"A friendly power."

The superintendent, suspecting irony, ignored this. "A Madam Vercollas of 17 Rue de la Pierre Blanche, St Amand d'Huiss… Huisse…" Leeyes gave up the unequal struggle to pronounce Huisselot. "Anyway she's here in

Berebury now, which is all that matters to us."

"Keeps it simple," agreed Sloan.

"Nothing like your own patch." The superintendent's xenophobia was well known to embrace the next county to Calleshire as well as the next country to England. He had always been one to equate stranger with enemy.

"And the French would like her back would they, sir?" asked Sloan, getting out his notebook.

"They would," growled Leeyes. He pushed the Extradition Order from the Home Office across the desk. "She's wanted on a charge of murdering her husband, Louis Vercollas, at a place called Corbeaux last September."

Sloan picked up the paper. "I take it, sir, that the fine detail isn't anything to do with us."

"Not really," said the superintendent a trifle wistfully. Murder didn't crop up all that often in Calleshire, and anyway he always liked to have a finger in any pie that was going.

"Just a matter of handing her over to the French, then?"

"That's all. The Home Office has agreed to her extradition." Leeyes sounded regretful at this. It went against the grain with him for the British to co-operate with any foreign power, but especially with the French. The superintendent blamed metrication entirely on Napoleon Bonaparte. "It should be all quite straightforward..."

"Does she speak English?"

"She *is* English," said Leeyes. "It's her husband who was French."

"I see, sir."

"And Sloan..."

"Sir?"

"You might as well take Crosby with you. It'll get him off my back for the afternoon."

If possible, Detective Constable Crosby was even more insular than the superintendent. "Do we have to deport her ourselves?" he asked as they drove down Berebury High Street.

"She's not being deported," explained Sloan patiently. "Deportation's when we're kicking someone out of this country. Extradition's when they're being asked for by another country with which we have a treaty."

"*Vive la différence*!" said the constable, changing gear.

In due course the police car reached a neat semi-detached house in a quiet street in a residential area of the town. The doorbell was answered by a pleasant-faced, middle-aged woman.

"Madame Vercollas?" began Sloan.

The woman shook her head. "That's my sister. I'm Anne Pickford. Come in and I'll get her for you." She led the way into the sitting room, calling out "Laura, someone to see you! Can you come?"

Madame Vercollas was a younger edition of the woman who had answered the door. "Good afternoon…"

Sloan explained the nature of their errand. Laura Vercollas sat down rather suddenly in one of the armchairs. Her sister murmured something about a cup of tea and retreated to the kitchen.

"I'm sorry to be silly, Inspector," said Laura Vercollas wanly. "I ought to have known why you had come. My notary in Huisselot warned me to expect all this."

"Quite so," said Sloan.

"But he didn't know how long the formalities would take."

Sloan cleared his throat. "Well, the due processes of the law have been gone through now and I must warn you that…"

"Yes, yes," she interrupted quickly. "I do understand the procedure." She twisted her lips into an awkward smile. "In a way, Inspector, it's a relief that you've come and the waiting's over."

He nodded with suitable gravity. Just as sometimes it was better to travel hopefully than to arrive, sometimes it was a relief when the axe fell… He pulled himself together, glad he hadn't spoken aloud. He wasn't at all sure if they still used the guillotine across the Channel.

"At least," said Madame Vercollas stoutly, "I shall have a chance to tell the court that I didn't kill my husband, in spite of what they say."

"Can you prove it, though?" asked Detective Constable Crosby with interest.

She turned her gaze in her direction. "I don't know. My husband was – well – rather older than I, and not a well man. He died in a strange hotel from a massive dose of a narcotic, and the French police say that I gave it to him."

"Tea," said Anne Pickford, coming into the room with a tray and dispelling any lingering doubts that Sloan might have had that both sisters were English.

"And you say you didn't poison him," said Crosby, leaning forward with the air of one trying to get something clear.

Madame Vercollas nodded gently. "I didn't kill Louis."

"The evidence…" began Crosby, to whom the arm's-length nature of an Extradition Order had not been explained.

"Is all against me," she said at once.

"Now, now, Laura," said her sister, "you mustn't be defeatist."

Detective Inspector Sloan, who prized realism for its own sake, hitched his shoulders forward and said, "You understand, Madam, that it is the French authorities who..."

"I understand all right," she said calmly, "and I don't blame them for thinking as they do. For one thing, we were strangers in Corbeaux. I'd never even seen the place before."

"How did you come to be there?" asked Sloan.

"We were staying in a resort about twenty miles away – Louis thought a holiday might do him good – when suddenly something or somebody there upset Louis and he insisted on leaving the hotel there and then and finding somewhere else that very night." She hesitated. "He was like that."

"A difficult man," pronounced Anne Pickford judiciously.

Laura Vercollas didn't deny this. She said, "That's something else they're holding against me: that he wasn't easy to live with..."

"And you just happened on Corbeaux?" asked Sloan, interested in spite of himself.

"Louis pointed to the map and said, 'We'll try there.'"

"He drove?"

"I drove and he directed me," she said. "It was practically dark by the time we arrived but he must have had a map because he steered me through the town all right – except for a one-way street that I had to reverse out of. He told me when to stop and I found we were outside the Hotel Coq d'Or in the Place Dr. Jacques Colliard."

"He went in?"

"I went in, Inspector. Louis didn't move about more than he had to. Not since his last illness. He told me to book a room for five nights, and so I did."

"Why five?"

"I don't know. But in the end, oddly enough, I was there for the five."

"You had dinner there?"

She twisted her lips wryly. "That's something else the police are holding against me. I think they think I'm another Madame de Brinvilliers. Louis wanted to have dinner in our room so they brought it up. We ate alone. You can see how their minds work, can't you?"

"More tea?" asked Anne Pickford.

Laura Vercollas was not diverted. "Corbeaux is one of those *bastide* towns with a war memorial and fountain in the middle of the square. We had our meal looking out onto the Place. It was lit up and rather nice. And in the morning when I woke up Louis was dead in bed."

"Had you had snails?" enquired Crosby, who could not have been described as exactly Francophile. "Or frogs' legs?"

The ghost of a smile crossed her face. "*Potage* and *boeuf bourgignon*. Nothing likely to upset anyone." She paused. "Louis had been ill – I think I told you – and he was always careful what he had in the evening in case it kept him awake. He slept badly enough anyway and he had a lot of nightmares when he did get to sleep. He often used to call out for the doctor in the night, but it was in his sleep. He talked a lot in his sleep," she said flatly.

"What about?" asked Sloan. In his book talking while asleep was a passkey to the subconscious mind.

"It was double Dutch to me," said the Englishwoman of the Frenchman. "Names mostly. Hercule, Jean-Paul, François – they were always cropping up."

"Did you never ask him who they were?"

"Once," she said in a reserved manner.

"And?"

"He moved into the second bedroom." She clasped her hands rigidly in her lap. "You must understand, Inspector, that he was much older than me and I was his second wife."

"That saying," put in her sister truculently, "about it being better to be an old man's darling than a young man's slave, isn't true."

Laura Vercollas flushed. "Let us say it was a marriage of convenience."

"*His* convenience," added Anne Pickford tartly.

"What happened next?" asked Crosby, who was still a bachelor.

"The hotel proprietor sent for the doctor. I explained about Louis's illness and showed him all the medicines he had been having for it. He said that since we were strangers in Corbeaux he would telephone our doctor in Huisselot."

"Then what?"

"At first everything was all right – well, straightforward anyway. I saw the undertaker and so forth and went to have a look at the cemetery – the French make rather a thing of their cemeteries."

Sloan nodded. Even he had heard of *pompe funèbre*.

"It was outside the town and I couldn't find Louis's map in the car, but I got there in the end." She looked at the two policemen. "There was no point in my taking him back to Huisselot. It hadn't been his home town or anything, and when I came to think of it I didn't even know where his parents and sister were buried. It had never cropped up, and in any case he was a very secretive man."

"Quite so," said Sloan.

"All I knew was their names – Henri Georges and Clothilde Marie. The sister was Clémence…" Her voice trailed away as if she had just remembered something.

"What is it?" asked Sloan sharply.

"Nothing." She shook her head. "I arranged the funeral and ordered some of those marble *éternelles* that aren't allowed in England, and then…"

"Then?" prompted Sloan.

"Then the doctor said that there would have to be a post-mortem after all. All of his sleeping draught had gone, you see."

"That's when they found out about the narcotic poisoning?" said Sloan soberly. She nodded.

"Didn't the fools think about suicide?" said Crosby, forgetting all about the professional *Entente*

Cordiale that was supposed to exist between national police forces.

"There was no note," said Laura Vercollas with the air of one repeating a well-rehearsed list. "There had been no threats to end his life at any time. He wasn't in pain, and generally speaking physically ill people don't do it. To say nothing," she added painfully, "of its being a funny time and place to choose – the first night in a strange hotel in a strange town."

"Looks black, doesn't it," agreed Crosby ingenuously.

"Louis wasn't exactly poor either." Laura Vercollas apparently couldn't resist piling Pelion upon Ossa. "That interested the French police a lot."

"I'll bet," said the constable warmly.

"That's all very well," said Laura Vercollas with spirit, "but I didn't put that sleeping draught into the wine or the soup, no matter what anyone says."

Had Crosby been French he might have said "*Bravo*" to that. Instead he looked distinctly mournful. "They've got everything on a plate, though, haven't they?"

"A strange hotel in a strange town," said Sloan slowly, "and yet your husband found it easily enough."

"He had a map."

"No," said Sloan quietly. "You couldn't find the map, could you?"

She stared at him.

"And the only mistake he made in getting to the hotel was directing you up a one-way street."

"Ye…es," she said uncertainly.

"Streets that have been two-way can be made one-way."

"What do you mean?"

"When you mentioned your husband's parents' names just now," said Sloan swiftly, "you were going to say something else."

"It was nothing, Inspector. Only a coincidence."

"Coincidence and circumstantial evidence sometimes go hand in hand," said Sloan sternly, hoping that he might be forgiven by an unknown number of defence counsels for picking one of their best lines.

"It was when I was in the cemetery," said Laura Vercollas. "I wandered about a bit, as one does, and I just happened to notice a tombstone to another husband and wife called Henri Georges and Clothilde Marie, that's all. Not the same surname. It was just a coincidence."

"And Clémence?" asked Sloan softly.

She shook her head. "There was a Clémence but in another part of the ceme..." She stopped and stared at him.

"Madame Vercollas," he said, "think carefully. You arrived in Corbeaux after dark."

"Yes."

"You yourself went into the hotel and arranged the room. Not your husband."

"Yes."

"You had your meal not in the dining room but in your bedroom."

"Yes."

"Who answered the door to the waiter who brought it up?"

"I did."

"Did he see your husband?"

"No. He was in the bathroom when he came."

"So no one in Corbeaux actually saw your husband?"

"No one."

"Did that not strike you as very strange?"

"I hadn't thought about it."

Sloan watched her face intently. "Had your husband ever mentioned Corbeaux in the past?"

"He never mentioned the past at all, Inspector," responded Laura Vercollas.

"The Occupation?"

"He wouldn't talk about the war at all except to say that he wanted to forget it."

"So he might," said Sloan vigorously. "And he succeeded, didn't he? Except perhaps," he added meaningfully, "when he was asleep."

"Those names, you mean?"

"Hercule, Jean-Paul, François," said Sloan.

"And the doctor," put in Crosby.

"Madam," said Sloan, "you told us the address of the hotel, didn't you?"

"Yes, I did," she replied quickly. "It was Le Coq d'Or, Place Dr. Jacques Colliard... Place Dr. Jacques Colliard." She stiffened. "Inspector, there was a plaque in the square. I noticed it particularly."

"Yes?" said Sloan into the sudden silence that had fallen in the neat sitting room in suburban Berebury.

Madame Vercollas's voice had sunk to a whisper. "It said 'Place Dr. Jacques Colliard, Martyr de la Résistance'."

"The doctor," said Crosby almost under his breath.

"If what I am suggesting is so," said Sloan carefully, "there will be other memorials too. Such men are not forgotten in France."

She moistened her lips. “You mean Louis arranged to go back to Corbeaux to die? But why didn’t he just…”

Sloan put the thought delicately: “Perhaps he wouldn’t have been welcome.”

She looked up.

“Perhaps,” he went on, “if they had known in Corbeaux who he was they wouldn’t have had him in their churchyard…”

“Are you saying, Inspector, he might have betrayed those men?”

“They were hard times in France,” said Sloan obliquely. “No one knows what sort of unimaginable pressure…”

“The names he couldn’t stop dreaming about.”

“The Gestapo,” said Sloan evenly, “might have gone on a ‘shopping expedition’, so to speak, that he would have found it hard to resist. Who are we to judge, Madam? We are too young to know.”

“It would explain how he knew the way in the dark,” she said.

“And why he would never come to England,” said Anne Pickford intelligently, the teapot still in her hand.

Crosby looked puzzled.

“Vercollas wouldn’t have been his real name and he couldn’t have got a passport,” she said.

Laura Vercollas was sitting very still. "Inspector, if those names that Louis couldn't stop remembering in his sleep are on the Corbeaux war memorial, the French police will have to think again, won't they?"

"They will." Sloan relaxed. "There's something you mustn't say to them, though, Madam."

"What's that?"

"*Honi soit qui mal y pense*."

Doctor Theatre

Simon Brett

"MARTIN CHEYNEY'S been poisoned!"

Charles Paris was alone in the Green Room of the Kean Theatre in Shaftesbury Avenue when the panic-stricken Assistant Stage Manager burst in with this devastating announcement. He was having an unrewarding tussle with the *Times* crossword, wondering whether his inability to untangle the clues was due to nerves about the First Night of *Richard II* that lay ahead that evening or the two large Bells' he'd managed to sneak in at lunchtime.

He knew he shouldn't drink before a performance. While the custom might have been acceptable – even expected – for actors in the heyday of the Richards Burton and Harris, it was heavily frowned on in the Perrier-swigging, gym-toned theatre of the twenty-first century. But Charles Paris found old habits hard to break.

And it wasn't as though he had a very big part, he reasoned jesuitically to himself. Had he been playing Richard or Bolingbroke, then OK, he would have laid off the sauce. But the Gardener, who only appeared in Act Three Scene Four… the odd Bells wasn't going to do much harm to that performance, was it? Hard to go wrong with rustic exhortations like 'Go, bind thou up yon dangling apricocks' and a lot of heavy-handed comparisons of the state of England to an untended garden. And as for the court scenes, where he had to fill out the stage as a non-speaking 'Noble'… well, that wasn't going to be too much of a challenge, was it? All he had to do was to stand up straight.

Anyway, Charles Paris had frequently been described as an actor who was 'BWP' ('better when pissed'). In the nineteen-eighties he'd done a long tour as Horatio in *Hamlet* ('stolidly supportive' – *South Wales Echo*) and not drawn a sober breath the entire six months. But of course he'd been younger then, he'd bounced back from the hangovers quicker.

Charles tried to remove from his mind the certainty that, before that night's performance of *Richard II*, he'd have had a few more swigs from the half-bottle of Bells secreted in his dressing room. He'd always said drinking was a habit he could easily break, but he was becoming decreasingly sure about the accuracy of that claim.

Anyway, no time for such gloomy introspection. If what the ASM had just announced was true, there was a big question mark as to whether the First Night of *Richard II* would actually take place.

"Poisoned?" Charles echoed. "Martin?"

"Yes. He's in his dressing room in a terrible state. Len on the Stage Door's rung for an ambulance."

"I'll go up and see if there's anything I can do."

The girl was distraught, tears welling on her eyelids. Early twenties, though he couldn't recall her name. Charles had clocked during rehearsals that she was very pretty in the short skirts and contour-hugging leggings that seemed to be obligatory uniform for young women of her age. He used the excuse of her distress to give her a big hug on his way out of the Green Room, and felt uncomfortably like a dirty old man as he hurried up the backstage stairs.

* * *

The Number One Dressing Room was on the first floor, and of course Martin Cheyney had the Number One Dressing Room. He was a very big name. He'd not only served his time in ever-grander roles at the RSC and the National, he'd also gained international recognition by playing a regular character in a series of movies about youthful wizards. Martin Cheyney was one of the few names big enough to guarantee healthy advance sales in the hazardous business of putting Shakespeare on in the West End. Couple him with the latest *wunderkind* director Andy Smoker, restrict the run to three months and you had the nearest thing to a Box Office certainty that the theatre could offer.

Most London dressing rooms are small and shabby, but the Number One Dressing Room at the Kean Theatre lived up to its billing. Though it would have been too camp actually to have a star stuck on the door, the place still left no one in any doubt about the status of its incumbent. Spread across half of the first floor backstage, it incorporated a separate bathroom and bedroom. What's more, before the run of *Richard II* started, the Number One Dressing Room had been specially redecorated for Martin Cheyney's occupancy. The management patently wanted to keep on the right side of their lead actor.

Charles passed through the main space, where the gorgeous costumes of the King were hung on rails, and into the back room, where he found the star writhing on the bed in paroxysms of agony. Watching him anxiously from the doorway was his dresser, an infinitely reliable dumpy ageing woman called Milly. Sitting at the side of the bed was Imogen Clay, the young actress who had won her way through the rounds of a television talent contest to gain the part of Richard's Queen. She kept trying to hold Martin Cheyney's hand, but it kept being snatched away from her as another spasm shuddered through the actor's body.

The phone in the main room rang. Milly answered it instantly. The call was short. "Stage Door," she announced. "Ambulance has just arrived. They'll be up in a minute." She moved towards the corridor, presumably to greet the ambulance men.

"I'd better go," said Imogen Clay. She bent down and managed to plant a kiss on the stricken star's temple, then moved quickly out of the dressing room. Charles Paris, along with everyone else in the company, knew that there had been something going on between the girl and Martin Cheyney. Though he had a beautiful actress wife and two adorable children whom he wheeled out regularly for magazine photo shoots, the star prided himself on his reputation as a ladies' man. And if he fancied a fling, everything was conveniently laid on for him in the Kean Theatre. It was not for nothing that the Number One Dressing Room was affectionately known as 'the star's knocking-shop'. Over the years it had served that purpose many times and for many stars of many sexual orientations.

Charles tried to catch Imogen Clay's eye as she hurried past him, but she kept her gaze studiously averted.

He moved forward to Martin Cheyney's bed. The actor's face was screwed up with pain, but the eyes registered his new visitor. "Charles…" he murmured. "Thank God that bloody Imogen's gone."

"Oh?"

"You have a nice no-strings bit of fun with some bloody woman and she thinks it's a full-on love affair, that you're going to break up your marriage and…" Martin winced and was unable to finish his sentence.

"What's happened to you? What's wrong?"

Martin Cheyney nodded towards a tall glass on the bedside table. It was empty, though some greenish vegetable residue clung to the inside. Charles recalled that the star was, like many actors, somewhat faddish about his diet and seemed to subsist on smoothies to whose ingredients he gave much thought, research and public discussion. Martin Cheyney could bore for England on the subject. Charles had often heard him chuntering on to groups of starstruck younger actors about how the right combinations of fruit, vegetables and herbs could cure all common ills. "I'm my own doctor," he would constantly assert. "I haven't seen a traditional doctor for over twenty years." Well, from the green tinge to his complexion it looked as though that record might be about to be broken.

On a shelf on the other side of the room stood the electric machine in which Martin Cheyney took great pride in mixing his own elixirs.

"Someone poisoned my smoothie," he gasped.

"How do you know?"

"Because nothing else has passed my lips all day except for a Starbucks Americano at breakfast." He clutched at his stomach as another surge of pain twisted his guts.

"Would it be easy for someone to get poison into the smoothie?"

"I'm not in the habit of locking my dressing room door, Charles. The top was off the smoothie maker. I'd put in oranges, blueberries, celery and kale. I added the other ingredients and the ice later, just before I liquidised them." He froze and fought for breath as he suffered another convulsion. "Anyone could have put anything in there."

"When?"

"You know we were called for notes at two. I got into the theatre about one and was in the Green Room till we were called on stage."

"But who might have—?"

Charles neither managed to finish the question nor get an answer. The ambulance men came into the dressing room and took over.

He lingered on the landing, as if ready to offer help, but his services weren't required. Once the ambulance men had manhandled the stretcher loaded with the gasping Martin Cheyney down the narrow stairs, he moved back inside.

Charles Paris reckoned he was too old to be part of the smoothie generation. To him the very word conjured up the image not of a liquidised fruit drink but of a slick lounge lizard – and he'd met a good few of them during his long career in the theatre.

He looked again at the glass by the side of the bed and then turned his attention to the smoothie maker itself. The smell that rose from the debris round its slicing blade was like something scraped up from the bottom of a duck pond. Charles Paris's nose wrinkled. He'd prefer a large Bells any day.

A few shreds of vegetable matter had survived the electronic pulping. There were some orange pips, a few filaments of celery… and some scraps of skin from what must have been the blueberries Martin Cheyney had referred to.

Except that, rather than blue, the scraps of skin appeared to be black.

To his surprise, because it had been more than fifty years ago, Charles Paris found himself remembering the stern words of his grandfather showing the young boy round the large family garden in Pinner. "Now I know it's very tempting, Charlie, but I don't want you stealing any fruit from the fruit cage, none of the strawberries or raspberries or red currants or black currants. Do you understand, Charlie? Grandpa'll be very cross if he finds out you've done that. And even more important – don't you ever try eating the berries from *this* plant. If you eat these, you'll get a very bad tummy ache indeed, Charlie boy."

And his grandfather had pointed out to him the *atropa belladonna*, commonly known as 'deadly nightshade'. In his mind's eye Charles could still see the shiny round black toxic berries.

* * *

Charles Paris was thoughtful as he climbed the stairs to the second floor where the smaller dressing rooms clustered. These were tiny compared to the lavishness of the Number One Dressing Room, but at least they were single occupancy. Nobody had to share. These were the dressing rooms for the supporting actors – Bolingbroke, John of Gaunt, Aumerle and so on.

(Charles Paris, by way of contrast, found that his role as the Gardener entitled him to share a long, low garret under the leaded eaves of the third floor, which was also peopled by those members of the *Dramatis Personae* who appear under the heading: 'Lords, Heralds, Officers, Soldiers, Gardeners, Keeper, Messenger, Groom, and other attendants'. Bagot and Green, two of the 'Servants to King Richard' – in fact two of his favourites – also roosted in this crowded communal space. The third favourite, Bushy, however, for some reason had a dressing room to himself on the floor below.)

Charles reckoned his next port of call had to be Imogen Clay. The entire *Richard II* company was convinced that she and Martin Cheyney had been having an affair, though what the star had said to Charles implied that anything of that sort might be over. Which news would probably not have been music to the ears of Imogen Clay. And hell notoriously hath no fury… etc., etc.

Charles paused for a moment on the landing outside her dressing room and marshalled what he knew about Imogen Clay. The main impression he had of the girl was that she was incredibly ambitious. She had trained at a little-known drama school and was doing no better than any other jobbing actress just out of her teens until television catapulted her to fame. Every West End show these days, it seemed to Charles, had to have its televised 'Search for a Star' component, and the one from which Imogen Clay had benefitted was called *Queen for a Play*.

For six weeks the British public had gawped at the trials, tribulations, tantrums and hysterics of the young contenders as they were put through ever tougher, but entirely pointless, theatrical exercises. The show was presented by a Geordie comedian with an ego-shrivelling line in vicious repartee, and other familiar television faces were brought in to act as 'mentors' for the hapless aspirants. There was much saccharine interviewing of their parents, who insisted that Such-and-Such's talent had been clear at age three when she'd done her hilarious impression of a teapot. She would therefore make a perfect Queen for Martin Cheyney's King.

To add an unthreateningly camp component to the programme's mix, Andy Smoker was part of the judging process, because of course it was his production of *Richard II* for which the untried Queen was being sought. He squealed, flapped his arms around and fluttered his eyelashes in a way that delighted the audience at home. And when the contenders were whittled down to the final two, the popular star of stage, film and television Martin Cheyney himself appeared in the final programme to have the casting vote in the casting.

The actress who had best negotiated all the hoops and been awarded the coveted role of Queen to King Richard had turned out to be Imogen Clay. Charles Paris was yet to be convinced of her acting talent, but there was no doubting the girl's resilience and ambition.

He tapped gently on her dressing room door and received permission to enter. Imogen Clay sat in front of her mirror, reading. Charles was struck again by how exceptionally pretty she was. She wore tight expensive-shabby jeans and a red t-shirt which left one shoulder bare. Her short hair was natural blonde and she had a face the camera loved. On screen she looked somehow fuller, more voluptuous. Close to her reality, Charles was aware of the thinness of her lips and the hardness in her deep blue eyes.

She looked up from her book. “What do you want?”

“I was just worried about Martin. Wondered if you knew anything about how he got ill…?”

The girl shrugged. “I went to his dressing room at three. He was already gasping and choking when I got there.” Given that she was supposed to be having an affair with Martin Cheyney, she seemed callously unaffected by his suffering.

“Was Milly there?”

“No.”

“Why were you going to see Martin?”

Imogen Clay didn’t reply, she just turned her hard blue eyes on him. Their message seemed to be: if you can’t work that out, Charles, then you’re stupider than I thought you were. The implication was that Imogen and Martin definitely were having an affair, and that she had gone to his dressing room at three for a pre-arranged sexual encounter between Andy Smoker’s note-giving and the First Night of *Richard II*.

“You know he was saying he was poisoned?”

That got no more than another shrug by way of response. “Given all that muck he liquidises into his smoothies, I can’t say I’m that surprised.”

Reconciling herself – without great enthusiasm – to the fact that Charles wanted to have a conversation, Imogen Clay closed her book and put it down on the neat table in front of her mirror. To his surprise, he saw that she had been reading *The Tree and Shrub Expert* by D.G. Hessayon.

"I didn't know you were interested in gardening," he said.

"I would imagine there are quite a lot of things you don't know about me, Charles." The actress gave him another of her hard stares. "A state of affairs which I am quite happy to allow to continue."

"It just seems an unusual book for someone of your age to be reading."

"You reckon? Then you probably don't know there's a new series of *Celebrity Gardening* coming up?"

Charles had to admit she was right. He didn't bother saying that the programme title managed to combine two of the subjects that interested him least in the world.

"Well, my manager reckons, on the back of my *Queen for a Play* profile, with the publicity surrounding this *Richard II* show and the kind of fan-base I'm getting on Facebook, I'd be a shoo-in for *Celebrity Gardening*."

Thinking back wistfully to the days when actors just used to act, Charles Paris asked, "But do you know anything about gardening?"

"How difficult can it be?" She gestured to her book. "I can learn it up."

"Do you have a garden?"

"My manager can arrange one for me."

There was a silence. Then Charles suddenly asked, "Do the words *atropa belladonna* mean anything to you?"

"Is it a kind of pizza?"

Now of course the girl could have been playing a very elaborate double bluff. But Charles didn't think she was that good an actress. He inclined more to the view that she really had never heard of *atropa belladonna*.

"No, it's a sort of herbaceous shrub. You'll probably come across it in that book. It's also called 'deadly nightshade'."

"Is it?" She leant across and jotted the information down in a small notebook on her table. Nothing was wasted in the life of Imogen Clay. If knowing the folk name for *atropa belladonna* might improve her chances of appearing in *Celebrity Gardening*, then it became a relevant piece of career-building.

"Martin didn't look too good when he was taken off to the ambulance," Charles observed, in a manner calculated to sound casual.

"No," Imogen agreed without much interest.

"If it's really serious… I mean, if he were to die… I imagine that would have quite an effect on you."

The girl looked up at him, not face to face, but making eye contact in the mirror. "What do you mean?" Then her puzzlement cleared. "Yes, of course. There's bound to be publicity." She clearly wasn't averse to the idea. "Hm, because we had been seen together a few times. The *Daily Mail* and the *Sunday Telegraph* both ran stories hinting there was something going on between us. But if Martin actually dies…" The idea was appealing to her more and more. "Yes. I mean, of course I'd deny it absolutely. I wouldn't want to cause pain to his wife and children, but there are ways of denying things which leave nobody in any doubt as to what was really going on…"

Charles thought it was time to break into her enchanting vision of burgeoning self-publicity. "Martin also implied," he said sharply, "that someone might have poisoned him."

"Oh?" Evidently this was a new idea to Imogen Clay.

"Someone who had a grudge against him, someone who felt he had treated them badly."

"Well, don't look at me, Charles."

"Martin did imply to me that your affair was over."

"So? Do you expect me to be heart-broken and collapse into a little wet heap? Look, I'd got everything I was going to get out of a relationship with him. I'd been seen out with Martin, at the Wolseley, at the Ivy – though going out for dinner with someone who takes their own smoothies with them is perhaps not the perfect date. Still, don't knock it. The gossip-mill had started up, it's raised my profile very nicely thank you." She grinned a small self-satisfied grin. "There are plenty of men out there who'd get turned on by the idea of shagging someone who's shagged Martin Cheyney."

"Particularly if he's by then the *late* Martin Cheyney?"

"It wouldn't hurt." She began to see other benefits in the situation. "Then again it does simplify the business of actually ending the relationship. None of those awkward loose ends. And it'll give me the opportunity to do a bit of the emotional stuff for the press. You know… 'Martin was such a *dear, dear* friend… He was a kind of *mentor* to me… so much more than a *dear, dear* friend…'"

Before Imogen Clay got too carried away in her imagined interview to the world's press, Charles reckoned it was time to leave. As he moved to the door, he asked, "So you can't think of anyone who might have wanted Martin dead?"

"I've done a *Midsomer Murders*," the girl replied, "and a *Touch of Frost*, and in both the episodes I did the detective said, in more or less exactly the same words, 'To find out who's done the murder, the first thing you have to ask yourself is: who stands to benefit from the death?' Well, in Martin's case it's pretty obvious, isn't it?"

"Not obvious to me yet."

"Oh, come on, Charles, join the twenty-first century. Tonight is the First Night of a production of *Richard II* which has already had a huge amount of publicity. If Martin dies, the publicity will be even greater. And the person who'll benefit from all that publicity is…?"

"Still not there."

"Charles, the play is called *Richard II*. Martin is not going to be playing Richard the Second. But somebody else is."

"You mean his understudy?"

"Well done, Charles. I thought we'd never get there."

And he left Imogen Clay to her dreams of perpetually increasing celebrity.

* * *

Charles Paris knew the *Richard II* understudy schedule inside out. Because of his advanced years, he himself was understudying John of Gaunt, a role currently occupied by the infinitely vain actor George Burkitt, with whom he'd worked many times over the years. Charles felt pretty sure, if called upon to stand in, he knew the famous 'silver stone set in a silver sea' speech, but his hold on the rest of John of Gaunt's lines was a little more tenuous.

There had even been a couple of half-hearted understudy rehearsals conducted by Andy Smoker's much-ignored Assistant Director. But, as ever in the run-up to a West End First Night, such precautionary activities had taken second place to the greater imperative of getting the show to open with the cast whose names appeared on the playbills.

So Charles knew that the actor understudying Martin Cheyney was Hal Westmacott, a good-looking boy playing one of the King's favourites, Bushy – the one who, unlike his fellows Bagot and Green, had a second-floor dressing room to himself.

Charles tapped on the door and was greeted by a preoccupied "Yes?" from inside. He entered, to find Hal Westmacott, like so many young actors these days, poring over the screen of his laptop. Charles Paris had never really got into computers. His wife Frances and his daughter Juliet kept urging on him the benefits of the new technology, but he remained as semi-detached from it as he did from his marriage.

He had eventually succumbed to a mobile phone, though. It was impossible these days to conduct a career as an actor without one. Details of rehearsal calls and so on were all sent out in messages and texts from the stage management. And it was impossible to conduct any kind of sexual relationship in the twenty-first century without frequent use of the mobile. Some actors maintained that they'd be lost without their phones because they never knew when their agents might call with urgent summonses to attend auditions. Charles Paris, whose agent was the notoriously lethargic Maurice Skellern, did not suffer from such anxieties. Maurice never called about anything.

But Charles could manage his bog standard mobile fairly well. He only used it for making and receiving calls. Its other functions – the ability to take photographs and so on – were untouched. And Charles did the minimum of texting. His fingers seemed too big – and in the mornings often too shaky – to home in on the right tiny key to form a coherent message.

As his visitor entered the dressing room, Hal Westmacott closed his laptop. Not quite quickly enough, though, to prevent Charles Paris from seeing that he had been googling the name 'Hal Westmacott'. Wonderful how computers had opened up whole new broad pastures for thespian egos to gambol in. Googling their own names was for actors the equivalent of authors checking their Amazon sales rankings on an hourly basis.

The young man looked up at him. He was tall, slender, with greenish eyes and a high forehead, over which flopped a drape of dark brown hair. As well as the laptop on his dressing room table was an open and heavily annotated paperback copy of *Richard II*. "What can I do for you, Charles? Have you come to congratulate me?"

"Congratulate you on what?"

"Oh, don't play dumb, sweetie. This is my big breakthrough. I'm going to be giving my Richard tonight...

due to the indisposition of that distinguished theatrical name and all-round shit, Martin Cheyney."

Charles knew that news travelled fast backstage, but he was surprised that Hal Westmacott had already been given the go-ahead to step into the sick man's shoes.

"Is it definite that Martin won't be able to do it? I'd have thought they'd wait to hear from the hospital when he's been checked out."

"Andy assured me that I was going on tonight," said the delighted understudy with some smugness. "And if the director says something's going to happen, then it's going to happen." He looked round his dressing room. "Andy's always been very generous to me."

"Are you saying Andy arranged for you to be in here, rather than stuck up in the communal dressing room with Bagot and Green?"

"Bagot and Green and you, Charles. Don't forget *you*. I was lucky. I did just happen to mention to Andy that I don't like mixing with the riff-raff."

There was no point in rising to the insult. Charles Paris had been the butt of many worse during his long career. Besides, he was more interested in investigating the poisoning of Martin Cheyney. "Rather convenient for you then, isn't it – Martin's illness?" he asked, quoting a line from *The Milkman Delivers Murder*, a creaky old thriller in which he'd played the Inspector who appears in Act Three ('I've seen mahogany sideboards that were less wooden than Charles Paris' – *Northampton Chronicle & Echo*).

"Good luck generally comes to those who deserve it," came the complacent reply. "Though of course you can help things along," Hal Westmacott went on, "by making your own luck."

"Are you saying you made your own luck in this instance?"

"What do you mean by that, Charles?"

"Martin Cheyney reckons he was poisoned."

Hal's response was much the same as Imogen Clay's had been. "No great surprise, given all that liquidised pondweed muck he lives on."

"No, he meant that he had been deliberately poisoned. That someone had poisoned him."

"Oh, really?" Either Hal Westmacott was a very good actor or this was a new idea to him. But then again, unlike Imogen Clay, Hal Westmacott *was* a very good actor. Charles had seen enough of the young man's range during rehearsals to think that he would probably make a very good fist of Richard the Second that evening.

"Poor Martin," Hal went on. "Never the most popular soul around the company – nobody with an ego that size could be – but I wouldn't have thought he'd have built up enough resentment for anyone to want to do away with him." Then he had a new, rather comforting, thought. A small smile crept across his face as he murmured, "Unless, of course…"

"Unless, of course, what?"

"Ooh, no, I don't think he would…" He played with the new thought, enjoying teasing it out. "Though I suppose it *is* just possible…"

"What are you talking about, Hal?"

"Charles, it wouldn't be right for me to spread suspicion about another member of the *Richard II* company, now would it?" But Hal Westmacott was far too caught up in the galloping thoughts to succumb to anything so boring as discretion. "How do you think I got this part, Charles?"

"The same way as most of us did. The Casting Director put your name on a list, you were called and auditioned by Andy, he decided you were the best person to play Bushy."

"Yes, that's more or less how it happened. But Andy was *very* insistent that I should be in the company."

Charles Paris thought he understood the implication and looked to Hal Westmacott for confirmation. "Yes, my fatal charm. I'm afraid Andy Smoker took a shine to me in rather a big way. He's been trying to get inside my knickers ever since we started rehearsal."

"But I didn't know you were gay."

"I'm not." The young actor was mildly offended by the suggestion.

"The rest of the company think you're having it off with that Kelly-Anne, you know, the one who's playing 'Lady attending on the Queen'."

"Oh dear. It's so difficult to have any secrets in the theatre, isn't it?"

"So you and Kelly-Anne are…?"

"A mild flirtation, no more. A flirtation that, it has to be said, does involves frequent exchange of bodily fluids, nothing more serious than that, though."

"But since everyone in the company knows about it, Andy must know too, so he must realise his advances to you—"

"Oh, don't be so old-fashioned, Charles. Of course Andy knows about Kelly-Anne and me, but I have made it clear to him that I'm not a one-woman man… nor indeed a one-man man. You have to be flexible in this business. I'd have thought, given the amount of time you've been around in it, you would have known that."

"Yes, but—"

"Charles, Charles… Right now Andy Smoker is an extremely hot name in the theatre. He can do me a lot of good. In fact he already has done me a lot of good. Thanks to him, I will be playing Richard the Second in a First Night that's going to get saturation media coverage. I think Andy may reckon he deserves a little thank-you from me for that. And I think it might be churlish of me to deny him that little thank-you." The green eyes looked straight into Charles's. "We all need help on our passage through life, and it's up to us to choose which passage we take advantage of." The innuendo was quite deliberate and, in case Charles might have missed it, was punctuated by a snigger.

"Are you suggesting that Andy Smoker might have deliberately poisoned Martin Cheyney to, as you put it, 'get inside your knickers'?"

The young actor preened in front of his mirror. "He *is* very besotted with me, you know."

"But surely—?"

Charles Paris was interrupted by a knock on the dressing room door. It was Martin's dresser Milly. She looked as if she might have been crying. Over her arms were draped her first load of resplendent costumes for Richard the Second.

And to confirm the understudy's elevation, the dressing room speaker at that moment crackled into life. The Stage Manager announced that, due to the indisposition of Martin Cheyney, the part of Richard would be played that night by Hal Westmacott. The entire company was required onstage in ten minutes to do a quick top-and-tail rehearsal with the revised casting. And strict secrecy about the news was to be observed. The Company Manager didn't want the news of Martin Cheyney's replacement to be leaked to the press any sooner than it had to be.

* * *

The top-and-tail rehearsal took longer than had been expected. Hal Westmacott's assumption of the role of Richard meant that his part of Bushy had to be taken over by one of the 'Attendants' with whom Charles Paris shared the upstairs dressing room. And that Attendant's part had to be filled by one of the male ASMs. A great deal of Andy Smoker's elaborate choreography of the large-cast scenes had to be run through and reorganised. The top-and-tail rehearsal even threatened to run into 'the half', that sacred time thirty-five minutes before a performance is due to start, by when all of the actors were contractually obliged to be in the theatre ready. And that particular night being a First Night, the show went up at seven, in theory to give newspaper critics time to file their review copy, so the time pressure was even greater.

As a result of all this confusion, Charles Paris did not get a chance to confront Andy Smoker until very near to curtain-up. 'Beginners' had been called over the Tannoy, and that meant most of the company. Act One Scene One of *Richard II* opens with the entrance of 'KING RICHARD, attended; JOHN OF GAUNT, and other Nobles." In that scene Charles was an 'other Noble'.

Dressed in his 'other Noble' costume, a bright tabard over heavy chain mail, he descended from the third floor and on the second landing met Hal Westmacott, glorious in his regalia, being escorted from his dressing room by Andy Smoker, who had a more-than-avuncular arm across the understudy's shoulders.

"You'll be great, Hal," the director was saying. "From the moment I heard you audition, I know you'd make a better Richard than Martin. He's got so stylised these days. And he just doesn't take notes – thinks he knows better than I do how to play the part. You're going to become a star tonight, Hal – a very big star indeed."

"I can't thank you enough for giving me the opportunity, Andy," said the young actor magnanimously. "I can't believe the way you've organised it all."

"Well, you know why I have, don't you, Hal?"

"Of course I do."

"And I'll get my reward, will I, after the First Night party?"

"You'll get your reward, Andy."

The men's hands clasped. Had there not been other actors making their way down the stairs to the stage, Charles Paris thought they might have kissed.

Still, what he'd heard was enough for him to challenge Andy Smoker. The director had virtually admitted to causing Martin Cheyney's illness. If the poison proved fatal, he had virtually admitted to committing murder. Time for a confrontation. Charles Paris stepped closer to the pair and tapped Andy Smoker on the shoulder.

They had reached the stage level. The director turned to see who had touched him, but before he could say anything to Charles, the door from the Green Room burst open to reveal a very fit-looking and extremely angry Martin Cheyney.

"Get out of my bloody costume, you little turd!" the star roared at his understudy. "I'm going on!"

* * *

The First Night of *Richard II* at the Kean Theatre in Shaftesbury Avenue went extremely well. The audience demographic was slightly younger than was usual for the West End, proving the value of the television publicity from *Queen for a Play*. The youngsters who cheered and whistled at Imogen Clay's first appearance as King Richard's consort clearly hadn't been to a Shakespeare play before.

Charles Paris managed to stand up straight in his various appearances an 'other Noble', and his scene as the Gardener went very well. Though he tried not to admit it to himself, he was actually very nervous before it started, but once he'd got out his first line – 'Go bind thou up yon dangling apricocks' – he was away. He felt the audience being moved as he told the young Queen the news of her husband's deposition. It was moments like that that reminded him why he had become an actor, and he felt warmed by the knowledge that his wife Frances was in the audience.

And it was only at the curtain call Charles Paris realised that, because of the excitements of the afternoon, he'd done the whole show without recourse to the half-bottle of Bells in his dressing room. So maybe that was a kind of good news.

Rising to the standard set by their star, the other actors also triumphed. And if anyone noticed a rather petulant expression on the face of Bushy... well, Bushy, Bagot and Green were meant to be petulant characters, anyway.

For Martin Cheyney as Richard the Second the evening was a triumph. The audience gave him a standing ovation and called him back for ten solo calls.

* * *

The First Night party was held in the Rose Langton room of the Century Club on Shaftesbury Avenue. Charles Paris's wife Frances was looking stunning, and it was one of those many occasions when he couldn't imagine why he hadn't been more efficient in staying properly married to her. He knew that in the past other women had been part of the problem, but... He must really work on getting the two of them permanently back together.

At the party Frances had met the agent of one of the actors, who turned out also to be a member of her book group in Muswell Hill, so while the two women talked, Charles looked around the milling throng, all of whom were glowing with the undoubted success of the evening.

Only Andy Smoker appeared out of sorts. In spite of constant flamboyant hugging accolades from actor friends, theatre management and sponsors, his eye kept moving disconsolately across to the corner where Hal Westmacott was making extremely unambiguous advances to Kelly-Jane, the young actress who played the 'Lady attending on the Queen'.

As Charles looked towards the couple, an extremely excited Martin Cheyney crossed his vision. The star was loudly toasting everyone with what was clearly not his first glass of champagne.

Charles managed to get close enough for a whispered word. "Are you all right, Martin?"

"All right? What do you mean?"

"The last time I saw you you were being rushed off to hospital in agony."

"Oh, yes. I'd forgotten about that." And he sounded as if he genuinely had. "Yes, bloody painful it was," he said quickly, to assert the genuineness of his suffering. "But it went as soon as it got to the hospital."

"Well, it didn't seem to affect your performance tonight. Bloody brilliant."

"Bless you, Charles. We do our humble best." He raised his glass. "To Doctor Theatre!"

Charles echoed the toast. 'Doctor Theatre' was the term actors use to explain the way they can be feeling terminally ill moments before they step on stage, then make their first entrance, forget their illness for the duration of the play and give the performance of their lives.

Martin Cheyney hadn't been poisoned, Charles reflected. The pain had all been in his mind, First Night nerves. And as he turned back towards his wife Frances, Charles Paris felt glad that he hadn't actually got as far as accusing any member of the *Richard II* company of murder.

Tour New Zealand in Five Easy Murders

Yvonne Eve Walus

The 3rd one, Christchurch

When I tell people I'm a criminal profiler, respectful silence falls on the conversation. I know what they're thinking: Sherlock Holmes, challenging cases, complex scientific methods.

That image is about as close to the truth as prostitution is to a glam way of spending your evenings with cocktails and distinguished gentlemen.

Speaking of prostitution, there's been another killing. That's why they called me in. I was shuffling my usual load of dusty files, with trails as cold as winter sand, when the boss stuck his head into my cubicle.

"Fuck all that, Cupcake," he said. "We have a live one here."

An ironic choice of words, given the state the victim was in.

It's difficult to be a woman in this job. "You won't have the stomach," they'd said when I applied. What they'd meant was, I wouldn't have the imagination. Getting into the mind of a serial killer (and I'm not being sexist here when I say they're all male) is difficult enough for any so-called normal person, but for a woman to try to get inside such a man's head… that's next to impossible.

Up till now, the only head I'd needed to get into was my boss's when I wanted a raise – which I managed; and my ex boyfriend's – which I did not. Profiling the home invaders, the restaurant arsonists and the small-scale extortionists didn't require a lot of imagination. I would study the crime scenes (mostly from photographs) and the statistics (mostly from tedious reports), I would pore over the evidence and produce profiles good enough for positive ID.

Up till now.

"That's the third one this year and it follows the pattern," I heard moments later in the emergency meeting. "A prostitute on her night off, a back street, a strike to the head hard enough to stun, followed by strangulation. In each case, autopsy revealed a first-class dinner eaten a few hours beforehand. As to sexual activity—"

"What did they eat?" I interrupted.

A few faces smirked. Trust a woman to ask that, especially just as we were getting to the sex part. Fuck, we'll be discussing shoes next if we let her say anything else.

"I presume the local police followed up on it?" I continued. "Like if it was snapper, then which restaurant served snapper on the night?"

The boss shrugged. It was his favourite way of side-stepping concerns. "Detective work is not your area. You are supposed to profile the perp, not the dining scene."

All the brown noses chuckled obediently.

The meeting went on and on. The first victim was in Invercargill, way down at the southern tip of the South Island. The second one in Dunedin, moving up north along the east coast. And now the third in Christchurch, as though the killer were taking a sightseeing trip of New Zealand's cities, starting right at the bottom and continuing up the tourist map.

The conference room chair felt like an anthill. I just wanted to be left alone with the evidence. Three victims, all prostitutes. No trace of sexual activity. I knew that was telling. I just wasn't sure yet *what* it was telling me.

That evening, when I'd climbed the stairs to my flat, I found a letter stuck into the tiny space between the door and the jamb. I recognised the handwriting in the single word on the envelope. I read the letter three times, cried twice, then went inside, smoothed out the sheet and put it deep in the knickers drawer, together with all the others.

That night, I dreamt about my ex. I don't call him by his name anymore. All that's important is his status: he was mine once, and now he isn't.

* * *

The 4th one, Wellington

I was right. The bastard is travelling up the map. Yesterday he crossed over to the North Island and did the capital city.

I had a busy week. First, I got to fly around the country, checking the dinner lead in Invercargill, Dunedin and Christchurch. Invercargill was sunny and cold, Dunedin was Scottish and cold, and Christchurch was its usual twee self.

I got several gourmet meals out of it, all compliments of the taxpayers, but no restaurant could recall seeing any of the murdered girls. Most owners shook their heads 'no' before they even glanced at the photos. I can understand that – some publicity can be bad publicity. When news came of the Wellington murder, I didn't even bother with the restaurants, although I did fly in to examine the murder scene itself, which looked like the rest of the capital city: windy and wet.

Second, I worked out what we knew of the perpetrator so far. Most serial killings are about control and power and – yes – sexual pleasure, whether or not any sexual assault has actually taken place. The fact that he first stunned his victims could point to inferior physical strength, or to cunning in not wanting to leave evidence that would have resulted from a struggle, the most obvious being his skin under the victim's fingernails. Then there was the geographical spread of the killings: years of experience were shouting that this was an important clue.

Third, I analysed the victims. We use victimology to discover the motives of the killer – profiling the victims to profile the killer, so to speak. Four women, prostitutes, all wined and dined and sexually untouched. Why?

I compared the photographs of the four. No obvious physical similarities, although all the victims were of European descent and on the plump side. I noticed that last point because my mental image of a call girl is slim curves and legs as slim as a man's, not the familiar portly lines I see in the mirror every night. There were no further points of intersection. The hair, for example, ranged from sandy to mousy, and there was nothing in the faces to suggest a fetish for small noses or heavy jaw lines or freckles.

"Cupcake, meet your new assistant." The boss's head was in my cubicle again, peering over the partition. How was I supposed to concentrate with him asking for progress updates every five minutes? "His name is Neil."

"What bloody assistant?"

"This isn't arson or a series of petty thefts, Cupcake. It's murder."

"Gee, thanks. I wouldn't have noticed myself."

The boss shrugged – I know because I saw one of his shoulders bob over the partition. "I'll leave you two to get acquainted."

My new assistant (he must be short not to show above the partition, I mused, as I kept my eyes on the latest pathology report) entered the cubicle and settled his arse comfortably between my coffee mug and the photographs. I raised my head from the paperwork in a studied theatrical gesture.

A sudden jolt. Heart in mouth. Knees that buckled even though I was sitting. Breathe, girl, breathe. Take a good look. See, the resemblance is just superficial.

"Hi," he said. Fortunately, the voice was nothing like my ex's.

"Bugger off, Nick. This is my case."

"Neil."

"Yeah, whatever."

I'd met my ex at a party. It was more of a booze-up than a party, really, which is not exactly my scene. I sat on the porch with a bottle of mineral water and wondered what to do with the rest of my Saturday night.

"Has anyone ever told you how gorgeous you look when you frown?" said a voice behind me.

For a pickup line, it wasn't the worst. And as the evening progressed, I discovered that he had a knack for words and always said the very thing I wanted to hear. I went home with him that night.

He was a dream to listen to, but crap in bed.

"I know there are two things I excel at," he said when he was done. "This, and my job."

I chose not to comment on the excelling-at-this part. "What's your job?"

"Chess instructor. You?"

"I'm with the police," I didn't go into the details of freelance contracting. "A criminal profiler."

We spent the rest of the night talking about my work and what an amazing person I was. By the time the sun came up, I was in love.

"So what do you make of the locations?" Neil was still perched on my desk.

"A tourist perhaps. Or a businessman. Or a trucker."

"I don't mean the geography. I mean the back streets."

I hadn't considered that. "He drove her there ostensibly to have sex? Nah, doesn't gel, they were too high class to do it in the street, be it business or pleasure. Plus, they weren't even killed in a car. They were killed in the street."

"Exactly," Neil's mouth said. His mouth looked so much like… I couldn't concentrate.

When my ex drove me to his flat that first night, he asked: "What are you thinking right now?"

"That I hope you're not planning to kill me. Or if you are, that you'll at least have the decency to fuck me first," I answered. I had no idea where that came from.

I mean, true, he was a stranger and I was riding in his car through deserted streets, but still. The job's shadow on my private life, I thought.

"I've never killed anyone," he replied gravely.

Something inside me churned. What sort of a comment was that?

"Well, that's good," I replied.

"I started a few fires, though," he added.

I flinched. Many serial killers play around with arson before they move onto murder. Arson allows the offender to feel the power and control, to observe the flames and the smoke and the commotion he created.

"By accident, of course," he said.

"I guess we both need to chew on it." Neil jumped off my desk. "I'll be next door if you need anything."

What I need, I reflected, is to know why the killer is not sticking to one city, thank you very much. And why he's targeting prostitutes.

"Have you ever been paid for sex?" he asked. We were lying in bed, but it wasn't afterglow. Despite ten minutes of vigorous pounding, I'd failed to get off, and, strangely enough, so had he. I faked. He didn't.

"No," I laughed. "Have you?"

"Me? You reckon I should be paid?" But it wasn't a question.

I ducked the issue. "I meant, have you ever paid for sex?"

"That would be disgusting."

So why mention it, I thought.

He pulled me towards his chest. "You're the most beautiful person I know," he whispered into my hair. "We are soul mates. I want to be with you forever."

I forgot the lousy sex and the weird conversation. I thought my heart would break with so much happiness.

I split up with him a month later.

* * *

The 5th one, Palmerston North

"We simply have to stop him before he gets to Auckland."

"Why? There are no major cities north of us." It slipped out of my mouth before I could stop it, so I followed up with "Sir."

"Ah, Miss Profiler." No *Cupcake* today. "Will we be able to make positive id based on all your sightseeing of the last fortnight?"

"Yes."

"Oh?"

"I just need one more day."

In fact, I only needed one email.

Before the meeting, as soon as I'd heard the news of the fifth murder, I looked up New Zealand chess championships on the Internet. As I suspected, they had been taking place in Palmerston North in the last couple of days. I couldn't find anything for Invercargill or Christchurch, but there had been an informal chess tournament in Dunedin on the exact day when the murder took place.

"Very well. One more day."

I split up with him when he tried to kill a pigeon.

We were sitting on a park bench, an idyllic picture of thigh to thigh and hand in hand. A few birds pecked at the ground nearby.

"Shoo, shooo," he shouted. Then his hand left mine and picked up a large stone.

I was quicker. "Don't!"

He held me close. "You have such a kind heart. You are a truly wonderful person. I don't deserve you. I'm evil."

It was my turn to say all the right things.

I did.

But that night I split up with him.

A week later, the first body was found.

Neil squeezed my arm in the corridor.

"Sure you know what you're doing? We haven't had a chance to catch up and I've discovered a few clues—"

"I'm sure. But thanks."

"Any time. You know where—"

"To find you, yes. Now, I have an email to write."

I had to type in his email address from memory because I'd deleted it from the address book when we broke up. The message itself was simple. I outlined the current case, I presented the facts and the profile, I accused him.

Then I sat in front of my screen waiting for the reply.

"Sorry to bother you—"

"Bugger off, Neil."

"At least you remember my name now." A quick wink, so quick I may have imagined it. "Listen, there is something you absolutely have to take a look at. I've been wondering about the locations, and then it hit me.

There is an airport in every one of the cities where the killings took place—"

"The cities? What about the back streets? That was your big idea."

Neil waved his hand. "Didn't pan out. We probably won't know until we have him. If then. Perhaps he has a cul-de-sac fetish, who knows? Meanwhile, it was your idea of geographical locations that struck gold. I first thought ports and sailors, you know, because the stereotype kind of goes hand in hand with prostitution—"

"But Palmerston North is not on the sea, so then you did a mental jump to airports?"

"Exactly. I checked all the aircrews stationed in the cities during the key times. One name is on every list."

I was off my feet. "Did you check out his background? How well does he fit the profile?"

"I left that for you. You're the expert."

By the end of the day, we had our man. Just like I'd promised the boss.

He was a pilot, a small guy with big issues.

But not nearly as big as the issues I had. Talk of egocentric: I imagined that just because I ditched a guy he'd go on a killing spree. Yeah right.

I'd almost screwed up my first big case.

But all the facts fitted: cruelty to animals, the fires, the ego, the problems in bed. The typical profile of a potential serial killer, if I ever saw one.

I was still sitting in front of the computer, typing in the final report and telling myself what an idiot I'd been, when the email came.

"I understand where you're coming from," my ex said. "And your email has given me an idea. An idea I'm very excited about. Let's have dinner tonight so that we can develop it further."

Such simple words. I didn't know why they sent a shiver down my back.

"You're still here?" Neil smiled as he squeezed into my cubicle. It was a kind smile. I didn't know how I could ever think there was any resemblance to… to *him*. "Fancy grabbing a bite to eat?"

"No thanks," I heard myself say. My tongue was dry. "I already have dinner plans."

Fedora

John Harvey

WHEN THEY HAD first met, amused by his occupation, Kate had sent him copies of Hammett and Chandler, two neat piles of paperbacks, bubble-wrapped, courier-delivered. A note: *If you're going to do, do it right. Fedora follows.* He hadn't been certain exactly what a fedora was.

Jack Kiley, private investigator. Security work of all kinds undertaken. Ex-Metropolitan Police.

Most of his assignments came from bigger security firms, PR agencies with clients in need of babysitting, steering clear of trouble; solicitors after witness confirmation, a little dirt. If it didn't make him rich, most months it paid the rent: a second-floor flat above a charity shop in north London, Tufnell Park. He still didn't have a hat.

Till now.

One of the volunteers in the shop had taken it in. "An admirer, Jack, is that what it is?"

There was a card attached to the outside of the box: *Chris Ruocco of London, Bespoke Tailoring.* It hadn't come far. A quarter mile, at most. Kiley had paused often enough outside the shop, coveting suits in the window he could ill afford.

But this was a broad-brimmed felt hat, not quite black. Midnight blue? He tried it on for size. More or less a perfect fit.

There was a note sticking up from the band: on one side, a quote from Chandler; on the other a message: *Ozone, tomorrow. 11am?* Both in Kate Keenan's hand.

He took the hat back off and placed it on the table alongside his mobile phone. Had half a mind to call her and decline. Thanks, but no thanks. Make some excuse. Drop the fedora back at Ruocco's next time he caught the overground from Kentish Town.

It had been six months now since he and Kate had last met, the premiere of a new Turkish-Albanian film to which she'd been invited, Kiley leaving halfway through and consoling himself with several large whiskies in the cinema bar. When Kate had finally emerged, preoccupied by the piece she was going to write for her column in the *Independent*, something praising the film's mysterious grandeur, its uncompromising pessimism – the phrases already forming inside her head – Kiley's sarcastic "Got better, did it?" precipitated a row which ended on the street outside with her calling him a hopeless philistine and Kiley suggesting she take whatever pretentious arty crap she was going to write for her bloody newspaper and shove it.

Since then, silence.

Now what was this? A peace offering? Something more?

Kiley shook his head. Was he really going to put himself through all that again? Kate's companion. Cramped evenings in some tiny theatre upstairs, less room for his knees than the North End at Leyton Orient; standing for what seemed like hours, watching others genuflect before the banality of some Turner Prize winner; another mind-numbing lecture at the British Library; brilliant meals at Moro or the River Cafe on Kate's expense account; great sex.

Well, thought Kiley, nothing was perfect.

* * *

Ozone, or to give it its proper title, Ozone Coffee Roasters, was on a side street close by Old Street station. In full view in the basement, industrial-size roasting machines had their way with carefully harvested beans from the best single-estate coffee farms in the world – Kiley had googled the place before leaving – while upstairs smart young people sat either side of a long counter or at heavy wooden tables, most of them busy at their laptops as their flat whites or espressos grew cold around them. Not that Kiley had anything against a good flat white – twenty-first-century man, or so he sometimes liked to think, he could navigate his way round the coffee houses in London with the best of them.

Chalked on a slate at the front of one of the tables was Kate Keenan's name and a time, 11:00, but no Kate to be seen.

Just time to reassess, change his mind.

Kiley slid along the bench seat and gave his order to a waitress who seemed to be wearing mostly tattoos. Five minutes later, Kate arrived.

She was wearing a long, loose crepe coat that swayed around her as she walked; black trousers, a white shirt, soft leather bag slung over one shoulder. Her dark hair was cut short, shorter than he remembered, taking an extra shine from the lighting overhead. As she approached the table her face broke into a smile. She looked, Kiley thought, allowing himself the odd ageist indiscretion, lovelier than any forty-four-year-old woman had the right.

"Jack, you could at least have worn the hat."

"Saving it for a special occasion."

"You mean this isn't one?"

"We'll see."

She kissed him on the mouth.

"I'm famished," she said. "You going to eat?"

"I don't know."

"The food's good. Very good."

There was an omelette on the menu, the cost, Kiley reckoned, of a meal at McDonald's or Subway for a family of five. When it came it was fat and delicious, stuffed with spinach, shallots and red pepper and bright with the taste of fresh chillis. Kate had poached eggs on sourdough toast with portobello mushrooms. She'd scarcely punctured the first egg when she got down to it.

"Jack, a favour."

He paused with his fork halfway to his mouth.

"Graeme Fisher, mean anything to you?"

"Vaguely." He didn't know how or in what connection.

"Photographer, big in the sixties. Bailey, Duffy, Fisher. The big three, according to some. Fashion, that was his thing. Everyone's thing. Biba. *Vogue.* You couldn't open a magazine, look at a hoarding without one of his pictures staring back at you." She took a sip from her espresso. "He disappeared for a while in the eighties – early seventies, eighties. Australia, maybe, I'm not sure. Resurfaced with a show at Victoria Miro, new work, quite a bit different. Cooler, more detached: buildings, interiors, mostly empty. Very few people."

Skip the art history, Kiley thought, this is leading where?

"I did a profile of him for the *Independent on Sunday*," Kate said. "Liked him. Self-deprecating, almost humble. Genuine."

"What's he done?" Kiley asked.

"Nothing."

"But he is in some kind of trouble?"

"Maybe."

"Shenanigans."

"Sorry?"

"Someone else's wife; someone else's son, daughter. What used to be called indiscretions. Now it's something more serious."

Following the high-profile arrests of several prominent media personalities, accused of a variety of sexual offences dating back up to forty years, reports to the police of historic rape and serious sexual abuse had increased fourfold. Men – it was mostly men – who had enjoyed both the spotlight and the supposed sexual liberation of the sixties and later were contacting their lawyers, setting up damage limitation exercises, quaking in their shoes.

"You've still got contacts in the Met, haven't you, Jack?"

"A few."

"I thought if there was anyone you knew – Operation Yewtree, is that what it's called? – I thought you might be able to have a word on the quiet, find out if Fisher was one of the people they were taking an interest in."

"Should they be?"

"No. No."

"Because if they're not, the minute I mention his name, they're going to be all over him like flies."

Kate cut away a small piece of toast, added mushroom, a smidgeon of egg. "Maybe there's another way."

Kiley said nothing.

As if forgetting she'd changed the style, Kate smoothed a hand across her forehead to brush away a strand of hair. "When he was what? Twenty-nine? Thirty? He had this relationship with a girl, a model."

Kiley nodded, sensing where this was going.

"She was young," Kate said. "Fifteen. Fifteen when it started."

"Fifteen," Kiley said quietly.

"It wasn't aggressive, wasn't in any sense against her will, it was... like I say, it was a relationship, a proper relationship. It wasn't even secret. People knew."

"People?"

"In the business. Friends. They were an item."

"And that made it OK? An item?"

"Jack..."

"What?"

"Don't prejudge. And stop repeating everything I say."

Kiley chased a last mouthful of spinach around his plate.

The waitress with the tattoos stopped by their table to ask if there was anything else they wanted and Kate sent her on her way.

"He's afraid of her," Kate said. "Afraid she'll go to the police herself."

"Why now?"

"It's in the air, Jack. You read the papers, watch the news. Cleaning out the Augean stables doesn't come into it."

Kiley was tempted to look at his watch: ten minutes without Kate making a reference he failed to understand. Maybe fifteen. "A proper relationship, isn't that what you said?"

"It ended badly. She didn't want to accept things had run their course. Made it difficult. When it became clear he wasn't going to change his mind, she attempted suicide."

"Pills?"

Kate nodded. "It was all hushed up at the time. Back then, that was still possible."

"And now he's terrified it'll all come out…"

"Go and talk to him, Jack. Do that at least. I think you'll like him."

Liking him, Kiley knew, would be neither here nor there, a hindrance at best.

* * *

There was a bookshop specialising in fashion and photography on Charing Cross Road. Claire de Rouen. Kiley had walked past there a hundred times without ever going in. Two narrow flights of stairs and then an interior slightly larger than the average bathroom. Books floor to ceiling, wall to wall. There was a catalogue from Fisher's show at Victoria Miro, alongside a fat retrospective, several inches thick. Most of the photographs, the early ones, were in glossy black and white. Beautiful young women slumming in fashionable clothes: standing, arms aloft, in a bomb site, dripping with costume jewellery and furs; laughing outside Tubby Isaac's Jellied Eel Stall at Spitalfields; stretched out along a coster's barrow, legs kicking high in the air. One picture that Kiley kept flicking back to, a thin-hipped, almost waif-like girl standing, marooned, in an empty swimming pool, naked save for a pair of skimpy pants and gold bangles snaking up both arms, a gold necklace hanging down between her breasts. Lisa Arnold. Kate had told him her name. Lisa. He wondered if this were her.

* * *

The house was between Ladbroke Grove and Notting Hill, not so far from the Portobello Road. Flat-fronted, once grand, paint beginning to flake away round the windows on the upper floors. Slabs of York stone leading, uneven, to the front door. Three bells. Graeme Fisher lived on the ground floor.

He took his time responding.

White hair fell in wisps around his ears; several days since he'd shaved. Corduroy trousers, collarless shirt, cardigan wrongly buttoned, slippers on his feet.

"You'll be Kate's friend."

Kiley nodded and held out his hand.

The grip was firm enough, though when he walked it was slow, more of a shuffle, with a pronounced tilt to one side.

"Better come through here."

Here was a large room towards the back of the house, now dining room and kitchen combined. A short line of servants' bells, polished brass, was still attached to the wall close by the door.

Fisher sat at the scrubbed oak table and waited for Kiley to do the same.

"Bought this place for a song in '64. All divided up since then, rented out. Investment banker and his lady friend on the top floor – when they're not down at his place in Dorset. Bloke above us, something in the social media." He said it as if it were a particularly nasty disease. "Keeps the bailiffs from the sodding door."

There were photographs, framed, on the far wall. A street scene, deserted, muted colours, late afternoon light. An open-top truck, its sides bright red, driving away up a dusty road, fields to either side. Café tables in bright sunshine, crowded, lively, in the corner of a square; then the same tables, towards evening, empty save for an old man, head down, sleeping. Set a little to one side, two near-abstracts, sharp angles, flat planes.

"Costa Rica," Fisher said, "'72. On assignment. Never bloody used. Too fucking arty by half."

He made tea, brought it to the table in plain white mugs, added two sugars to his own and then, after a moment's thought, a third.

"Tell me about Lisa," Kiley said.

Fisher laughed, no shred of humour. "You don't have the time."

"It ended badly, Kate said."

"It always ends fucking badly." He coughed, a rasp low in the throat, turning his head aside.

"And you think she might be harbouring a grudge?"

"Harbouring? Who knows? Life of her own. Kids. Grandkids by now, most like. Doubt she gives me a second thought, one year's end to the next."

"Then why…?"

"This woman a couple of days back, right? Lisa's age. There she is on TV, evening news. Some bloke, some third-rate comedian, French-kissed her in the back of a taxi when she was fifteen, copped a feel. Now she's reckoning sexual assault. Poor bastard's picture all over the papers. Paedophile. That's not a fucking paedophile." He shook his head. "I'd sooner bloody die."

Kiley cushioned his mug in both hands. "Why don't you talk to her? Make sure?"

Fisher smiled. "A while back, round the time I met Kate, I was going to have this show, Victoria Miro, first one in ages, and I thought, Lisa, I'll give her a bell. See if she might, you know, come along. Last minute, I couldn't, couldn't do it. I sent her a note instead, invitation to the private view. Never replied, never came."

He wiped a hand across his mouth, finished his tea.

"You'll go see her? Kate said you would. Just help me rest easy." He laughed. "Too much tension, not good for the heart."

* * *

Google Maps said the London Borough of Haringey, estate agents called it Muswell Hill. A street of Arts and Crafts houses, nestled together, white louvred shutters at the windows, prettily painted doors. She was tall, taller than Kiley had expected, hair pulled back off her face, little make-up; tunic top, skinny jeans. He could still see the girl who'd stood in the empty pool through the lines that ran from the corners of her mouth and eyes.

"Lisa Arnold?"

"Not for thirty years."

"Jack Kiley." He held out a hand. "An old friend of yours asked me to stop by."

"An old friend?"

"Yes."

"Then he should have told you it's Collins. Lisa Collins." She still didn't take his hand and Kiley let it fall back by his side.

"This old friend, he have a name?" But, of course, she knew. "You better come in," she said. "Just mind the mess in the hall."

Kiley stepped around a miniature pram, various dolls, a wooden puzzle, skittles, soft toys.

"Grandkids," she explained, "two of them, Tuesdays and Thursday mornings, Wednesday afternoons. Run me ragged."

Two small rooms had been knocked through to give a view of the garden: flowering shrubs, a small fruit tree, more toys on the lawn.

Lisa Collins sat in a wing-backed chair, motioning Kiley to the settee. There were paintings on the wall, watercolours; no photographs other than a cluster of family pictures above the fireplace. Two narrow bookcases; rugs on polished boards; dried flowers. It was difficult to believe she was over sixty years old.

"How is Graeme?"

Kiley shrugged. "He seemed OK. Not brilliant, maybe, but OK."

"You're not really a friend, are you?"

"No?"

"Graeme doesn't do friends."

"Maybe he's changed."

She looked beyond Kiley towards the window, distracted by the shadow of someone passing along the street outside.

"You don't smoke, I suppose?"

"Afraid not."

"No. Well, in that case, you'll have to join me in a glass of wine. And don't say no."

"I wasn't about to."

"White OK?"

"White's fine."

She left the room and he heard the fridge door open and close; the glasses were tissue-thin, tinged with green; the wine grassy, cold.

"All this hoo-ha going on," she said. "People digging up the past, I'd been half-expecting someone doorstepping me on the way to Budgens." She gave a little laugh. "Me and my shopping trolley. Some reporter or other. Expecting me to dig up the dirt, spill the beans."

Kiley said nothing.

"That's what he's worried about, isn't it? After all this time, the big exposé, shit hitting the fan."

"Yes."

"That invitation he sent me, the private view. I should have gone."

"Why didn't you?"

"I was afraid."

"What of?"

"Seeing him again. After all this time. Afraid what it would do to all this." She gestured round the room, the two rooms. "Afraid it could blow it all apart."

"It could do that?"

"Oh, yes." She drank some wine and set the glass carefully back down. "People said it was just a phase. Too young, you know, like in the song? Too young to know. You'll snap out of it, they said, the other girls. Get away, move on, get a life of your own. Cradle-snatcher, they'd say to Graeme, and laugh."

Shaking her head, she smiled.

"Four years we were together. Four years. Say it like that, it doesn't seem so long." She shook her head again.

"A lifetime, that's what it was. When it started I was just a kid and then..."

She was seeing something Kiley couldn't see; as if, for a moment, he were no longer there.

"I knew – I wasn't stupid – I knew it wasn't going to last forever, I even forced it a bit myself, looking back, but then, when it happened, I don't know, I suppose I sort of fell apart."

She reached for her glass.

"What's that they say? Whatever doesn't kill you, makes you strong. Having your stomach pumped out, that helps, too. Didn't want to do that again in a hurry, I can tell you. And thanks to Graeme, I had contacts, a portfolio, I could work. David Bailey round knocking at the door. Brian bloody Duffy. *Harper's Bazaar*. I had a life. A good one. Still have."

Still holding the wine glass, she got to her feet.

"You can tell Graeme, I don't regret a thing. Tell him I love him, the old bastard. But now..." A glance at her watch. "Mr. Collins – that's what I call him – Mr. Collins will be home soon. Golf widow, that's me. Stops him getting under my feet, I suppose."

She walked Kiley to the door.

"There was someone sniffing round. Oh, a good month ago now. More. Some journalist or other. That piece by Kate Moss had just been in the news. How when she was getting started she used to feel awkward, posing, you know, half-naked. Nude. Not feeling able to say no. Wanted to know, the reporter, had I ever felt exploited? Back then. Fifteen, she said, it's very young after all. I told her I'd felt fine. Asked her to leave, hello and goodbye. Might have been the *Telegraph*, I'm not sure."

She shook Kiley's hand.

When he was crossing the street she called after him. "Don't forget, give Graeme my love."

* * *

The article appeared a week later, eight pages stripped across the Sunday magazine, accompanied by a hefty news item in the main paper. 'Art or Exploitation?' Ballet dancers and fashion models, a few gymnasts and tennis players thrown in for good measure. Unhealthy relationships between fathers and daughters, young girls and their coaches or mentors. The swimming pool shot of Lisa was there, along with several others. Snatched from somewhere, a recent picture of Graeme Fisher, looking old, startled.

"The bastards," Kate said, vehemently. "The bastards."

Your profession, Kiley thought, biting back the words.

They were on their way to Amsterdam, Kate there to cover the reopening of the Stedelijk Museum after nine years of renovations, Kiley invited along as his reward for services rendered. "Three days in Amsterdam, Jack. What's not to like?"

At her insistence, he'd worn the hat.

They were staying at a small but smart hotel on the Prinsengracht Canal, theirs one of the quiet rooms at the back, looking out onto a small square. For old times' sake, she insisted on taking him for breakfast, the first morning, to the art deco Café Americain in the Amsterdam American Hotel.

"First time I ever came here, Jack, to Amsterdam, this is where we stayed."

He didn't ask.

The news from England, a bright 12 point on her iPad, erased the smile from her face. As a result of recent revelations in the media, officers from Operation Yewtree yesterday made two arrests; others were expected.

"Fisher?" Kiley asked.

She shook her head. "Not yet." When she tried to reach him on her mobile, there was no reply.

"Maybe he'll be OK," Kiley said.

"Let's hope," Kate said, and pushed back her chair, signalling it was time to go. Whatever was happening back in England, there was nothing they could do.

From the outside, Kiley thought, the new extension to the Stedelijk looked like a giant bathtub on stilts; inside didn't get much better. Kate seemed to be enthralled.

Kiley found the café, pulled out the copy of *The Glass Key* he'd taken the precaution of stuffing into his pocket, and read. Instead of getting better, as the story progressed things went from bad to worse, the hero chasing round in ever-widening circles, only pausing, every now and then, to get punched in the face.

"Fantastic!" Kate said, a good couple of hours later. "Just amazing."

There was a restaurant some friends had suggested they try for dinner, Le Hollandais; Kate wanted to go back to the hotel first, write up her notes, rest a little, change.

In the room, she switched on the TV to catch the news. Over her shoulder, Kiley thought he recognised the street in Ladbroke Grove. Officers from the Metropolitan Police arriving at the residence of former photographer, Graeme Fisher, wishing to question him with regard to allegations of historic sexual abuse, found Fisher hanging from a light flex at the rear of the house. Despite efforts by paramedics and ambulance staff to revive him, he was pronounced dead at the scene.

A sound, somewhere between a gasp and a sob, broke from Kate's throat, and when Kiley went across to comfort her, she shrugged him off.

There would be no dinner, Le Hollandais or elsewhere.

When she came out of the bathroom, Kate used her laptop to book the next available flight, ordered a taxi, rang down to reception to explain.

Kiley walked to the window and stood there, looking out across the square. Already the light was starting to change. Two runners loped by in breathless conversation, then an elderly woman walking her dog, then no one. The tables outside the cafe at right angles to the hotel were empty, save for an old man, head down, sleeping. Behind him, Kate moved, businesslike, around the room, readying their departure, her reflection picked out, ghostlike, in the glass. When Kiley looked back towards the tables, the old man had gone.

Les Inconnus

Kate Ellis

"NO WINDOW in Paris attracts more onlookers than this."

Jules Seurot ignored the remark. He stared at the scene behind the huge plate glass window feeling no revulsion, only a mild, detached curiosity.

The corpses lay on a row of slabs behind the glass, propped up slightly so that their features were clearly visible to the viewers. They were naked, their modesty covered by a small board upon which was written the details of where and when they had been found. Their clothes hung above them, dangling from a rail, providing a pathetic splash of colour in that white chamber of death.

The man who had spoken to Seurot was small with a shock of dark hair and a pair of spectacles perched precariously on the end of his nose. He was dressed like a clerk, neat but shabby in dusty black.

Seurot turned to him. "Where do they come from?"

"They are pulled from the Seine and brought here to the morgue in the hope that someone will claim them. Allow me introduce myself, Monsieur. My name is Charles Mery and it is my unhappy duty to investigate the deaths of these unfortunates. It is your first time in this place?"

"Indeed, Monsieur."

"You are not from Paris?"

Seurot wondered if his small-town ways had betrayed him in some way. He was painfully aware that the sophisticated Parisians saw him for what he was; a middle-aged provincial with an expanding belly and thinning hair.

"No, Monsieur. Although it is my wife's wish to move to the city. I am in search of an apartment."

"I wish you luck." Charles Mery inclined his head politely and gave the henpecked husband a look of pity. "I must take my leave, Monsieur. I have matters to attend to."

Seurot watched him disappear through a green painted door. Mery seemed amiable enough, although he was sure that he had detected a note of mockery in his voice.

The crowd before the window was growing fast. Mothers had brought their children to stare at the unfortunates behind the plate glass and the young seemed as entranced by the spectacle as their elders. People chattered and laughed as they gawped at the unseeing dead. Seurot had heard it was the best show in Paris, not to be missed, and it seemed that the rest of the city thought likewise. All classes of Paris society thronged into the morgue: from well-heeled gentlemen in silk hats arm in arm with their plump wives, to rough matelots and ladies of a certain calling with their cheap bright plumage and hard, pinched faces. Death fascinates all manner of men and women.

Seurot mopped his brow: the place was oppressive with too many bodies, alive and dead. He turned to go: he would view the great cathedral of Notre Dame nearby before continuing his search for an apartment that would satisfy Madeleine's exacting requirements.

He glanced at the large notice on the wall as he was leaving. "The public is requested to declare to the Morgue Clerk the name of any individual they recognise." Seurot continued on his way. The notice did not concern him as all Parisians were strangers.

As he reached the morgue's main door, he collided with a roughly dressed man who mumbled an apology and hurried on his way. It wasn't until he entered the portals of Notre Dame that Jules Seurot felt in his pocket and realised that his wallet was missing.

* * *

The Seurots lived just outside the centre of the small town of Moret, east of Fontainebleau. Jules returned from Paris to find the shutters open but no sign of life. Madeleine was out, which wasn't unusual. There were times Jules suspected that she had a lover, that she and Maitre Michet, the lawyer, were more than friends. However Moret – unlike Paris – was a small place where everyone knew each other's business and if his wife were unfaithful the town gossips would be bound to know of it.

And Madeleine's ardent desire to move to Paris reassured Seurot that there was no lover to keep her there. He understood her longing for city life: she had endured years trapped in Moret's dull provincial world by the need to be near her ageing and miserly father. But now her father was dead and she had come into her considerable inheritance. Soon they would be in the city, in the centre of things where Madeleine could show off the jewels and fine gowns she could now afford.

As Jules opened the front door a girl scurried from the back of the house. She bobbed a curtsey and smiled coquettishly. The sun had brought out the freckles on her turned up nose: Jules liked that. And he liked the swell of her breasts beneath her starched white apron.

"Where is your mistress, Chantal?"

Chantal looked him in the eye, too boldly for maid and master. "Visiting Madame Benot. Boasting of how she will soon be playing the grand lady in Paris."

Jules flinched. "You mustn't speak like that?"

"Why not?" Chantal reached out and drew him towards her. A few moments later he was kissing her, tasting her lips and running his fingers through her fine fair hair, dislodging her white linen cap. He broke away, breathless. "Not now, Chantal. It is not the time or the place."

The girl pouted. "But when we're in Paris…"

Jules's heart was pounding. He put his finger to her lips. "We must be careful. My wife must have no inkling of…"

Chantal caught his finger and kissed it. "Trust me," she whispered.

The sound of footsteps on the stone steps leading up to the front door heralded Madeleine's arrival. Chantal ran down the hallway and opened the door, bobbing a curtsey meekly to her mistress who barely acknowledged her presence. Jules breathed deeply, his heart still thumping in his chest. Deception was an exhausting game.

"My dear, how well you look," he said forcing a smile. He kissed his wife on the cheek but she hardly seemed to notice as she was busying herself with a hat box.

"What news of Paris? Did you find...?"

"I found the most beautiful apartment near the Rue Saint Honore. It has every luxury – such a bathroom. And it is spacious and light: you will love it." He looked round and saw that Chantal had disappeared into the servants' quarters below stairs.

"And what did you get up to in Paris?" Madeleine asked, narrowing her eyes.

"I saw the sights, of course... Notre Dame; the Louvre and... I lost my wallet. I fear it was stolen."

Madeleine looked at her husband disapprovingly. She put him in mind of an overripe fruit – plump and past her best. She frowned and he could see the fine lines radiating from her pursed lips.

"You should be on your guard in the city."

"It was your idea to live in Paris, my dear."

She ignored the remark. "Did you report the loss?"

"I returned to the morgue and the gentleman I spoke to there was most agreeable in spite of his grim calling. He said that there had been many such thefts there and that the gendarmes have been alerted. But he held out little hope of getting it back. Paris is full of pickpockets."

Madeleine's face was a mask of horror. "You went to the morgue?"

"In Paris it is quite an attraction. Whole families go to view the corpses pulled from the Seine. I will take you when we move to the city."

He watched her face, enjoying her expression of disgust.

"I would never set foot in such a place."

"How was Madame Benot? And her revolting little dog?"

"Both well. Although her nephew, that so-called artist, still causes her much worry. She fears that his immoral behaviour will scandalise all of Moret."

Jules fought back a smile. "What a trial it is to have scandalous neighbours. You do realise that in Paris it is possible that all our neighbours will be scandalous?"

Madeleine gave a snort of disapproval and swept off to try on her new hat. Jules watched her ample backside disappear through the doorway.

He was looking forward to Paris. In fact he could hardly wait.

* * *

A city, any city, bestows a certain anonymity upon its inhabitants. But Paris possessed a body of women who considered it their right and duty to know the business of others. The concierge was queen of her domain and observed all the comings and goings in her kingdom. Madame Dubois dwelt in her dark quarters on the ground floor beneath the Seurots' new apartment like a spider waiting in its web. Jules Seurot, who had never before lived in the capital, found her constant, vigilant presence disconcerting.

Seurot moved into the first-floor apartment in a small street off the Rue Saint Honore on the last Wednesday in November. Madeleine was to follow at the weekend as she had business to attend to in Moret. Jules knew that this involved spending time alone with Maitre Michet and he still had an uneasy feeling that there was something between them. The lawyer was much younger that he was, a tall and attractive man, and last week at Mass he had been staring in the direction of their pew. Madeleine was still what some would call a handsome woman, rendered even more handsome by her substantial fortune. And Gaston Michet knew exactly how much she was worth, down to the last centime.

But soon Michet wouldn't bother them. Madeleine and their maid, Chantal, were due in Paris on Saturday at three o'clock and Seurot was to meet them at the station. On Saturday afternoons the concierge, Madame Dubois, visited her aged mother and as he waited on the platform at the Gare de Lyon he congratulated himself that he had timed his wife's arrival to perfection.

When the train arrived in a cloud of billowing steam, he watched as Madeleine strutted confidently along the crowded platform towards him; the new Parisienne preparing to explore her adopted city with the zeal of a convert. Behind her walked Chantal carrying a valise and a hatbox. Madeleine wore blue silk and Chantal plain brown; a sparrow in the wake of a peacock.

Madeleine stared wide-eyed out of the carriage window as they trotted along the Rue de Rivoli past the great bulk of the Louvre. When they arrived at the apartment,

Seurot studied Madame Dubois' windows but saw no telltale twitch of curtains. The horse that had pulled their carriage to its destination looked at him with soulful eyes and Jules patted the animal's nose absentmindedly. He liked horses; horses didn't ask questions.

He paid the driver and hesitated before entering the building. He knew what had to be done. And it had to be done quickly before Madame Dubois returned.

When Jules entered the apartment, he found Chantal busy in the bedroom unpacking her mistress's clothes. She hurried to and fro, avoiding his eyes; tense, frightened. He felt like taking her in his arms. But he had to be patient.

Madeleine was exploring each room, making noises of approval. "What do you think of the apartment, my dear," he asked, playing the dutiful husband.

"It will do very nicely… for now. But when we begin to entertain, we may need somewhere larger."

Jules didn't reply. He studied his feet for a few moments.

"I thought we could take a stroll down to the river while Chantal unpacks," he said casually. "Then we shall dine out to celebrate your arrival: there are many fine restaurants in the vicinity."

She looked like a cat who had just caught sight of a desirable bowl of cream. "Why not? I am no longer a dull provincial woman so why should I not eat at the best restaurants in Paris." She laughed, the tinkling laugh that set his teeth on edge. "But it is almost dark."

"Paris is at its best in the dark."

"Very well, Jules, let us take our stroll. Chantal can manage here."

Madame Dubois had not returned so they left the apartment unobserved and walked arm in arm in the fading light through the bustling crowds, towards the Quai des Tuileries. And as they walked Madeleine Seurot took in every new sight, sound and smell, and stared round in wonder like a child in a toy shop.

* * *

"Is it done?"

Seurot nodded. "I saw the concierge return as I was coming in. She asked me if my wife had arrived safely."

"And how did you answer?"

"I said she liked the new apartment." Jules Seurot breathed deeply and realised that his hands were still shaking. "Shall we dine out?" he asked, hoping his voice sounded normal, untroubled.

"I have nothing to wear."

"You shall have the finest gowns now that you are…"

"Madame Madeleine Seurot?" Chantal tilted her head to one side. "Are you sure we shall not be discovered?"

"Do you think I have not taken precautions? There is no reason why anybody here should suspect that you are not who you say you are."

"What about Maitre Michet?"

"What about him?" Seurot snapped. Was there something he had overlooked?

"Nothing. He has been dealing with Madame's affairs, that is all."

"He won't trouble us. He has said on many occasions that he never visits Paris. But it would be as well to find a new apartment soon, just in case Madeleine has given anyone this address."

"You think of everything," she said admiringly before kissing him on the lips. "And… and Madame? Did she…?"

Seurot tried to smile. "What a blessing it is to have a wife who can't swim."

"And nobody saw you?"

"It was quite dark by the time we reached the river and I made sure there was nobody about."

"And when she is found? They might identify her and…"

He stroked her hair, like a parent comforting a child. "It is impossible, my darling. I visited the morgue. Many bodies pulled from the Seine are never claimed – I have seen it for myself. *Les inconnus* – the unknown ones – are common in a great city. Nothing can go wrong. As far as all Paris is concerned you are Madame Madeleine Seurot. I shall take you downstairs soon and introduce you to Madame Dubois as my wife."

Chantal fluttered her eyelids as her hand travelled down his body. "And tomorrow we will go shopping. I have nothing to wear and if we are to…"

"You shall have the finest clothes Paris can offer," he muttered as he led her to the bedroom.

* * *

Chantal was everything Jules Seurot had ever dreamed of in a woman; passionate and uncomplaining, her slender body excited him in a way that Madeleine's never had. But after a week he began to find lust rather exhausting. And he wasn't sleeping well.

Each night Madeleine's face appeared in his dreams, drowned, bloated and accusing. Her murder had been so easy. She had been off her guard, excited at seeing the river she had heard so much about. One shove and it was over: a splash, a muffled cry, then her heavy clothes had dragged her down and the murky river claimed another victim.

Now he had control of Madeleine's money and Chantal's body. But he felt uneasy, as though Madeleine was about to rise, dripping, from her watery grave and bring him to justice. Perhaps if he saw the body, if he reassured himself that everything was going as planned, he would feel better.

One morning when he suggested to Chantal that they venture out to explore their new city, she pouted sulkily and stated that she would rather buy a new hat.

"My dear, you have enough hats. And as for gowns, why don't you have some of..." He hesitated. "Why don't you have some of Madeleine's gowns altered? There are many good dressmakers in Paris."

Chantal stared at him in horror. "I would never wear a dead woman's clothes." She turned away from him. That was her last word on the subject.

Jules said nothing. He was beginning to discover that Chantal, so compliant at first, possessed a stubborn streak – and that after surviving for so many years on a servant's slender wages she was becoming all too adept at spending money.

He would go out alone, which was probably best. There was one place he needed to visit again. He had to know if Madeleine had been found.

The first time he had visited the Paris morgue, he had been filled with curiosity. This time his only emotion was dread. But he couldn't rest until he knew that Madeleine was lying there, anonymous and unclaimed, awaiting her pauper's grave.

Even though he knew he would find her there, naked and bloated, behind the plate glass window, the first sight of her body shocked him and his heart began to pound uncontrollably. As he stood in the milling crowd, breathing in the scent of the rich mingled with the stench of the poor, he couldn't take his eyes off her waxy, lifeless face.

He had never loved Madeleine: he had married her because he knew that one day she would be a very rich woman. And when she was visiting her dying father he would lie with Chantal in her narrow attic bed formulating the great plan: the plan that could not fail. Once they were in Paris, Madeleine would die but nobody would know because Chantal would take her identity, steal her life. It had seemed so simple. But now he was faced with the reality of what he had done, he felt sick and afraid.

"Ah, good morning, Monsieur Seurot. I had not thought to see you again so soon."

The voice made Seurot jump. He swung round and saw Charles Mery smiling at him, a suspicious and mirthless smile.

"You remember me?" he muttered.

"I have a remarkable memory, Monsieur. I never forget a face. I have some news for you. The gendarmes arrested a pickpocket here this morning. It may be the man who stole your wallet. He may say what he has done with it and…"

"Don't worry about it, Monsieur. There was nothing of great value in it," Seurot replied quickly , anxious to get away. He was aware of Madeleine, lying behind the glass a few yards away.

"You have moved to Paris now?"

"Yes."

"Perhaps you would give me your address, Monsieur – in case the wallet is found."

It was a direct question that Seurot couldn't avoid answering. And in his panic, it never occurred to him to lie. He gabbled his address and was gratified to see that Mery did not write it down.

Mery smiled again. "And how do you like our city?"

"Very much." Seurot took his gold watch from his waistcoat and made a great show of studying it. "I am late for an appointment, Monsieur. If you will excuse me..."

"Of course. You do not recognise any of our cadavers today?"

Seurot shook his head and made a swift exit. Before going home to Chantal, he needed a drink.

* * *

Seurot tried to put Madeleine out of his mind, but in his dreams she still rose from her slab behind the plate glass and pointed an accusing finger at her murderer. His stomach lurched every time he thought of that dark building in the shadow of Notre Dame. He would never go near the morgue again.

But Chantal, like a butterfly, had emerged from the chrysalis of the submissive maidservant and was spreading her beautiful wings. She walked past the concierge, Madame Dubois, with her nose in the air and she had discovered the delights of the Moulin Rouge and other fashionable haunts. The late nights were tiring Seurot out and he wondered how long he could keep up with a beautiful woman young enough to be his daughter. But they were tied together forever by what he had done. Neither of them could escape.

Then, a few days later on a damp Tuesday evening, the visitor arrived.

Jules answered the door, thinking it would be Madame Dubois. But when the door opened he saw a familiar figure silhouetted against the gaslight on the stairs. Maitre Michet's hat and coat glistened with rain and he looked weary, as though he had spent the day trudging around the city.

His smiled as he took off his hat. "Monsieur Seurot, it is so good to see you. May I come in?"

Jules opened and closed his mouth, uncertain what to do next. This was something he hadn't expected. He told himself to keep calm, to think clearly. Then he remembered that Chantal was in the drawing room wearing a fine gown of red silk, hardly the attire of a maidservant. Somehow he had to warn her that she had to resume her former role.

"I'm surprised to see you, Maitre. I understood that you never visited the city." Seurot hoped that the terror he felt didn't show on his face.

"There are times when it is inevitable, Monsieur. Your wife is at home?"

"I'm afraid she is not here. She's visiting an old friend in Rheims," he said, hoping he sounded convincing.

Michet looked disappointed. "I'm sorry to have missed her. I wished to speak with her."

"I understood that her affairs could be dealt with in Paris."

Michet smiled. "Indeed, Monsieur. But this concerns, er, a delicate, private matter. In Madame's absence, you might be able to help me. If I may come in…" He shivered and looked at Seurot expectantly.

Seurot had no option. He stood aside and the lawyer stepped into the hallway. Thinking quickly, he opened the door to the dining room, praying that Chantal wouldn't wander in: she had a habit of seeking him out when she was bored that was beginning to irritate him. "Please step in here, Maitre Michet," he said in a loud voice, hoping she would hear and be on her guard. "If you would excuse me one moment."

He closed the dining room door, leaving the unwanted guest alone. Then he rushed to the drawing room. It was empty. Perhaps Chantal had heard Michet's arrival after all and was in the bedroom putting on one of her old, plain gowns; something more suitable for a maidservant.

But as he left the drawing room, he saw to his horror that Chantal, in her finery, was at the dining room door. Before he could attract her attention she swept into the room as though she were mistress of the place. Seurot froze as he imagined the look on Michet's face.

He stood, paralysed with terror as he watched her make a rapid retreat, closing the dining room door noisily behind her. She spotted him hovering in the doorway and their eyes met. They slipped quietly into the drawing room. Something had to be done.

"You didn't tell me he was there," she accused.

"I didn't have a chance. Did he look surprised to see you?"

"Yes." Her eyes widened in panic, verging on hysteria. "My gown. I saw him look... I'm certain he suspects something. What shall we do?"

Seurot looked down at her upturned face and touched her cheek gently. He suddenly felt calm, in control. "Do not worry. I will deal with Maitre Michet. Go and get ready: we will visit the Moulin Rouge tonight if you wish."

"But..."

"You are not to worry." He patted the padded silk of her bustle. "Run along." He watched her leave the room, feeling the first tingling of desire, and he realised that the danger had excited him.

He took a deep, calming breath before returning to the dining room where Michet was waiting.

The lawyer spoke first. "Your wife has not taken her maid to Rheims?" The suspicion in his voice was almost palpable.

Michet looked his host straight in the eye and Seurot knew that he had seen through their charade. He had come this far; taken so many risks. He had killed once and he had heard it said that murder was easier the second time.

Now Jules Seurot recognised the sprawling, crowded city as his friend. If Michet joined *les inconnus* at the morgue, what did it matter? He had to kill again to keep his secret – to keep Madeleine's money and Chantal in his bed.

He smiled at Michet. "I have a slight headache and I am in need of some fresh air. Perhaps you would walk with me. Paris is very beautiful at night – particularly the river."

Chantal stood in the bedroom, her ear pressed to the door, listening to their departure.

* * *

An hour later Chantal rushed to answer the door. "Is it done?" she whispered.

"It was easy. He suspected nothing."

"I can't believe it has worked out so well."

"We must move from here quickly."

"To a bigger and better apartment?"

"We can afford it."

They kissed, tentatively at first, then passionately.

"We are rich," Chantal announced in triumph.

Gaston Michet smiled. "And Jules never suspected?"

"He thought you and Madame Seurot..."

Michet snorted in derision. "I have better taste." He kissed her head. "I was afraid Jules would lose his nerve."

"Once I suggested the plan, it was easy. He was all too eager to get rid of her. She led him a dog's life: never let him forget who had the money."

"So to everyone in Paris you are Madame Seurot?"

"Yes. The money is ours." She put her arms around his neck. "When are you returning to Moret?"

"Tomorrow – I must finalise my affairs. All Madeleine's money must be transferred to a Paris bank. You have been practising her signature?"

Chantal nodded. "I think I could fool anyone."

"In that case I have some papers for you to sign." He smiled and kissed her nose. "And I have put it about in Moret that I am moving to Lyons to care for my aged mother. You must move to a new apartment at once before that old concierge downstairs begins to ask questions and I will join you as soon as I can."

"Did she see you return?"

"I don't think so."

"And Jules? You are sure he is..."

He took her hand. "Don't worry. Jules put up a fight but he went in the river. When his body is found they will think he is just be another suicide – another victim of the city who ended up choosing the Seine to take their worthless life. But forget him. We are now Monsieur and Madame Jules Seurot." Gaston Michet shivered. "I am cold. The air by the river was damp."

"Then take a bath. We have every luxury here." She kissed him, her tongue exploring his mouth. "And we have the whole night ahead of us."

The water was running in the bathroom and the pipes in the apartment gurgled so noisily that Chantal didn't hear the first knock on the door. When the second knock came she froze, wondering who it could be at that late hour. Then came another knock, louder this time: the caller was persistent. Chantal hesitated. It was probably Madame Dubois who would know that there was somebody at home. She had no choice but to answer the door.

But it wasn't Madame Dubois who stood there in the corridor. It was a small man with a shock of dark hair. The spectacles perched on the end of his nose made him look older than his years. He grasped a hat with both hands and was turning it round nervously.

"Pardon me for intruding, Madame, but the concierge confirmed that I had the correct address. It is Madame Seurot, is it not? Wife of Monsieur Jules Seurot."

Chantal's heart was beating fast. She nodded.

"I had the pleasure of meeting your husband recently, Madame. Is he at home?"

Gaston Michet chose that moment to call from the bathroom, asking her to join him. His voice echoed against the green tiles. Too loud. Too suggestive.

"My husband is in the bath, Monsieur, and it is late." She was surprised at how calmly she said the words.

The little man bowed his head. "No matter, Madame. If you would tell him that his wallet has been found. The gendarmes apprehended the thief who has revealed where he disposed of his ill-gotten gains. The gendarme is a friend of mine and I offered to return your husband's property. The money has gone, alas but the name inside confirmed that it was his. If you would give it to him, Madame, with my compliments. My name is Charles Mery."

As Chantal took the damp, crumpled wallet from him she hoped he wouldn't see that her hand was shaking. She watched as he hurried away down the stairs; just another clerk. Now she had tasted riches, she was starting to feel contempt for such people. But as she had assumed that nobody in Paris knew Jules or where he lived, the encounter disturbed her. The sooner they moved to another district, and took advantage of the anonymity the city offered, the better.

"Chantal." The voice from the bathroom was urgent.

She walked slowly down the hallway. There was no need to tell Gaston about Monsieur Mery. The man was a nobody, she told herself. And she didn't want to spoil their first night in Paris together.

* * *

"Have we any new guests today, Pierre?" Charles Mery asked as he bustled into the morgue the next morning.

A large man with a face like a death's head was sweeping the floor. He looked up. "Just three, monsieur. Two girls, one with her throat cut, and a well-dressed gent."

"I'd better make their acquaintance."

Pierre nodded and led the way into a white tiled chamber. Mery passed the naked remains of a young female and bowed his head reverently. A prostitute probably, he thought; another victim of the city. She looked so young, so vulnerable.

He came to the second corpse and stopped.

"He was pulled out of the river by a couple of sailors yesterday evening," said Pierre. "Hadn't been in long, by the look of him. They thought he was a jumper but I reckon he'd been in a fight. Look at the bruises."

But Charles Mery was looking at the face. He never forgot a face. Or anything else come to that.

"I know him," he said quietly. "I called at his apartment last night at ten o'clock and a woman who claimed to be his wife – although she was young enough to be his daughter – said that he was home and in the bath. I heard a man's voice call out to her." He frowned. "What time was he pulled from the river?"

Pierre ambled over to a high desk and consulted an open ledger. "Half past nine, Monsieur."

"You are certain?"

"Yes, Monsieur. It is recorded in the book."

Mery stared at the body of Jules Seurot for a few moments then moved on to the third corpse. Another young woman, and this time the yawning wound on her neck told Mery exactly how she had met her death. He stared at her in disbelief.

"Pierre, this is most curious. This woman is Madame Seurot. I saw her last night at Seurot's apartment. And now she is…" He paused, deep in thought. "Pierre, my friend. I have a call to make."

He walked out of the building and breathed in the smoky air. This time perhaps he could do something to bring the killer of Jules Seurot and his wife to justice.

It was what he wished he could do for all his *inconnus* – all the unknown ones of Paris.

* * *

Gaston Michet congratulated himself as the carriage crossed the Pont Neuf. Everything had gone as planned. Now he had control of Madeleine Seurot's fortune and he didn't even have to share it with the tiresome Chantal, who had served her purpose well.

He sat back and listened to the clip clop of the horse's hoofs on the cobbled city streets. This was his reward for the dull respectable years in Moret. Soon he would be at the apartment he had rented near the

Palais du Luxembourg; a rich young man with Paris at his disposal.

The great, noisy, city sprawled around him, hiding all manner of evil deeds. For Gaston Michet, life was just beginning.

A Bridge Too Far

Zoë Sharp

I WATCHED with a kind of horrified fascination as the boy climbed onto the narrow parapet. Below his feet, the elongated brick arches of the old viaduct stretched, so I'd been told, exactly one hundred and twenty-three feet to the ground. He balanced on the crumbling brickwork at the edge, casual and unconcerned.

My God, I thought, *He's going to do it. He's actually going to jump.*

"Don't prat around, Adam," one of the others said. I was still sorting out their names. Paul, that was it. He was a medical student, tall and bony with a long almost Roman nose. "If you're going to do it, do it, or let someone else have their turn."

"Now now," Adam said, wagging a finger. "Don't be bitchy."

Paul glared at him, took a step forwards, but the cool blonde-haired girl, Diana, put a hand on his arm.

"Leave him alone, Paul," Diana said, and there was a faint snap to her voice. She'd been introduced as Adam's girlfriend, so I suppose she had the right to be protective. "He'll jump when he's ready. You'll have your chance to impress the newbies."

She flicked unfriendly eyes in my direction as she spoke but I didn't rise to it. Heights didn't draw or repel me the way I knew they did with most people, but that didn't mean I was inclined to throw myself off a bridge to prove my courage. I'd already done that at enough other times, in enough other places.

Beside me, my friend Sam muttered under his breath, "OK, I'm impressed. No way are you getting me up there."

I grinned at him. It was Sam who'd told me about the local Dangerous Sports Club who trekked out to this disused viaduct in the middle of nowhere. There they tied one end of a rope to the far parapet and brought the other end up underneath between the supports before tying it round their ankles.

And then they jumped.

The idea, as Sam explained it, was to propel yourself outwards as though diving off a cliff and trying to avoid the rocks below. I suspected this wasn't an analogy with resonance for either of us, but the technique ensured that when you reached the end of your tether, so to speak, the slack was taken up progressively and you swung backwards and forwards under the bridge in a graceful arc.

Jump straight down, however, and you would be jerked to a stop hard enough to break your spine. They used modern climbing rope with a fair amount of give in it but it was far from the elastic gear required by the bungee jumper. That was for wimps.

Sam knew the group's leader, Adam Lane, from the nearby university, where Sam was something incomprehensible to do with computers and Adam was the star of the track and field teams. He was one of these magnetic golden boys who breezed effortlessly through life, always looking for a greater challenge, something to set their heartbeat racing. And for Adam the unlikely pastime of bridge swinging, it seemed, was it.

I hadn't believed Sam's description of the activity and had made the mistake of expressing my scepticism out loud. So, here I was on a bright but surprisingly nippy Sunday morning in May, waiting for the first of these lunatics to launch himself into the abyss.

Now, though, Adam put his hands on his hips and breathed in deep, looking around with a certain intensity at the landscape. His stance, up there on the edge of the precipice, was almost a pose.

We were halfway across the valley floor, in splendid isolation. The tracks to this Brunel masterpiece had been long since ripped up and carted away. The only clue to their existence was the footpath that led across the fields from the lay-by on the road where Sam and I had left our motorbikes. The other cars there, I guessed, belonged to Adam and his friends.

The view from the viaduct was stunning, the sides of the valley curving away at either side as though seen through a fish-eye lens. It was still early, so that the last of the dawn mist clung to the dips and hollows, and it was quiet enough to hear the world turning.

"Hello there! Not starting without us, are you?" called a girl's cheery voice, putting a scatter of crows to flight, breaking the spell. A flash of annoyance passed across Adam's handsome features.

A young couple was approaching. Like the other three DSC members, they were wearing high-tech outdoor clothing – lightweight trousers you can wash and dry in thirty seconds, and lairy-coloured fleeces.

The boy was short and muscular, a look emphasised by the fact he'd turned his coat collar up against the chill, giving him no neck to speak of. He tramped onto the bridge and almost threw his rucksack down with the others.

"What's the matter, Michael?" Adam said, his voice a lazy taunt. "Get out of bed on the wrong side?"

The newcomer gave him a single, vicious look and said nothing.

The girl was shorter and plumper than Diana. Her gaze flicked nervously from one to the other, latching onto the rope already secured round Adam's legs as if glad of the distraction. "Oh *Adam*, you're never jumping today are you?" she cried. "I didn't think you were supposed to—"

"I'm perfectly OK, Izzy darling," Adam drawled. His eyes shifted meaningfully towards Sam and me, then back again.

Izzy opened her mouth to speak, closing it again with a snap as she caught on. Her pale complexion bloomed into sudden pink across her cheekbones and she bent to fuss with her own rucksack. She drew out a stainless steel flask and held it up like an offering. "I brought coffee."

"How very thoughtful of you, Izzy dear," Diana said,

speaking down her well-bred nose at the other girl. "You always were so very accommodating."

Izzy's colour deepened. "I'm not sure there's enough for everybody," she went on, dogged. She nodded apologetically to us. "No one told me there'd be new people coming. I'm Izzy, by the way."

"Sam Pickering," Sam put in, "and this is Charlie Fox."

Izzy smiled a little shyly, then a sudden thought struck her. "You're not thinking of joining are you?" she said in an anxious tone. "Only, it's not certain we're going to carry on with the club for much longer."

"'Course we are," Michael said brusquely, raising his dark stubbled chin out of his collar for the first time. "Just because Adam has to give up, no reason for the rest of us to pack it in. We'll manage without him."

The others seemed to hold their breath while they checked Adam's response to this dismissive declaration, but he seemed to have lost interest in the squabbles of lesser mortals. He continued to stand on the parapet, untroubled by the yawning drop below him, staring into the middle distance like an ocean sailor.

"That's not the only reason we might have to stop," the tall bony boy, Paul, said. "In fact, here comes another right now."

He nodded across the far side of the field. We all turned and I noticed for the first time that a man on a red Honda quad bike was making a beeline for us across the dewy grass.

"Oh shit," Michael muttered. "Wacko Jacko. That's all we need."

"Who is he?" Sam asked, watching the purposeful way the quad was bearing down on us.

"He's the local farmer," Paul explained. "He owns all the land round here and he's dead against us using the viaduct, but it's a public right of way and legally he can't stop us. That doesn't stop the old bugger coming and giving us a hard time every Sunday."

"Mr. Jackson's a strict Methodist you see," Izzy said quietly as the quad drew nearer. "It's not trespassing that's the problem – it's the fact that when the boys jump, well, they do tend to swear a bit. I think he objects to the blasphemy."

I eyed the farmer warily as he finally braked to a halt at the edge of the bridge and cut the quad's engine. The main reason for my caution was the elderly double-barrelled Baikal shotgun he lifted out of the rack on one side and brought with him.

Jackson came stumping along the bridge towards us with the kind of rolling, twitching gait that denotes a pair of totally worn-out knees. He wore a flat cap with tar on the peak and a tatty raincoat tied together with orange bailer twine. As he closed on us he snapped the Baikal shut, and I instinctively edged myself slightly in front of Sam.

"'Morning Mr. Jackson," Izzy called, the tension sending her voice into a high waver.

The farmer ignored the greeting, his eyes fixed on Adam. It was only when Michael and Paul physically blocked his path that he seemed to notice the rest of us.

"I've told you lot before. You've no right to do this on my land," he said gruffly, clutching the shotgun almost nervously, as though suddenly aware he was outnumbered. "You been warned."

"And you've been told that *you* have no right to stop us, you daft old bugger," Adam said, the derision clear in his voice.

Jackson's ruddy face congested. He tried to push closer to Adam, but Paul caught the lapel of his raincoat and shoved him backwards. With a fraction less aggression the whole thing could have passed off with a few harsh words, but after this, there was only one way it was going to go.

The scuffle was brief. Jackson was hard and fit from years of manual labour but the boys both had thirty years on him. It was the shotgun that worried me the most. Michael had grabbed hold of the barrel and was trying to wrench it from the farmer's grasp, while *he* was determined to keep hold of it. The business end of the Baikal swung wildly across the rest of us.

Izzy was shrieking, ducked down with her hands over her ears. I piled Sam backwards, starting to head for the end of the bridge.

The blast of the shotgun discharging stopped my breath. I flinched at the pellets twanging off the brickwork as the shot spread. The echo rolled away up and down the valley like a call to battle.

The silence that followed was quickly broken by Izzy's whimpering cries. She was still on the ground, staring in horrified disbelief at the blood seeping through a couple of small holes in the leg of her trousers.

Paul crouched near to her, hands fluttering over the wounds without actually wanting to touch them. Sam had turned vaguely green at the first sign of blood, but he unwound the cotton scarf from under the neck of his leathers and handed it over to me without a word. I moved Paul aside quietly and padded the makeshift dressing onto Izzy's leg.

"It's only a couple of pellets," I told her. "It's not serious. Hold this against it as hard as you can. You'll be fine."

Michael had managed to wrestle the Baikal away from Jackson. He turned and took in Izzy's state, then pointed the shotgun meaningfully back at the shaken farmer, settling his finger onto the second trigger.

"You bastard," he ground out.

"Michael, stop it," Diana said.

Michael ignored her, his dark eyes fixed menacingly on Jackson. "You've just shot my girlfriend."

"*Michael!*" Diana tried again, shouting this time. She had quite a voice for one so slender. "Stop it! Don't you understand? *Where's Adam?*"

We all turned then, looked back to the section of parapet where he'd been standing. The lichen-covered wall was peppered with tiny fresh chips but the parapet itself was empty.

Adam was gone.

I ran to the edge and leaned out over it as far as I dared. A hundred and twenty-three feet below me, a crumpled form lay utterly still on the grassy slope. The blood was a bright halo around his head.

"Adam!" Diana yelled, her voice cracking. "Oh, God. Can you hear me?"

I stepped back, caught Sam's enquiring glance and shook my head.

Paul was already hurrying towards the end of the bridge to pick his way down beneath the arches. I went after him, snagged his arm as he started his descent.

"I'll go," I said. When he looked at me dubiously, I added, "I know First Aid if there's anything to be done and if not, well—" I shrugged, "—I've seen dead bodies before."

His face was grave for a moment, then he nodded. "What can we do?"

"Get an ambulance – Izzy probably needs one even if Adam doesn't – and call the police." He nodded again and had already started back up the slope when I added, "Oh, and try not to let Michael shoot that bloody farmer."

"Why not?" Paul demanded bitterly. "He deserves it." And then he was gone.

It was a relatively easy path down to where Adam's body lay. Close to, it wasn't particularly pretty. I hardly needed to search for a pulse at his outflung wrist to know the boy was dead. Still, the relatively soft surface had kept him largely intact, enough for me to tell that it wasn't any shotgun blast that had killed him. Gravity had done that all by itself.

I took off my jacket and gently laid it over the top half of the body, covering his head. It was the only thing I could do for him, and even that was more to protect the sensibilities of the living.

When I looked up I could see half of the rope dangling from the opposite side of the bridge high above my head, its loose end swaying gently. The other end was still tied around Adam's ankles. It had snapped during his fall, but why?

Had Jackson's shot severed the rope at the moment when Adam had either lost his balance and fallen, or as he'd chosen to jump?

I got to my feet and followed the rope along the ground to where the severed end lay coiled in the grass. I used a twig to carefully lift it up enough to examine it.

And then I knew.

The embankment seemed a hell of a lot steeper on the way up than it had on the way down. I ran all the way and was totally out of breath by the time I regained the bridge. But I was just in time.

Diana was crouched next to Izzy, holding her hand. Paul and Sam were standing a few feet behind Michael, eyeing him with varying amounts of fear and mistrust. The thickset youth had the shotgun wedged up under Jackson's chin, using it to force his upper body backwards over the top of the parapet. Michael's face was blenched with anger, teetering on the edge of control.

"He's dead, isn't he?" He didn't take his eyes off the farmer as I approached.

"Yes," I said carefully, "but Jackson didn't kill him, Michael."

"But he must have done." It was Paul who spoke. "We all saw—"

"You saw nothing," I cut in. "The gun went off and Adam either jumped or fell, but he wasn't shot. The rope gave out. That's why he's dead."

"That's ridiculous," Diana said, haughty rather than anguished. "The breaking strain on the ropes we use is enormous. No way could it have simply broken. The shot must have hit it."

"It didn't," I said. "It was cut halfway through. With a knife."

Even Michael reacted to that one, taking the shotgun away from Jackson's neck as he swivelled round to face me. I could see the indentations the barrels had left in the scrawny skin of the old man's throat.

Chances like that don't come very often. I took a quick step closer, looped my arm over the one of Michael's that held the gun and brought my elbow back sharply into the fleshy vee between his ribs.

He doubled over, gasping, letting go of the weapon. I picked it out of his hands and stepped back again. It was all over in a moment.

The others watched in silence as I broke the Baikal and picked out the remaining live cartridge. Once it was unloaded I put the gun down, propped against the brickwork, and dropped the cartridge into my pocket. Michael had caught his breath enough to think about coming at me, but it was Sam who intervened.

"I wouldn't if you know what's good for you," he said, his voice kindly. "Charlie's a bit of an expert at this type of thing. She'd eat you for breakfast."

Michael favoured me with a hard stare. I returned it flat and level. I don't know what he thought he saw but he backed off, sullen, rubbing his stomach.

"So," I said, "the question is, who cut Adam's rope?"

For a moment there was total silence. "Look, we either have this out now, or you get the third degree when the police arrive," I said, shrugging. "I assume you *did* call them?" I added in Paul's direction.

"No, but I did," Sam said, brandishing his mobile phone. "They're on their way. I've said I'll wait for them up on the road. Show them the way. Will you be OK down here?"

I nodded. "I'll cope," I said. "Oh and Sam – when they arrive, tell them it looks like murder."

Nobody spoke as Sam started out across the field. He eyed the quad bike with some envy as he passed, but went on foot.

"I still say the old bastard deserves shooting," Michael muttered.

"I didn't do nothing," Jackson blurted out suddenly. Relieved of the immediate threat to his life he simply stood looking dazed with his shoulders slumped. "I never would have fired. It was him who grabbed my hand! He's the one who forced my finger down on the trigger!"

He waved towards Michael, who flushed angrily at the charge. I replayed the scene again and recalled the way the stocky boy had been struggling with Jackson for control of the gun. It had looked for all the world like a genuine skirmish but it could just as easily have been a convenient set-up.

When no one immediately spoke up in his defence, Michael rounded on us.

"How can you believe anything so *stupid*?" he bit out. "Adam was a good mate. I would have given him my last cent."

"Didn't like sharing your girlfriend with him, though, did you?" Paul said quietly.

Izzy, still lying on the ground, gave an audible gasp. I checked to see how Diana was taking the news of her dead boyfriend's apparent infidelity but there was little to be gleaned from her cool and colourless expression.

A brief spasm of what might have been fear passed across Michael's face. "You can't believe I'd want to kill him for that?" he said and gave a harsh laugh. "Defending Izzy's honour? Come on! I knew right from the start that she's not exactly choosy."

Izzy had begun to cry. "He loved me," she managed between sobs, and it wasn't immediately clear if she was referring to Michael or Adam. "He told me he loved me."

Diana sat back, still looking at Izzy, but without really seeing her. "That's what he tells – told – all of them," she said, almost to herself. "Wanted to hear them say it back to him, I suppose." She smiled then, a little sadly. "Adam always did need to be adored. The centre of attention."

"You're just saying that but it wasn't true," Izzy cried. "He loved me. He was going to give you up but he wanted to let you down gently, not to hurt your feelings. He was just waiting for the right time."

"Oh Izzy, of course he wasn't going to give me up," Diana said, her tone one of great patience, as though talking to the very young, or the very slow. "He used to come straight from your bed back to mine and tell me all about it." She laughed, a high brittle peal. "How desperately keen you were. How eager to please."

"And you didn't *mind*?" I asked, fighting to keep the disbelief and the distaste buried.

"Of course not," Diana said, sounding vaguely surprised that I should feel the need to ask. She sighed. "Adam had some… interesting tastes. There were some things that I simply drew the line at, but Izzy—" her eyes slipped away from mine to skim dispassionately over the girl lying cringing in front of her, "—well, she would do just about anything he asked. Pathetic, really."

"Are you really trying to tell me that you *knew* your boyfriend was sleeping around and you didn't care at all?"

Diana stood, looked down her nose again in that way she had. The way that indicated I was being too bourgeois for words. "Naturally," she said. "I understood Adam perfectly and I understood that this was his last fling at life while he still had the chance."

"What do you mean, while he still had the chance?" I said. I recalled Michael's jibe about Adam having to pack in the dangerous sports. "What was the matter with him?"

There was a long pause. Even Jackson, I noticed, seemed to be waiting intently for the answer. Eventually, Izzy was the one who broke the silence.

"He only told us a month ago that he'd been diagnosed with MND," she said. Her leg had just about stopped bleeding but her face had started to sweat now as the pain and the shock crept in. When I looked blank it was Paul who continued.

"Motor Neurone Disease," he said, sounding authoritative. "It's a progressive degeneration of the motor neurones in the brain and spinal cord. In most cases the mind is unaffected but you gradually lose control of various muscle groups – the arms and legs are usually the first to go. You can never quite tell how far or how fast it will develop because it affects everyone in a different way. Sometimes you lose the ability to speak and swallow. It was such rotten luck! The chances of it happening in someone under forty are so remote, but for it to hit Adam of all people—" He broke off, shook his head and seemed to remember how none of that mattered anymore. "Poor sod."

"It was a tragedy," Izzy said, defiant. "And if I gave him pleasure while he could still take it, what was wrong with that?"

"So," I murmured, "was this a murder, or a mercy killing?"

Diana made a sort of snuffling noise then, bringing one hand up to her face. For a moment I thought she was fighting back tears but then she looked up and I saw that it was laughter. And she'd lost the battle.

"Oh for God's sake, Adam didn't have Motor Neurone Disease!" she cried, jumping to her feet, hysteria bubbling up through the words. "That was all a lie! He *wanted* you to think of him as the tragic hero, struck down at the pinnacle of his youth. And you all fell for it. All of you!"

Paul's face was blank. "So there was nothing wrong with him?" he said faintly. "But he said—"

"Adam was diagnosed HIV-positive six months ago," Diana said flatly. "He had AIDS."

The dismay rippled through the group like the bore of a changing tide. AIDS. The bogeyman of the modern age. I almost saw them edge away from each other, as though afraid of cross-contamination. No wonder Adam had preferred the pretence of a more user-friendly affliction.

And then it dawned on them, one by one.

Izzy realised it first. "Oh my God," she whispered. "He never used…" She broke off, lifting her tear-stained face to Michael. "Oh God," she said again. "I am *so* sorry."

Michael caught on then, reeling away to clutch at the bridge parapet as though his legs suddenly wouldn't support him any longer.

Paul was just standing there, staring at nothing. "Bastard," he muttered, over and over.

Michael rounded on him in a burst of fury. "It's all right for you," he yelled. "You're probably the only one of us who hasn't got it!"

"Ah, that's not quite the case, is it, Paul?" Diana said, her voice like chiselled ice. "Always had a bit of a thing for Adam, didn't you? But he wasn't having any of that. Oh, he kept you dangling for years," she went on, scanning Paul's stunned face without compassion. "Did you really not wonder *at all* why he suddenly changed his mind recently?"

She laughed again. A sound like glass breaking, sharp and bitter. "No, I can see you didn't. You poor fools," she said, taking in all of their devastated faces, her voice mocking. "There you all were debasing yourselves to please him, hoping to bathe in a last little piece of Adam's reflected glory, when all the time he was spitting on your graves."

Michael lunged for her, reaching for her throat. I swept his legs out from under him before he'd taken a stride, then twisted an arm behind his back to hold him down once he was on the floor. *Come on Sam! Where the hell were the police when you needed them?*

I looked up at Diana, who'd stood unconcerned during the abortive attack. "Why on earth did you stay with him?" I asked.

She shrugged. "By the time he confessed, it was too late," she said simply. "There's no doubt – I've had all the tests. Besides, you didn't know Adam. He was one of those people who was a bright star, for all his faults. I wanted to be with him, and you can't be infected twice."

"And what about us?" Paul demanded, sounding close to tears himself. "We were your friends. Why didn't you tell us the truth?"

"Friends!" Diana scoffed. "What kind of friends would screw my boyfriend – or let their girlfriends screw him – behind my back? Answer me that!"

"You never got anything you didn't ask for," Jackson said quietly then, his voice rich with disgust. "The whole lot of you."

Privately, part of me couldn't help but agree with the farmer. "The question is," I said, "which one of you went for revenge?"

And then, across the field, a new-looking Toyota Land Cruiser turned off the road and came bowling across the grass, snaking wildly as it came.

"Oh shit," Paul muttered, "it's Adam's parents. How the hell did they get to hear about it so fast?"

The Land Cruiser didn't stop by the quad bike but came thundering straight onto the bridge itself, heedless of the weight-bearing capabilities of the old structure. It braked jerkily to a halt and the middle-aged couple inside flung open the doors and jumped out.

"Where's Adam?" the man said urgently. He looked as though he'd thrown his clothes on in a great hurry. His shirt was unbuttoned and his hair awry. "Are we in time?"

None of the group spoke. I let go of Michael's wriggling body and got to my feet. "Mr. Lane?" I said. "I'm terribly sorry to tell you this, but there seems to have been an accident—"

"*Accident?*" Adam's mother almost shrieked the word as she came forwards. "Accident? What about this?" and she thrust a crumpled sheet of paper into my hands.

Uncertain what else to do, I unfolded the letter just as the first of the police Land Rover Discoveries began its approach, rather more sedately, across the field.

Adam's suicide note was brief and to the point. He couldn't face the prospect of the future, it said. He couldn't face the dreadful responsibility of what he'd knowingly inflicted on his friends. He was sorry. Goodbye.

He did not, I noticed, express the hope that they would forgive him for what he'd done.

I folded the note up again as the lead Discovery reached us and a uniformed sergeant got out, adjusting his cap. Sam was in the passenger seat.

The sergeant advanced, his experienced gaze taking in the shotgun still leaning against the brickwork, Izzy's blood-soaked trousers, and the array of staggered faces.

"I understand there's been a murder committed," he said, businesslike, glancing round. "Where's the victim?"

I waved my hand towards the surviving members of the Dangerous Sports Club. "Take your pick," I said. "And if you want the murderer, well—" I nodded at the parapet where Adam had taken his final dive, "—you'll find him down there."

The Reluctant Dueller

Bill Knox

"YOU WILL, of course, be aware of Scottish law relating to duelling," said Mr. Deathstone. The Glasgow solicitor's thin, elderly features crinkled into a frown of calvinistic disapproval. "If two men fight a duel by arrangement and one is killed, then the survivor is guilty of murder."

Cam Gordon raised an eyebrow in barely concealed surprise. Mr. Deathstone had a habit of posing the unusual, but what the heck did duelling have to do with a private detective?

"The situation is – ah – delicate," sighed Mr. Deathstone. "Our client, Sir Randolph, is in a difficult position. If this ridiculous business goes on, he stands to lose either way."

"He gets killed, or he gets charged with murder,"

agreed Cam. "Why don't you get the police to throw a scare into both parties?"

The solicitor shook his head. "Sir Randolph is gifted, stubborn and – well, eccentric. That applies equally to his opponent. But the result of their foolishness would be unfortunate to – ah – certain interests. I want it stopped, without fuss or publicity.

"Miss Taylor will travel with you. Sir Randolph is anxious that certain minor changes be made in his will. She has the new copy ready for signature."

Sir Randolph Mitchell's home was just outside Perth. Cam took his time on the drive, puzzling over the set-up. "People just don't do that sort of thing any more," he declared, as the dark green Mercedes purred through Stirling. "It's old-fashioned."

Beth Taylor, old Deathstone's attractive red-headed secretary, curled back against the seat cushions. "Sir Randolph has quite a reputation. He may be an eccentric, but he practically invented electronics."

"OK, he's a genius," accepted Cam. "But if he wants this duel then he's off his little pointed head."

Sir Randolph's home was a medium-sized mansion standing in its own grounds. Cam crunched the Merc up the gravel driveway, a cheerful middle-aged housekeeper met them, and they were ushered into the electronics expert's study.

"Glad you could come," boomed Sir Randolph, a large tubby figure with a spade beard. "Well, ladies first, eh?" His twinkling-eyed appreciation of Beth made it apparent that though he might be on the wrong side of sixty he still hadn't let go of the finer things in life.

The will signed and witnessed, he turned to Cam. "Now then, young fellow – Deathstone seems to think there's a chance you can sort out this affair. What do you want to know?"

"For a start, who's the other man?" queried Cam.

"A pig-headed old fool called Nathan – Jonah Nathan," said Sir Randolph. "He came storming in here yesterday, accused me of breaking into his home and stealing his blasted pepperpot..."

"Pepperpot?"

"Kind of pistol – antique," said Sir Randolph brusquely. "Collector's item. I've been trying to get one for years – so's Nathan." He strode across to a big display cabinet and swung open the doors. Inside was an array of pistols, muskets and similar warlike museum pieces. "I told him he was a dam' fool. One thing led to another, then he challenged me to a duel." He paused, ruefully. "That's when I became a bigger fool – I said yes!"

"You could call it off," urged Beth.

"'Fraid not, m'dear," growled Sir Randolph. "Fellow would be sure I'd stolen it – go round calling me a coward as well as a thief. No, I've got to do this – unless Gordon here can prove I didn't take the blasted thing."

Cam pondered. "This duel – what's arranged?"

"It's tomorrow – at dawn, of course."

"Pistols for two, coffee for one sort of thing?"

Sir Randolph nodded, and took an old-fashioned rifle from the cupboard collection. "My choice of weapons, of course – was going to phone him today. We'll use these – Nathan has its twin. Enfield single-shot muzzle-loader, 'bout one hundred and twenty years old."

His visitors blinked.

"Does it still work?" queried Cam.

"Work? Fires a .577 lead bullet," declared Sir Randolph, looking somewhat unhappy as he added, "It could stop an elephant."

Half an hour later, Cam arrived at Jonah Nathan's home, a converted farmhouse set overlooking the silver thread of the River Tay. Nathan was tall, thin, grey-haired, and equally stubborn. He greeted his visitor with scant courtesy.

"Sir Randolph's second, eh?" He learned the choice of weapons, and gave a grunt. "It's his funeral. Tell him I'll have Ashencombe act for me." He pressed a buzzer on his desk and a younger man, slim, self-assured, a small well-trimmed moustache on his upper lip, came into the room with a confident stride.

Ashencombe, it seemed, was Nathan's nephew, who also acted as his secretary. His mission explained to him, he looked pained.

"The whole thing's ridiculous, Uncle," he protested. "Sir Randolph may have stolen your pistol, but..."

"The penalty for murder doesn't alter much," murmured Cam.

"He accepted my challenge," snorted Nathan. "Charles and yourself will be the only two people who know the details, and if Sir Randolph is accidentally shot while we're experimenting with antique firearms, that's the end of it."

Cam tried again. "How can you be sure it was Sir Randolph?"

"He's been greedy for a pepperpot for years – that's proof enough. I know only one man who'd be fanatically jealous enough to steal it. I'll show you how he got in."

First, there was the window in a small ground-floor cloakroom, smashed and broken. Then, along the short corridor, the door leading to the basement was lying forced.

"I keep my collection down there," explained Nathan. "Charles and I have a small target range fitted up – we keep the door locked because there's powder and shot lying around."

Cam examined the door. On the inside the lock had been held in place by four rusted screws. Forcing the door inwards had smashed the lock free and splintered the surrounding wood. The four screwnails lay on the floor where they'd been thrown.

When he got back to Sir Randolph's home, the electronics expert was offering Beth yet another glass of sherry. There was little about the elderly gentleman's manner to show that he could have an appointment with a bullet the following morning. Cam settled for a small whisky.

"I think I can get you off the hook," said Cam thoughtfully. "But Beth and I will have some work to do first."

* * *

They gathered at dawn the next morning. The spot was well chosen, a clearing in a quiet stretch of woodland near Gleneagles. Cam's Mere was already parked and waiting when Nathan and his nephew arrived in a dark blue saloon.

"You've got a last chance, Sir Randolph," said his opponent. "Admit you took it, return the pepperpot, and I'm satisfied."

Sir Randolph growled refusal. Nathan gave a nervous shrug, and they turned to preparing the guns. Carefully, each poured an exact quantity of powder from their horn flasks down the muzzles, then rammed in a greased lead bullet.

"Ready?" asked Ashencombe.

The two men nodded, each grasping his muzzle-loader.

"Whatever happens, it was an accident," warned Nathan.

Cam nodded, and glanced at the other man's nephew.

"Agreed," said Ashencombe slowly.

Back to back, Sir Randolph and Nathan stood waiting.

"Twenty paces forward, then turn and fire." Cam's voice was strained. "Ready – go."

The two elderly opponents strode away from each other as he counted... "Eighteen... nineteen... twenty!"

They turned. Two muzzle-loaders swept shoulderwards, two triggers were pulled – and there were two clicks, nothing more.

"But... but..." Nathan looked down at his weapon in disbelief. "Why didn't it fire?"

Sir Randolph gave a sigh of relief, and leaned against the nearest tree.

Cam stepped forward. "Now listen to me, both of you. The fact that you're two pompous idiots doesn't particularly concern me. But you've been acting like a pair of overgrown schoolchildren – and helping in an unscrupulous little game of murder."

"Don't try to put things off, young man," said Nathan shrilly. "We'll—" he licked dry lips, "—we'll reload."

Cam shook his head. "Sir Randolph didn't steal your pepperpot, Mr. Nathan, and I can prove it. Put down these overgrown popguns." He waited till the two muzzle-loaders were on the ground beside him.

"Sir Randolph was supposed to have come in through a window, then forced open the basement door," said Cam quietly. "Mr. Nathan, the cellar door may have been forced from the outside, but someone in your own house did it."

"That's ridiculous," protested Ashencombe. "I want to stop this duel too, Gordon, but this nonsense..." His voice died away before Cam's ice-flecked glare.

"The lock was held by four screwnails," said Cam. "Rusty screwnails. Two of them had small pieces of wood still in the thread, caught there when the door was forced. But the other two were clean of wood – and had fresh screwdriver marks on their heads. Whoever faked the forcing of that door loosened two of the screwnails first to make the job easier – didn't he, Ashencombe?"

Nathan's nephew had lost his usual self-assurance. He rubbed one finger nervously along his moustache. "Gordon, I warn you..."

Cam shook his head. "I don't believe in duels. Nor in using them as an alibi for murder." He stopped, and gave a faint smile of satisfaction as the noise of an approaching engine reached his ears. "You'll see what I mean in a moment or two."

An old-fashioned black saloon lumbered into the clearing and stopped. Beth Taylor got out first, followed by Mr. Deathstone. The elderly lawyer crossed over, sniffed as he took in the scene, then handed Cam a cloth-wrapped bundle.

Cam opened it up and nodded. The pepperpot pistol had been found.

"It was under a floorboard in his room," said Beth. "And the other stuff was there too."

Nathan came forward, sudden concern on his face. "What does it mean, Gordon?"

"This wasn't a duel, Mr. Nathan," said Cam. "You were going to be killed.

"Once I saw those screwnails I made some checks – and had Mr. Deathstone come up to help. Your nephew was short of cash – for a start, he owes the local bookie three hundred. He faked the theft of the pistol, planning to sell it, hoping you'd blame Sir Randolph. But when the duel came along, he couldn't have been happier. Your solicitor confirmed – indirectly, of course – that Ashencombe gets most of your money if you die.

"But what decided it was when Beth and I broke into your house last night." He let Nathan give a splutter, then went on, "That was Beth's idea. She said you were such a stubborn old devil that you needed a lesson. We emptied Sir Randolph's powder-horn first and refilled it with a nice harmless mixture of garden fertiliser whipped up by the local chemist. Then we went to do the same with yours – but somebody had beat us to it. I asked Mr. Deathstone and Beth to search Ashencombe's room as soon as you'd both left this morning.

"Only one gun was meant to fire, Mr. Nathan – and it wasn't yours."

Ashencombe turned to run. As he passed Mr. Deathstone the lawyer stretched out a long, thin leg and the younger man went sprawling.

When he rose, Cam smacked an arm-lock on him.

"Move if you like," he invited. But Ashencombe had more sense.

The two duellers looked at their muzzle-loaders, then at each other.

"We're a pair of old fools," said Nathan. "I'm sorry." Solemnly, they shook hands.

"What about this?" Cam pushed his captive forward. "Shall I deliver him to the local gendarmes?"

Nathan exchanged glances with Sir Randolph, and shook his head. "I'll drop him from my will and throw him out – that's punishment enough, and no scandal."

Ashencombe scrambled off.

"It would have made wonderful headlines," mused Cam watching him go. "No more duels, gentlemen?"

Nathan gave a shudder. "Don't even mention the word. I've never been so frightened."

"Mind you," Sir Randolph pondered. "I'm the better shot..."

Mr. Deathstone groaned aloud. They were at it again!

D.O.A.

Cath Staincliffe

JOHNNY SAW. Johnny saw blue.

Deep blue, blue as bone.

Cold.

Like some place deep in the ocean with little light, full of neon fish. Bill used to have fish in a tank like that at his place, he reckoned they were good for the head. If you were wired, losing it, paranoid or whatever Bill recommended a decent spliff, a carton of double chocolate ice-cream and an hour or so watching the fish dart and float in the tank.

Bill was away now. Someone had grassed him up and the Es in the back room got him four in Strangeways. Bill had asked Headcase to sort the house out but Headcase had got cabbaged in town and gone off to Blackpool with some girl who had a scam going. Time Headcase gets back the leccy's run out and all Bill's fish have frozen to death. Or boiled. Or suffocated. Something they needed from the little motor in the tank.

Johnny saw blue circles, spinning above, like light from a propeller. Loud light that whooped at him. Mint FX. Well cool. Maybe he was swimming except he couldn't feel water, no silky waves rocking him, no ripples or splashes, no chlorine or salt spray. Not warm. Not cold. Zero. Just the light above and below...?

...A snake of fear needled through him, left him lurching but when he tried to trace it, to name it, he came up empty...

...Below? The nearest he could get was air, like he was a hovercraft. Wished he could remember what he'd taken because this was a real mind-fucking trip.

* * *

Johnny spinning on a plate. Blue noise whipping him fast, like the lads on the Waltzers did with the talent: giving them a faster spin, something to get them squealing. All excited in among the hot smell of candy floss and the gut-thump of boom-boxes.

Johnny saw Lola spilling off the rides, breathless already, into his arms. Eyes teasing, violet eyes. Lola, legs apart and eyes wide open, moaning in her throat, hands on his back, on his arse.

Changed when she had Kim. He was made-up at first. Lovely girl like Lola, sweet baby. But it all unravelled. She was on at him all the time. Do this, do that, get this, get that. Endless bloody weeks of never enough of anything, never enough fags, or chips, or money. Not enough love. Dreams shrinking to the size of a crappy 14" repo set with a moody video.

Lola in tears or having a fit. Kim likewise. Did his best. Shifts at the airport, loading bags, seventeen years old, not even minimum wage. Job made no sense when Headcase or Bill could set him up with a nice little earner, score a month's pay in a night. Then Victor bloody Meldrew, supervisor in his poxy uniform accuses him of inefficiency. Jesus Christ, the bags got on or off or they didn't and he wasn't going to kill himself working up a sweat about it. Stuff the job.

Lola kicked him out at Christmas. Maybe he walked. Hard to tell.

You don't know how to be a father.

You never give me the chance.

Kim bawling.

Fuck off Johnny…

* * *

…Just like your fuckin' father.

His mam calling him now. But he wasn't. Wasn't anything like his dad who'd spent more time inside than out and spent his whole life being sorry, saying sorry, feeling sorry – for himself mainly. A wash-out of a man. No charm, no nouse, no bloody point.

I'm not, Johnny had yelled, nothing like him. Freaked at the way his voice cracked and his eyes stung. Turning away. She could at least have stuck up for him. Her only son. Seen that he had done his best, done what he could to be a man and provide for them in this shit-heap. What more could he have done? Even the robbin' was for them, wasn't it?

You never gave us a chance, he told his mam.

I had yer didn't I? Fed you, clothed you?

Not enough.

It wasn't easy for me either.

You owe me…

What Johnny? Just what exactly?

* * *

Johnny saw but couldn't speak. There were moths in his throat. Large and blurry and soft. Saw how it should have been. Felt it, in the space between his ribs, in the back of his skull and the pit of his belly, that he deserved more, if only…

…spike of fear again. The blue swimming red and Johnny closing his eyes. Not liking the gush of the red, the colour clotting his vision.

* * *

Johnny listened instead to the whirl of sound, a spiral like a wolf's cry. Baying for him. Johnny danced with the sound, arms flung out, head back, reeling. The two-tones slowing and Johnny heard Lola moaning as they fucked, Lola screaming before they took her in for the Caesarian. Kim's wail cracking a thinner sound. Two notes over and over. Johnny wheeling heard the horns play; saxophones and trumpets chasing round each other.

Played in a Silver Band once, when he was a little kid; French horn and a blue uniform. Marching round the estate, neighbours out and smiling. Didn't last. Half the time it sounded like he'd stepped on the cat's tail or farted.

Couldn't read the words never mind the music. Never got on with reading. And the bigger lads began to take the piss. They worked out this plan to nick the instruments. Johnny had to tell them what the set-up was. He told them about the padlocks and the metal cabinets and the bars across the doors. Not exactly a soft touch. They spent an hour at it with hammers and iron bars, Johnny as look-out. Then the neighbours came nosing and they were out of there. Total waste of time. And after, thinking where would they have got rid of twenty-three horns and bugles? Crap idea. Better stick to stuff that's easy to shift. VCRs, fags, sound systems, cameras, drugs, mobile phones.

In the whirl of sound Johnny heard an old train hooting. Then an owl. There'd been an owl in the park for a while where he and Lola went before Kim. Fuckin' spooky sound that. Made you think of wild places, moors and haunted houses not the city with the smell of rogan josh in the air and the drone of the traffic and carrier bags and takeaway trays blowing across the concrete.

Lola said it meant death, the cry of the owl.

For a mouse maybe…

Aw, fuck.

Johnny fell. Back into the space beneath him. Pictures tumbling through him like bloody Lottery balls.

A Beemer.

Headcase getting them in, disabling the alarm.

Not a job just a laugh. Go for a spin.

Barrelling down the Parkway. The city falling away behind them.

Some Ragga on the CD player. M56. Pretty quiet. Dark. Headcase gunning it. Johnny rolling a fat one. No plan. A buzz from the speed and the smoke and the cheek of it.

Headcase sees the Old Bill first, races away. Fast as fuck. A whump and they're flying. Outer space, stars like rain.

Falling.

Voices.

Stretcher.

Ambulance.

In the blue Johnny cartwheels up, a satellite revolving through the howling. Fear bucking, protest rising.

No. Fuck no. Not enough. Please.

Then the wolf falls quiet, the blue fades, bleaches to white. Crystal light. Fear gone. Hope gone. All gone.

Day or Night

Liza Cody

I'M SHAREEN MANASSEH. Sometimes I wish I had a plain name like Anna Lee which any fool can spell. Anna Lee is a good name – short, fits on a granite headstone in big gold letters. According to the date underneath she died two years ago. She's remembered – there were two fresh vases of daffodils and jonquils and a spray of yellow roses.

Rachel Silver said, "I should have come before now. I feel terrible." A slow tear rolled out from under her dark glasses and stuck quivering in the make-up on her left cheek. Her hands, in their beautiful suede gloves, fluttered. She seemed to be waiting for me to reassure her so I said, "It isn't easy for you."

"No. I don't come to the UK often. I was ill when she died – a basket case." Again she waited for me.

"You'd been through a lot," I supplied.

"No one gets it." She sighed. "When I first saw her… Anna… she was the first human being I'd actually *seen*… they told me… in nearly five months."

I said. "They told me that too."

"He kept me in total darkness. Can you imagine that, Shareen? I thought I was blind. You've no idea how badly light hurts the eyes."

Now her eyes were shielded by dark lenses. Her perfect hair was raked by a breath of early spring wind but it soon settled back into its smooth shape. She hunched her shoulders as if she were freezing. Why, I wondered, was she putting herself through this? It was like watching someone poke at an unhealed wound with a fork.

"I almost forgot." She took a round white pebble out of her pocket. "From Atlantic City," she said and placed it on Anna's black granite stone.

I followed her example. Before leaving home I'd picked up a mundane grey pebble from the stock I keep for my grandmother's grave. Even in the matter of stones this woman made me feel like a pauper.

I said, "Shall we get out of the cold?"

"It *is* pretty bleak," she agreed, surveying the grassy

ground with its network of narrow paths – a crematorium at one end and a chapel at the other. There were no lichen-covered stones, no Victorian angels or whimsical mausoleums. All the trees and dead people had been planted less than a decade ago.

"Soulless," I said without thinking.

She let out a sharp gasp and a brittle laugh.

We sat in her chauffeur-driven car with thick privacy glass between us and the driver. It embarrassed me. I wished my Chief Inspector had picked someone else to come to London for this assignment. I didn't know why it was a police job anyway. All he said was, "You've heard of hush-hush? Well this is hush-hush-hush."

Rachel Silver said, "He kept me in the dark. I didn't know what time it was. He fed me through a letterbox in the door, shoving food through like I was a dog."

The car had bullet-proof glass, a bomb-proof chassis and a security driver. I'd been issued with a regulation Glock sidearm. But Ms Silver did not look like a woman who would ever feel safe.

"First he gave me a ham sandwich." She shuddered. "I said, 'I can't eat this.' He said, 'You'll eat what I give you or you'll starve.' I made up my mind to starve. But I'm weak."

"That's not weakness. That's survival." I felt she'd put me in the place of her therapist or someone whose responses she could rely on for comfort.

But she rejected the comfort. "It was the thin end of the wedge. He said, 'You've been here a week' and I said, 'OK,' even when I was sure it was only a couple of days. And then it got so I wasn't sure. He'd shove a sandwich through the door and say, 'Lunch,' waking me up from a sleep so long I thought it must be breakfast. I'd say, 'Is it day or night?' just so I could hear a human voice. He said, 'It's what I say it is, stupid, dirty woman.' And that was better than when he said nothing at all."

Kept in the dark and lied to. A bit like what my last boyfriend did to me. He too was the kind of guy who could convince a woman that day was night. But he wasn't a terrorist so I had no reason to believe he was torturing me.

"He wouldn't let me wash," Rachel Silver went on, her head bowed. She seemed to be giving a speech she'd returned to over and over again. Maybe her therapist said, "Keep telling the story till it loses its power." You'd think if that was going to work it would've worked after two years.

I was uncomfortable sitting so close to a woman who'd been brainwashed and tortured. But the Chief Inspector said, "Do whatever it takes. The Deputy Commissioner in London doesn't want the Americans complaining we can't do a simple job right."

I tried to change the subject. "How did an English private detective get involved with this?"

"Anna Lee?" Rachel sounded as if she'd forgotten that she'd come all this way to visit her rescuer's grave. "She was working in the States and I guess my dad had her on salary. He likes the British. Maybe Military Intelligence kinda seconded her because she was an outsider. I don't know. The operation's still classified. Even from me. They think I'm a security risk."

"That's a bit unfair."

"They think I was 'turned'. They still monitor my calls in case *he* gets in touch. But he wasn't just one person. I think there were five of them but only one mattered. I had to call all of them 'Friend'. The real Friend escaped in the gunfire. They say he shot Anna Lee the next day. She was gunned down in the street, you know. It was like a regular LA gang drive-by, but they insist it was Friend because she was the only one who saw him and he was the only one who could possibly recognise *her*. He's still out there."

She was beginning to sound like a tired little girl. I said, "Do you want to go back to the hotel?"

"I'm exhausted." She took off her dark glasses and I turned to look out of the window.

I knew, because it was in the notes I'd been given, that when she was rescued, Rachel had an eye infection so bad that she lost the sight in one of her eyes and eventually it was removed. I didn't want to see it.

I couldn't understand the resentment I felt – the toxic twin emotions of pity and impatience. "Get over it," I wanted to say. "Your daddy's a senator. You're rich. You can afford all the therapy, all the security you'll ever need. What about the woman who got tangled up in US politics almost by mistake and lost her whole life? Is that what you rich important people do – hire someone to stand between you and the bullet that's meant just for you?" Because today it was me and my stupid little sidearm that I'd never actually used outside a firing range. We'd been chosen to stand between Rachel Silver and her own personal bullet.

* * *

I spent the night at her hotel in London because she wanted an escort to the airport the next day. Then she was gone.

After that, to my surprise, I was sent to a newly built office in South London to talk to a quiet man who called himself Mr. Franklin. I was warned that he would want to see my case notes. He stood with his back to the window reading and turning pages. I sat on a hard chair embarrassed about my spelling and handwriting which I'm sometimes told is 'chaotic'. He didn't comment on either. Nor did he give me back my notebook.

All he said was, "Thank you so much for your help on this one, Ms. Manasseh. In the unlikely event that anyone should ever approach you about this matter I'd appreciate it if you'd report back instantly to Deputy Commissioner Mead in the Met – not anyone from your home station. Is that clear?"

He pushed some papers across the desk, and that's how I found out that the previous day's assignment was an Official Secret.

* * *

I don't know how it happened – I never said anything to *anyone* about my trip to London – but word spread all the way back to Bristol.

A few nights later I was in the Cat-Man-Do bar with a couple of women from work. Teresa said, "We saw your ex last night, Shareen."

"Al?"

"How many exes you got?" Jude said. "You ain't *that* popular."

"Yes, Al," Teresa said. "He said you were on Special Assignment to MI5 in London."

I didn't know quiet Mr. Franklin was MI5, so unless Al was bullshitting Teresa, he knew more than me.

I said, "He's shitting you Teresa. It's what he does."

Jude said, "He was with Norm and Kill-Bill from the armoury. They said you were issued a sidearm."

How did they know that? The Glock was issued in London, not locally.

"It's a joke," I said. "I passed the basic course, that's all. *You're* both more qualified and experienced than I am."

Teresa said, "They told us it was cos you were baby-sitting that Jewish senator's daughter who was taken hostage by terrorists, remember? Because no one knows you in London."

"Al said they always pick an 'exotic' for a job like that," Jude added.

"*Exotic*?"

"Don't get all huffy," Teresa said. "It doesn't mean you're more expendable."

"Don't count on it," Jude said with a malicious grin. She tipped the last of her pint down her throat. She still looked thirsty.

"Never mind her," Teresa said, while Jude was at the bar getting the next round in. "Al was talking about you and she hates that. You're supposed to be history."

"I *am* history," I said sadly.

"That's not how Al sounded last night."

"Well, *he's* history," I said even more sadly, because he'd been gone for six weeks and I was lonely. It was dark in the bar, and 'Fix You' was playing on the sound system.

Al used to like me. Now he likes Jude. Or maybe it was exclusively about sex, and liking had nothing to do with it. I don't understand men at all.

Deputy Commissioner Mead told me that when Anna Lee freed Rachel Silver she ran into the underground bunker while a firefight was going on around her. He said that she had to dress Rachel in Kevlar and carry her out in her arms – not because Rachel was too weak to walk but because she didn't want to go.

As well as the eye infection, she was treated for multiple STDs. But according to the debriefing reports she never once, even to this day, described a rape. Deputy Commissioner Mead doesn't understand *women* at all.

Sitting in the Cat-Man-Do bar, listening to 'Fix You' and waiting for Jude who hates me to bring more drinks, I knew I should leave, phone Mead and tell him that the Official Secret wasn't a secret – that my colleagues, the men and women I'd been trained to protect and rely on, were asking questions.

Jude came back with a pint for Teresa, a pint for herself and nothing for me.

"*Jude!*" Teresa protested, laughing.

"She gets stupid and slutty when she's rat-arsed," Jude explained sweetly. "That's what Al told me."

"Al would never lie to *you*," I said. "You remind him too much of his mother."

Jude threw knives with her eyes. Clearly she knew as well as I did what Al thinks of his mother.

"We used to be mates," Teresa said. "There's way more interesting stuff to talk about than some twat-faced bloke."

"Like what?"

"Like what Shar was doing in London. Like, how does Rachel Silver look now? She used to be one of the Ten Best Dressed Women in Washington. Like were the terrorists really behind that private eye's murder or is it just another conspiracy theory?"

"Is she even dead?" Jude said. "Kill-Bill says she's prob'ly in some witness protection programme somewhere. She's the only one who actually saw the leader. He was long gone by the time the military stormed the bunker."

"They killed the other four," Teresa said. "Anna Whatsername can't be protected twenty-four-seven. Unless they fake her death and give her a new identity."

"Don't look at me," I said because they were both waiting for me to comment.

"You're involved."

"I'm *so* not involved. Where on earth are you getting your gossip from?"

"Already told you," Jude sighed impatiently. "Al said you never listen."

"Oh do shut up," Teresa said, but added, "Don't go, Shar. She's just trying to wind you up."

"Failing," I said. "I'm bored." And I left.

* * *

We drove to the underground car park behind the Watershed near the docks. He didn't speak until we were facing the water. Then he said, "Tell me everything, Shareen – verbatim if you can."

When I'd finished, he said, "Is that all?"

I was offended.

He said, "I know, he told you he was a Friend and threatened you and your family in very few words – I mean, what else has been happening?"

I'd thought about this question all day and prepared an answer. I said, "Everyone at my station and everyone at the Armoury knows about me escorting Rachel Silver in London. Everyone's speculating."

"Everyone? I'll need names." He looked at me. I looked at him.

He sighed and said, "Ms. Silver is still emotionally attached to the leader of the cell who kidnapped her. She was half blinded and so messed up inside that she will never be able to have children, but she's still loyal to him."

"She's frightened."

"So are you. Rightly. But because she persists in a bad choice there are some very dangerous people still out there. One of whom you spoke to last night."

"She didn't have a fair choice."

"Agreed. But choice about who you're loyal to should be reassessed in the light of new information. Mindless fidelity to a person, a group, a policy or a nation… well, you, Shareen Manasseh, should know better than most what that can lead to."

I was grateful to him for not naming the fascistic, extremist groups I might be afraid of. He gave me time to think.

In the end I said, "Is this why you always choose 'exotics'?"

"I beg your pardon?"

"Because we don't quite feel we belong? And so it's easier to persuade us that our friends aren't our friends?"

He looked me straight in the eye, holding contact till I looked away. His eyes were pale grey and his gaze was as frank and honest as Al's.

In the end I chose the family I'd left behind and I gave him the names he wanted. I gave up my friends.

As far as I know nothing at all happened to Teresa, Jude, Al, Norm or Kill-Bill. But I was transferred from Bristol to South London by the end of the month. I was given no choice.

I never heard another word from the so-called Friend.

Why had I thought the caller was Al? It wasn't Al but it might have been a voice I'd heard recently. An English voice. Like quiet Mr. Franklin's. So I began to wonder how 'Friendly' *he* was. Could the threat have been made just to manipulate me – to expose a leak? Was Mr. Franklin another man who could convince a woman that day was night? I wondered about this for quite a long time.

I never saw or heard from him again. And I still don't know who to be loyal to, unless it's to family – even though I left them behind long ago.

Owl Wars

Ann Cleeves

IT WAS ELEVEN O'CLOCK. At home, the pubs would be closing, the streetlights would be on, and people would be preparing for bed. Here, on the edge of the Arctic Circle, there was no night in June. It seemed that nobody slept, and birds would still be singing at three in the morning.

The small group outside the nature centre was edgy and awake. The Finnish guide sat in the minibus, smoking a cigarette, bored. He'd worked thirty-seven nights without a break. What did it matter to him, if they were a little late setting off?

But it did matter to the group. They wanted to see owls: Ural, pygmy and great grey. They'd seen hawk owl and Tengmalm's in Kuusamo and they needed to complete their lists. They gathered around Annie, expecting an explanation for the delay.

She was tempted to say, *Look, it's not my fault that he's not on time. You know what he's like. Just go without him.*

But she didn't think they'd go without Simon. He was their leader. As soon as he turned up their restiveness would disappear. They'd be all smiles and understanding then. He'd been late before, and they'd always forgiven him. He was like their surrogate son, their favourite nephew.

"Give me ten minutes," Annie said. "He might have gone to the tower to photograph the cranes."

She ran along the path cut through the reeds towards the orange sun, which would never quite set. She paused once to brush mosquitoes away from her face. They were everywhere, tormenting them all. When she looked back at the group, she saw that George, the oldest of the group, was watching her.

The track was made of stripped pine trunks, split in half and laid flat side up. The path was only two logs wide and uneven, so she had to watch her feet. It had been cut through birch scrub from the centre and then ran across the reed bed to the bay. Simon had brought them here earlier in the day while the sun was still hot. The watch tower was more than sixty feet high, three storeys, built of rough planks. It had steep wooden steps and was enclosed at the top by a single rail. From there, they'd looked over the reed bed to the sea. They'd watched flocks of cranes coming into the marsh and heard whooper swans.

Simon had pointed out, on rocky islands in the water, the huts where fishermen and hunters stayed. The space, flat and wild as far as she could see, had made her dizzy.

Now, lost in memory she had come, quite suddenly, to the base of the tower. Beyond it there was a wide ditch full of brown water. A rotting punt was tethered to a loose post. She heard a bittern wheezing, and footsteps behind her, though there was a curve in the path, and the reeds were too tall and thick for her to tell who it might be.

Then she saw Simon. He lay, crumpled and damp as if he'd been washed up the creek by the tide. He'd been the centre of her life for five months and she could tell without touching him that he was dead.

* * *

They'd met at the British Birdwatching Fair at Rutland Water, in the main marquee, which had that English summer smell of crushed grass, tarpaulin and rope. She saw *him* first. He was sitting on a stool by a stand, advertising natural history tours, talking earnestly to a middle-aged couple. No doubt he was selling, persuading, but the couple seemed not to mind. They listened, giving him their full attention, as if they were getting a story, not a sales pitch. Then he looked up and saw Annie. He gave a wide, flattering smile of appreciation. In that moment, she felt she knew everything about him. She knew, for instance, that he'd used that smile to get his own way since he was a baby.

And still, even knowing that, she didn't walk away. She took her time. She didn't rush over immediately to pretend an interest in Madagascar or Morocco. She had more sense than that. She picked up the recently published *Birds New to Britain* and admired the illustrations. She filled out a form to join the British Trust for Ornithology.

But from the corner of her eye, she was watching him, and she knew he was trying to catch her attention. She moved across the boarded floor of the marquee, a teasing minuet of approach and retreat, until she landed next to him. He wore a green polo shirt with the name of his company on the back and a badge: *Simon Webb.*

* * *

He said nothing and she thought that was unusual for him. He would earn his living by talking. Talking and travelling. From a distance, Annie had thought he was young. Younger even than she was. Now she could tell he was approaching middle age. That made him no less attractive. She saw him as a raffish and dashing adventurer, dangerous and a challenge. In the silence between them, the surrounding background noise seemed to fade.

"Will you take me to lunch?" she said.

He frowned and she wondered if she'd blown it.

"How long have you got?" he asked. "There's nowhere decent on site."

It was on the tip of her tongue to suggest somewhere indecent, but she was scared of frightening him off. "All afternoon. I'm on my own. I can please myself."

And he smiled again.

They sat in the back room of a pub. It was cool and shadowy, and the other diners were finishing as they arrived. She asked for a mineral water. Best, she thought, to keep a clear head. Everything was happening quickly, and she wanted to cry out, *I don't do this sort of thing.*

Not usually. I mean propositioning strange men. It's not me at all. But the speed excited her too, the sense that she'd started on a journey she could no longer control.

He asked her what line of work she was in. A peculiar phrase. Slightly old-fashioned.

"I teach English as a foreign language," she said. She waited for him to ask for more details, but he just looked at her, seeming to drink her in, and she had to continue. "I worked abroad for a couple of years, but now I'm in a language school. Cambridge."

Then, realising that some reciprocal information was required, he began talking about his company. There was, she was told, only someone to run the office and him.

"We specialise in small groups. Sometimes just three or four people. Expert birdwatchers with very specific requirements. People who would travel independently if they had the time or expertise to arrange it. We can give them individual attention. Make sure they get the species they really need." She raised her eyebrows and he grinned. "OK sorry. That was the sales pitch. Sometimes, you know, it just spills out."

He worked out of a cottage close to the reservoir, with an overgrown garden and a slow stream choked with weed.

"Terribly impractical," he said, "but I just fell in love."

That afternoon, the day of the Bird Fair, he took her there and led her up the uneven wooden stairs to the bedroom. His hand was resting on her head so she shouldn't hurt herself on the low doorway. He lay her on the bed and undressed her deliberately and told her that it was a willow warbler singing in the orchard and that kingfishers bred near the stream.

Again, she wanted to say, *I'm not this sort of woman.*

But she felt the sun on her eyelids and his tongue on her skin. When she spoke again, it was dark outside and perhaps she *was* that sort of person. Certainly, she was different.

They met as often as they could after that, which meant whenever he wasn't travelling. During the day she would work with her students, repeating the lessons she had prepared the year before for the previous cohort. She could tell that she performed well. They responded to her encouragement and laughed at her jokes. There was no real engagement though. She knew their names – the Marias and the Mai-Lins and the Berndts – but she didn't care about them in the least. All the time she would be thinking of her next meeting with Simon, what she would wear for him, how he would respond. She knew it was a madness, an obsession. He was obsessed too. That gave her hope and carried her on.

She decided on Northern Finland for her first trip away with him. He gave her a free choice. "Wherever you like," he said, waving his arm expansively.

They were sitting in the cottage. She'd cooked for him, and he'd drunk lots of the good red wine he'd brought back with him after a short break in the Cevennes. It was November, a damp and gloomy Saturday night and they'd lit the first fire of the winter. His face was flushed. He'd invited her to go on a trip with him before – once to the Coto Donana, once to Goa – but those invitations had followed last minute cancellations by punters, and she hadn't been able to arrange cover for her classes. Anyway, she'd said, hot places didn't appeal.

"Are you serious?" She was sitting on the floor, her arms wrapped around her knees.

"Of course." And he suddenly *became* serious and fetched her the brochure and maps and began making suggestions.

When she asked for Finland, she'd wondered at first if there might be a problem, because there'd been a moment of hesitation, then he gave that wonderful smile and said of course. Finland. Kuusamo first, then Oulu.

"I love owls," she told him, in explanation. She spoke tentatively, because wasn't that the sort of thing that a teenage girl might say? Owls were so easy to love, with their dense white feathers and their huge eyes. Wasn't it as unsophisticated as saying that she loved teddy bears.

But he only looked at her fondly. "Oh, I can promise you owls. I've got that side of things all set up with the locals. They take owls very seriously there. It brings in thousands of dollars in eco-tourism. They even have owl wars."

She didn't ask what he meant. Perhaps she should have done.

* * *

There were only six of them in the group. She and Simon and four paying punters: a middle-aged couple called Norman and Jean who had travelled with the company before, George, the elderly man, and a frail and beautiful woman named Emily.

Annie dismissed the Norman and Jean immediately as tedious. They came from Wolverhampton and talked at length, even on the plane, about the rare birds they'd seen, the distance they'd travelled to see them and the cost of each twitch. Simon attended to their stories with great courtesy, and she saw that his success must be based on this ability to pretend interest. There was something disturbing about the sight of his listening to them. She saw for the first time that he was a ruthless businessman and considered that he might lie to her if the situation demanded it.

George, it seemed was rather a famous birdwatcher. Simon had been excited when he'd booked.

"Everyone knows he has the biggest list in the UK, but he doesn't talk about it. He once found a seabird that was new to the world. Before he retired, he worked in the Home Office. Something to do with the police."

On the journey, the older man was very self-contained. He read all the way on the plane, and at the transfer in Helsinki, he brusquely rejected Simon's offer of help with his bags. Annie found him intimidating. He wouldn't be satisfied, like the couple from Wolverhampton, with smiling admiration and kind words.

Annie didn't know what to make of Emily, who said very little and had a distracted smile. Simon usually enjoyed the company of pretty young women, and Annie wondered why he didn't make more of a fuss of her. It occurred to her that Emily had been on one of his earlier trips, that perhaps there had been a brief romance, which he now preferred to forget. Certainly, in Annie's presence. In their hotel room in Kuusamo, she couldn't quite bring herself to enquire if he'd met Emily before. She hardly recognised Simon in work mode. Besides, the hotel itself cast a sinister gloss over everything and she didn't quite trust her judgement here.

It was a massive building constructed in a Soviet brutalist style. Everything was solid and dark. There was a huge desk at reception and the wood panelled walls had an almost black varnish. Yet, there were touches of kitsch which were playful and unsettling. Lava lamps on the bar. Two massive stuffed bears in the dining room. Red plush upholstery in the lounge, which made her think of a Victorian bordello. Everywhere – in the lifts and the saunas and the long straight corridors – lush arrangements of Burt Bacharach filtered through an invisible sound system.

"What do you think?" Simon was lying in the bath with a large glass of the gin he'd thought to bring from home. Booze in Scandinavia was outrageously expensive, he'd said, when she'd questioned the number of bottles he wrapped in his underpants to pack. And it was always useful as a present for the locals. An aid to negotiations when required.

"I'm not sure."

"Isn't it crazy? You can imagine western spies lurking here during the Cold War, setting honey traps for their Soviet colleagues. The border is only twenty miles away after all."

"Yes," she said. "That's just what it's like. An elaborate Cold War movie."

For the three days that they spent there, she felt she was an actor in the film. There were the brooding and atmospheric sets – miles of birch forests and long, grey lakes, distant mountains with patches of dirty snow. Even the weather, chill and gloomy for mid-summer, could have been ordered by a director. And there were incidents that seemed to have been designed only to add to the intrigue and further the plot.

Simon gave them a free afternoon to rest before the big push for owls. Annie felt she had to get away from the stifling hotel, and from Simon, and she wandered into the town. On a street corner she saw Emily, wrapped in a long, fur-trimmed parka, smoking a cigarette, obviously waiting for someone. It had started to rain, but still she lingered, the hood pulled low over her eyes. Annie stood in a doorway and watched. At last, a young man arrived in a small, battered car. He expected Emily to get in beside him. At first, she refused and there was a sharp and angry conversation. In Finnish. Then she relented and climbed in.

Back in the hotel, Annie recounted the scene to Simon. "Why didn't she tell us that she spoke the language? I mean, you'd think that she'd mention it."

"I don't know," he said, but she couldn't tell whether this was news to him or not.

The next night, when the rest of the group went to bed early, Simon told her that he couldn't sleep, that he'd go to the bar for a night cap. Sleepless herself, she dressed and followed him. He was sitting in a dark corner of the bar, drinking vodka and in earnest conversation with their local guide, a taciturn bear of a man called Olli. When Simon saw her, she thought she caught a frown of annoyance, before he turned on the wonderful smile.

But she could have been mistaken. They had stayed up the whole of the previous night to stumble through the forest. They'd glimpsed one owl swoop in to feed young and then another perched in silhouette on a pine tree. The group had been jubilant, too wired for real sleep. Norman and Jean had surprised her by their passion. They had the glitter of fanatics in their eyes. In the minibus back to the hotel, they'd listed the species they'd seen since the start of the trip. Misers counting hoarded gold. Annie thought that after only snatches of sleep, it was easy to make mistakes. Perhaps she saw mystery and intrigue where there was none. She was glad when they left Kuusamo and began the drive on the long straight road to Oulu.

In Oulu, the sun was shining, and the harbour and the beaches provided some relief from the endless birch forest and peat bog. There was warmth on their backs as they watched the cranes and the swans fly into the bay. Even Emily shed her anorak and and seemed to blossom in the sun. She smiled and became more expansive. She had grown up in Finland, she said. Her father had been a businessman and had seen the possibilities at the end of the Cold War. He'd imported luxury goods into the new ski resorts near Kuusamo and exported reindeer skins and handicrafts from Lapland. Now she'd taken over. She handed round her business card. The logo in the corner was a stylised owl.

They had lunch in the marketplace in Oulu, surrounded by elegant houses, sitting at the outside stalls, eating fried fish cooked in big flat pans shaped like dustbin lids. Annie felt for the first time that she was among friends.

* * *

But now, Simon was dead, and she couldn't trust these people who played themselves like actors. It came into her head that she would have to tell them that there would be no owls tonight.

She was kneeling beside Simon when she heard the footsteps again. Turning, she saw Olli. She realised she must have been there at the foot of the watchtower for some time and that she was crying. The tears seemed to have come from nowhere. Inside she felt frozen.

But now, she came to her senses and began shouting to him. Simon must have tripped! Was there anything that could be done? An ambulance? Perhaps it wasn't too late. She caught her breath, suddenly picturing Simon's plunge from the tower. Would he have felt, even for a moment, the exhilaration of a bird in flight? Like a tern, wings folded, diving into the waves. Or had there only been terror?

"It is too late," Olli said. Nothing more. She had learned that Finns never waste words.

"No," she whispered. She remembered the winter afternoons in the cottage and realised that now she was feeling sorry for herself. "What a waste. A senseless accident."

"Perhaps not an accident," Olli said quietly. He had lit another cigarette and was looking over the salt marsh. "Another victim of the Owl Wars."

* * *

He explained his words in the bar of the nature centre, where the group was staying that night. She had wanted to go home immediately. She longed to be a child again, tucked up by her mother between cool sheets in a dimly lit room, waiting for the fever to pass and reality to return, but there were no flights. Besides, the local police had politely asked that the party should stay at least for another day.

So, she sat with Olli in the bar, drinking vodka and beer, and he told her about the Owl Wars. It was very different from the bar in Kuusamo. No heavy furniture or wood panels here. This was Scandinavian minimalist, pine floor and low wooden tables, a view over the salt marsh to the viewing towers. It was still full of people despite the hour. All their group were there, watching her at a discreet distance. Simon had been their favourite and they owed it to him to take care of her.

"It's big business," Olli said. "The tour companies bring thousands of people to birdwatch in northern Finland in the spring. Mostly Germans and Americans, but Brits too. They pay for the certainty of seeing the owls. All our species. Luck isn't involved here. They don't understand luck. To provide certainty, we have to find where the birds breed. That knowledge is valuable. Do you understand?"

She nodded. She understood.

"For us, the guides, there is fierce competition. To find the nest site and then sell our skill to the highest bidder. It would be impossible for an outsider to locate the nest sites. The forests here all look the same. We don't allow maps or GPS. We do the driving. Even tour leaders who have been to the same spot three years in a row would never find their own way back there." He stopped talking, stared into the glass, and drank the shot of vodka in one go. "It's a short season. It's how we earn our living. You understand the competition can lead to conflict, even among friends. Between the tour companies, also." He stood up clumsily to go to the bar and she realised for the first time how drunk he was, how miserable.

"You said that Simon could be another victim," she said when he returned. "Who was the first?"

"A young man. Pekka Kapanen. A friend of mine. But greedy. He arranged to sell his information to one tour leader then broke the contract when he was offered more money. That was an accident too. A car accident. Apparently. He drove off a mountain road near Kuusamo. The police thought another driver was involved, but he was never found." Olli's face was mottled now, and his words were slurred. He stared moodily into his drink.

When the bar closed, Annie couldn't sleep. She followed one of the walkways at random into the marsh and sat on a bench looking over a small pool. The sun was further above the horizon and there was a breeze that made the reeds rustle and hiss like the sound of waves on shingle.

The footsteps startled her. She thought Olli must have followed. He would be drunk and slightly amorous and there would be an embarrassing encounter while she fended him off.

"I think we should talk."

It was George. She was more irritated than if it had been Olli. She had wanted to be alone, but the elderly birder stood, looking down at her. Because of his age and because Simon had admired him, she felt obliged to be polite.

"Of course."

"Why don't you tell me what happened?" He sat beside her.

She felt the wax on his jacket, clammy on the back of her hand, and could smell the apple in his pocket.

"I'm sorry?"

"I should have realised," he said. "I was distracted by the others. Everyone with guilty secrets. Everyone with something to hide. Norman and Jean cheat, you know. They haven't seen half the species on their lists. Hardly illegal, but they'd be mortified if anyone found out. It would kill them. Then there's Emily. She sells native art. If she can't get an export licence, she smuggles it out. It's her passion. I don't believe she does it entirely for the money. Is that an excuse, do you think?"

"I fell in love." It was a confession, her guilty secret.

He frowned as if he had guessed as much. "Of course you did. But not with Simon."

"I was teaching in a language school in Helsinki. There was a student from the north, Pekka." She tried to picture the man, but the image was blurred and all she had left was the story she'd repeated to herself for a year, about their meeting and his death. "He wanted better English for his work, but his first love was natural history. He worked as a guide, finding owls. He loved this landscape. Olli called him greedy, but it wasn't like that. Pekka didn't break his contract with the tour operator because he wanted more money from them. He tried to organise all the guides into a co-op. His idea was that they'd pool information."

"And keep the prices high."

"Why not? It was his country. He and the others did all the work. There would be no owl tours without him."

"And then he was killed?"

"Driven off a mountain road on an afternoon in early spring."

"How did you know that Simon was involved?"

"It became an obsession." Like Norman and Jean with their lists, she thought, and Emily with her Lapp art. "I tracked him down. He was in Kuusamo when it happened. The police here thought he was involved, but they couldn't prove anything. When I was sure, I came back to England and got a job in Cambridge. I waited for the right time."

"Did you ask Simon about Pekka's death?"

She nodded. "There, on the watch tower. Of course he denied it. If he'd told me the truth, perhaps I wouldn't have lost my temper, I wouldn't have pushed out at him." She closed her eyes, but she couldn't shut out the scene: the two of them, held on the top of the tower, space all around them. Simon's mouth open to speak words of reasonable explanation, which it would be a betrayal for her to hear. The push to stop him speaking, to stop herself listening. The cracking and shattering of the wooden handrail, his body, arms outstretched, flying.

"But that was what you intended all along. To kill him. That was why you set out to meet him." George's words brought her back to the present. She opened her eyes.

"Yes." But occasionally, in the cottage by the stream, she'd forgotten why she was there. There were times when she'd believed the fiction, got so caught up with the stories that she was no longer acting.

"Simon was telling the truth," George said. He wasn't looking at her. She couldn't tell what he was thinking. "Simon had nothing to with Pekka's murder. Olli killed Pekka. He didn't want to share his information with any co-op. He wanted to keep it and sell it to the tour companies himself. So, he drove Pekka off the road near Kuusamo. He was drunk. You saw what he was like tonight. That day, he was drunk and out of control. A crazy moment of rage. Simon hired me to investigate. He wanted to find out who had murdered Pekka. To put a stop to all the rumours."

Then she felt dizzy again, as she had looking out from the tower after her encounter with Simon. Above her, the cranes circled, carried by the morning thermals. She tipped back her head and watched them until George touched her elbow and walked with her through the reeds, back to the centre.

Arabella's Answer

Peter Lovesey

ANSWERS TO CORRESPONDENTS

January, 1878

ARABELLA. If you are serious in aspiring to elicit a reply from a reputable journal such as ours, you should take the elementary trouble to express yourself in legible handwriting.

March, 1878

ARABELLA. Your Papa is perfectly right. A young girl of fifteen should not be seen at a dinner party at which unmarried gentlemen are guests. Your protestations at being, as you express it, "confined" to your room do you no credit. A wiser girl would be content to occupy herself in some profitably quiet pastime, such as sewing, for the duration of the party. So long as you childishly persist in questioning decorum, you reveal your utter unreadiness for adult society.

October, 1879

ARABELLA. No gentleman sends flowers or any other presents to a young lady to whom he has not been introduced. Let him learn some manners and present his card to your parents if he entertains a notion of making your acquaintance. We doubt whether his conduct thus far will commend itself to your Papa.

December, 1879

ARABELLA. In common civility you are bound to receive the young gentleman if he has called on your Papa and satisfied him that his intentions are honourable. The “misgivings” that you instance in your letter are of no consequence. A gentleman should be judged by his conduct, not his outward imperfections. The protruding teeth and shortness of stature are no fault of his, any more than your tallness is of your making. We expect to hear that you have set aside these absurd objections and obeyed your parents, who clearly have a more enlightened apprehension of this young gentleman than yourself.

February, 1880

ARABELLA. We suspect that your anxieties are prompted by the shyness which is natural in a young girl, but which properly must grow into the self-possession of a lady. How can you possibly say that the gentleman's blandishments are unwelcome when you have met him only once in your parents' home?

June, 1880

ARABELLA. She who finds difficulty in making conversation with her escort should not despair. There are many talkers, but few who know how to converse agreeably. The art of conversation may be learned. Mark how the most accomplished of conversationalists avoid conceit and affectation. Their speech is characterised by naturalness and sincerity which may be spiced with humour, but never oversteps the limits of propriety.

August, 1880

ARABELLA. We are surprised by your enquiry. Kissing is not a subject that we care to give advice upon, particularly to members of the sex that may receive such tokens of affection, in certain circumstances, but ought never to initiate them.

January, 1881

ARABELLA. To give no answer if the young man proposes to marry you would not only be discourteous; it would not achieve the outcome you apparently expect. When the lady is so ill advised as to say nothing, the gentleman is entitled to publish the banns at once, for 'silence gives consent'. Have you really considered how the gentleman is placed? Making a declaration of love is one of the most trying ordeals he will experience in his life. We counsel you to give the most earnest consideration to the question, if you are so fortunate as to be asked it. Many are not, and live to regret it. Some have been known to say 'No' when they meant 'Yes'.

March, 1881

ARABELLA. Your letter reaffirms our faith in the innate wisdom of womankind. In conveying our felicities on your forthcoming marriage, we would advise you that a gown of ivory satin trimmed with lace and orange blossoms is *de rigueur*.

August, 1881

ARABELLA. We see no reason why you should object to cleaning your husband's boots, as you have no servant, but we cannot comprehend your meaning when you state that he "leaves them outside his bedroom door at night." Are we to gather from this that you occupy a different bedroom from your husband? If so, is this at your behest, or his?

October, 1881

ARABELLA. As we have frequently reiterated in this column, the joys of marriage grow out of duty, honesty and fidelity. If, as you assure us, you have not been negligent in any of these, you must ask yourself if there is not some other impediment in your behaviour, which, when remedied, will allow a happier intimacy to ripen. Have you considered whether your choice of clothes and the way you dress your hair are pleasing to your husband?

November, 1881

ARABELLA. As a rule we deprecate the recourse to powder and rouge as an enhancement to good looks. It is possible, however, that ill-health or the anxiety sometimes experienced in the first months of marriage may deprive the skin of its colour and complexion, and in such cases art may be called in as an aid to nature.

January, 1882

ARABELLA. We condemn in the strongest possible terms the practice of using drops of belladonna in the eyes. Belladonna is the extract from that noxious plant, the deadly nightshade (*atropa belladonna*). To keep it on one's dressing table would be dangerous and foolish. A pinch of boracic powder dissolved in warm water and used with an eye-cup is a safe and beneficial tonic that may be relied upon to bring a brightness to the eyes. A little vaseline or cocoa-butter well rubbed into the eyebrows and lashes at night will promote their growth. Frequent brushing with a small brow-brush is also efficacious.

March, 1882

ARABELLA. Your difficulties are more common among newly married wives than probably you realise.

May, 1882

ARABELLA. We think it most injudicious for a wife to listen to tale-bearing neighbours. The company a husband keeps is usually dictated by the duties and obligations of his professional and business life. To expect a man to pursue his manifold interests without ever communicating with the sex who make up half of humanity is to expect the impossible. Shut your ears to gossip. If you have genuine cause for concern, it will manifest itself in other ways. Hold fast to our previous advice. Endeavour to be as pleasant and engaging as possible, to keep your husband at home. Propagate the first shoots of affection as soon as they appear.

July, 1882

ARABELLA. The experience you describe is both regrettable and deplorable, and we trust that there has been no recurrence of the incident since you wrote your letter. If the gentleman concerned was a Frenchman, as you suppose, he may be unused to our British code of decorum. He may, to be as charitable as we can to our cousins from across the Channel, have been under a misapprehension as to your married state. Yet we are bound to observe that a gentleman who attempts to ingratiate himself with a lady, whether married or not, *in a public street*, is a disgrace to his nation. If he should importune you again, look straight onwards, ignore his addresses and tell your husband as soon as you get home. We assume, of course, that the Frenchman's conduct was not encouraged by any light manner on your part.

September, 1882

ARABELLA. We sympathise with your position. It is true that in a previous issue we gave our approval to the judicious use of rouge and powder to enhance your pale complexion in the expectation that it would please your husband. Now that he appears to blame the rouge-box for the excessive behaviour of the foreign gentleman who pesters you, we think you are bound to give up using it.

January, 1883

ARABELLA. We seem to remember cautioning you last year of the dangers attendant upon the use of belladonna drops and we are surprised that you should waste our time with a further enquiry. For the benefit of other readers we repeat that belladonna is a deadly poison and ought never to be used for cosmetic purposes.

March, 1883

ARABELLA. A bereavement such as you have so tragically and so suddenly suffered will strike a chord of sympathy in every young wife who has known that dread fear of impending tragedy when her husband is unwell. You may console yourself with the knowledge that you did all that was possible to comfort your brave consort in the throes of his delirium and convulsion. To have abandoned him even for a short time to summon a physician was unthinkable, and, from your account of the severity of the onset, would not have made a jot of difference. The proper dress materials for deep mourning are crepe and silk. We can recommend Messrs Jay of Regent Street, the London General Mourning Warehouse, for the most sympathetic assistance and advice on suitable costumes, mantles and millinery. Their advertisement will be found elsewhere on these pages.

July, 1883

ARABELLA. We are surprised that you should ask such a question. Velvet is utterly inadmissible for a widow in deep mourning.

September, 1883

ARABELLA. Certainly not. In the first year of mourning, a jersey would be unseemly in the extreme.

October, 1883

ARABELLA. Any person who has the temerity to address a widow of less than one year in familiar terms forfeits the right to the title of gentleman. The fact that he is

French is no mitigation of the offence. Indeed, if he is the same person of whom you had cause to complain on a previous occasion, he must be a blackguard of the deepest dye. On no account should you permit him to engage you in conversation. Avoid the possibility of meeting him again by varying the route you are accustomed to taking when walking to the shops. As the proverb wisely cautions us, better go round than fall into the ditch.

March, 1884

ARABELLA. Black beads are permissible in the second year of mourning, but gold or silver or pearls would be disrespectful. We cannot understand how any widow could consider adorning herself in jewellery so soon after the loss of the one to whom she pledged her entire life. We are shocked at your enquiry, and we can only ascribe it to an aberration consequent upon your grief. Set aside all thoughts of gratifying yourself by such vanities.

May, 1884

ARABELLA. It would be in the worst possible taste for a widow of fifteen months to "walk out" with a gentleman, whatever he professes in the name of sympathy for you and respect for the one you mourn. Let him show his sympathy and respect by leaving you to your private grief until at least two years have passed since your bereavement. As to the "restlessness" that you admit to feeling, this may be subdued by turning your energy to some useful occupation in the house or garden. Many a widow has found solace in the later stages of mourning by cultivating flowers.

July, 1884

ARABELLA. How can we proffer advice if you do not fully acquaint us with the circumstances in which you live? Of course you cannot employ your time in the garden if you live in a second-floor apartment without a garden, but there is no reason why you should not cultivate plants of the indoor variety. Contrary to a widely held belief, it is not necessary to have a conservatory for the successful rearing of plants in the home. Certain varieties of fern may be cultivated with gratifying success in, say, a drawing room or dining room. All that they require is a little water regularly given. We have seen some most attractive species growing under glass domes, and some prefer them to wax flowers.

September, 1884

ARABELLA. The variety known as maidenhair is in our opinion the prettiest. Perhaps you over-watered the lady fern.

November, 1884

ARABELLA. Since you seem unable to care adequately for the ferns we recommend, we suggest you try a hardier indoor plant of the palm variety, such as an aspidistra. The aspidistra will grow best in a pot of sufficient size to allow for the roots to develop. A brass plant-pot of the largest size supplied by Messrs Pugh & Martindale would be ideal. Their shop is not far from where you live. The address may be found in the advertisement on the back page of this issue.

January, 1885

ARABELLA. We are gratified to hear that you purchased a large brass pot for your aspidistra, as we suggested in our November issue, and that it is thriving. With regard to another matter that you mention, we wish it to be known that your letters until the latest did not make it clear that the French gentleman whose attentions to you appeared so importunate, is, in fact, the owner of the art gallery over which you live. Had we been privy to this information before, we might have taken a different view of his conduct. It is only civil for a neighbour to raise his hat and pass the time of day to a lady, and his invitation to "walk out", while still unthinkable, may now be seen in a more favourable light, with allowance for alien customs. Your own sentiments towards this gentleman must remain irreproachable.

February, 1885

ARABELLA. We did not expect that our altruistic comments in the last issue would encourage an effusion of such unseemliness. No man, however "handsome, immaculately tailored and charmingly civil towards the fair sex", be he from France or Timbuktu, ought to be described in such unbecoming terms by one who, not two years since, buried her dear departed husband. If you have a vestige of propriety left, dismiss him from your thoughts.

March, 1885

ARABELLA. Your latest communication unhappily confirms what we have for some time suspected: that you are suffering from the delusions of a foolish, infatuated female. How can you otherwise suppose that a lady who has chanced to stand below your window in the vicinity of the art gallery on one or two occasions has "designs" on the owner, even if he were "the most eligible man in London"? Clear your mind of such nonsense and attend to the horticultural interests we have been at such pains to foster.

April, 1885

It is with profound regret and a deep sense of shock that we announce the death of Miss Gertrude Smyth, who edited our *Answers to Correspondents* since this journal was founded six years ago. Miss Smyth was the victim last month of a singularly unfortunate and distressing accident in Chelsea, when she was struck on the head by a brass flower-pot that fell from an upper window ledge. Miss Smyth's sagacious and authoritative advice was of the greatest service to myriads of our readers. Out of respect for her memory, we are publishing no *Answers to Correspondents* this month. The column will be resumed in our next issue.

May, 1885

ARABELLA. We can see no impediment to your being married in September in Paris.

About the Authors

Anne Perry (1938–2023) won an Edgar Award in 2000 for her short story 'Heroes' (also nominated for a Macavity Award). Anne has also written introductions to Conan Doyle's *The Hound of the Baskervilles*, Wilkie Collins' *The Woman in White* and Baroness Orczy's *The Scarlet Pimpernel* for The New Modern Library, and has edited and contributed to a number of anthologies. She was awarded the Premio de Honor Aragón Negro in 2015, and selected by the *Times* as one of the twentieth century's '100 Masters of Crime'. In 2020 she was Guest of Honour at Bouchercon. Over 25 million copies of Anne's books have now been sold worldwide.

Before **Christine Poulson** turned to crime, she was an academic with a PhD in History of Art. She has written three medical thrillers, *Deep Water* (2016), *Cold Cold Heart* (2017), set in Antarctica, and *An Air That Kills* (2019) as well as three academic mysteries set in Cambridge. Her short stories have been published in Comma Press anthologies, *Ellery Queen's Mystery Magazine*, CWA anthologies, the *Mammoth Book of Best British Mysteries* and elsewhere.

They have been shortlisted for the Margery Allingham Prize, the Short Mystery Fiction Derringer, and the CWA Short Story Dagger. *Safe as Houses*, a collection of her short stories, will be published by Comma Press in December 2025. Find out more about her at christinepoulson.co.uk.

Andrew Taylor's crime novels include the William Dougal series, starting with the Dagger-winning *Caroline Minuscule*; the Roth Trilogy, televised as *Fallen Angel*; the Lydmouth series; the bestselling *The Ashes of London* and its sequels; and stand-alone novels such as *The American Boy* and *A Schooling in Murder.* He has won the Historical Dagger three times and also the Diamond Dagger, as well as received awards in Sweden and the US.

Amy Myers is best known for her Marsh and Daughter mystery series, featuring a writing team consisting of a wheelchair-bound ex-policeman and his daughter, and for another series, featuring a Victorian-era chef, Auguste Didier. She launched a third series in 2007 about a Victorian-era chimney sweep in East London, who solves crimes with his former apprentice. Her fourth series features a modern-day classic-car restorer in Kent, Jack Colby, and in 2024, she began another series, featuring Cara Shelley of the Happy Huffkin Café at the stately home of Tanton Towers. Amy has also written under the names Harriet Hudson, Laura Daniels and Alice Carr.

Judith Cutler was born and bred in the Midlands, one of her favourite locations for her fiction. A former lecturer in English and Creative Writing and one-time CWA secretary, Judith has written fifty novels and many short stories. She now blogs on behalf of a hedgehog on the Hedgehog Highways Facebook page. She is married to fellow crime writer, Edward Marston.

Gillian Linscott studied at Somerville College, Oxford, and worked as a journalist before becoming a crime writer. She won the CWA Ellis Peters Historical Dagger in 2000 for her novel *Absent Friends*, which featured her series character Nell Bray, a former suffragette. Gillian has also published a series of seven detective novels under the name Caro Peacock.

Martin Edwards's novels include the Lake District Mysteries and the Rachel Savernake books, most recently *Hemlock Bay*. His non-fiction includes a multi-award-winning history of crime fiction, *The Life of Crime*. He has received three Daggers, including the CWA Diamond Dagger, as well as two Edgars, and four lifetime achievement awards. A former Chair of the CWA, he is consultant to the British Library's Crime Classics and President of the Detection Club.

Bernie Crosthwaite is a novelist, playwright and short story writer. Her Ravenbridge Trilogy (*If It Bleeds*, *Body Language* and *The Hemp House*) features press photographer Jude Baxendale. Her plays and stories have been performed on national radio, and 'The Golden Hour' was shortlisted for the CWA Short Story Dagger Award. Bernie has worked as a newspaper reporter, a tour guide, and a teacher of English and creative writing. She lives and works in North Yorkshire.

Catherine Aird was the pen-name of Kinn McIntosh (1930–2024). She was the author of the Calleshire Chronicles, a series featuring Detective Inspector C.D. Sloan, which began with *The Religious Body* in 1966. She also published several collections of short stories. A former Chair of the CWA, she received the MBE in 1988. She received the Golden Handcuffs award (now known as the CWA Dagger in the Library) and also the CWA Diamond Dagger.

Simon Brett was educated at Dulwich College and Wadham College Oxford and subsequently worked as a producer with BBC Radio Light Entertainment and London Weekend Television, before becoming a full-time writer in 1979. He is the author of over a hundred books, including the Charles Paris, Mrs. Pargeter, Fethering and Blotto & Twinks series of crime novels, and his radio and TV series include *After Henry* and *No Commitments*. Another former Chair of the CWA, he has received the CWA Diamond Dagger and an OBE for services to literature.

Yvonne Eve Walus is a Doctor of Mathematics, business analyst, wife, mother and novelist. Until the age of 12, Yvonne grew up in communist Poland, which taught her to value uniformity and enjoy public transit before moving to South Africa for the next sixteen years. She now resides in New Zealand with her husband and children. Her novels include *The Wrong Girl* and *Murder @ Play*.

John Harvey has enjoyed a long and varied literary career, and high among his varied achievements are the Charlie Resnick crime stories, set in Nottingham, which began with *Lonely Hearts* in 1989. The series was adapted (by John himself) for television as *Resnick*, with the Oscar-nominated actor Tom Wilkinson playing the jazz-loving Charlie, and for radio. John's other major characters include Frank Elder and Jack Kiley, who features in 'Fedora', for which John won the CWA Short Story Dagger. He received the CWA Diamond Dagger in 2007.

Kate Ellis's first novel, *The Merchant House*, launched the long-running DI Wesley Peterson series set in Devon. She has also written five crime novels in an ongoing series featuring another cop, Joe Plantagenet, set in a fictionalised version of York, and a trilogy set in the immediate aftermath of the First World War as well as many short stories. She won the CWA Dagger in the Library in 2019. *The Devil's Priest* is a stand-alone historical mystery set in Liverpool.

Zoë Sharp spent her formative years living aboard a catamaran on the northwest coast of England. She started writing the Charlotte 'Charlie' Fox crime thriller series (currently under option for TV) after receiving death-threats in the course of her career as a photo-journalist. Her work has been nominated for numerous awards on both sides of the Atlantic, including the Barry for Best British Crime Novel and the CWA Short Story Dagger. She also writes two other crime series and stand-alone novels, including a collaboration with espionage thriller author John Lawton.

Bill Knox (1928–99) began his writing career as a journalist in Glasgow. He made many contributions to radio and television and was well-known to Scottish viewers as the writer and presenter for twelve years of the STV police liaison programme *Crime Desk*. Bill was a prolific crime writer under a variety of names, his best-known series being the Thane and Moss series; the last book, *The Lazarus Widow*, was completed by Martin Edwards.

Cath Staincliffe is a novelist, radio playwright, and creator of the ITV series *Blue Murder*. Her debut, *Looking for Trouble*, launched private eye Sal Kilkenny, a single parent juggling work and home, onto Manchester's mean streets and was the first of eight books in the series. More recently, *The Fells*, the first of her new Donovan and Young series, has been shortlisted for The People's Book Prize. She has been shortlisted (three times) for the CWA Dagger in the Library, and twice for the Short Story Dagger. In 2012 Cath was joint winner of the Short Story Dagger.

Liza Cody is an artist trained at the Royal Academy Schools of Art as well as a crime novelist. *Dupe*, her first novel, won the John Creasey Memorial Dagger, and launched a series about the female private investigator Anna Lee, which was televised with Imogen Stubbs in the lead role. She has also published the Bucket Nut Trilogy featuring professional wrestler Eva Wylie, as well as stand-alone novels such as *Rift*, *Gimme More*, *Ballad of a Dead Nobody*, *Miss Terry*, *Lady Bag*, *Crocodiles and Good Intentions*, *Gift or Theft*, and *The Short Order Detective*, and numerous short stories, which are collected in *Lucky Dip and Other Stories* and *My People and Other Crime Stories*. She has won a CWA Silver Dagger, an Anthony award, and a Marlowe award in Germany.

Ann Cleeves published her first crime novel in 1986. A series about amateur detectives and bird-watchers George and Molly Palmer-Jones was followed by a police-focused series featuring Inspector Ramsay. DCI Vera Stanhope was introduced in *The Crow Trap*, which was originally intended as a stand-alone but developed into a series adapted for TV as *Vera*, with Brenda Blethyn in the title role. Her series featuring Jimmy Perez and set on Shetland was equally popular, while *The Long Call*, the first book in her latest series, has also been adapted for television.

Peter Lovesey (1936–2025) had already published a successful book about athletics when he won a competition with his first crime fiction novel, *Wobble to Death*, which launched a series about the Victorian detective Sergeant Cribb. His many books and short stories since then went on to win or were shortlisted for nearly all the major prizes in the international crime writing world. He was presented with Lifetime Achievement awards both in the UK and the US, before passing away in April 2025.

Crime Writers' Association

The CWA was founded in 1953 by John Creasey – that's over seventy years of support, promotion and celebration of this most durable, adaptable and successful of genres. They run the prestigious CWA Dagger Awards, which celebrate the best in crime writing, and are proud to be a thriving, growing community with a membership encompassing authors at all stages of their careers. They are UK based, yet attract many members from overseas. Previous CWA anthologies published by Flame Tree and edited by Martin Edwards are *Vintage Crime*, *Music of the Night*, and *Midsummer Mysteries*.

About the Illustrator

Oliver Hurst (Frontispiece) graduated from Falmouth College of Arts in 2006 with a degree in Illustration. He has produced artwork for various publications, including the *Financial Times*, *Country Life*, The Folio Society and the previous CWA anthology *Midsummer Mysteries*. He paints in oils and his work is inspired by nineteenth- and twentieth-century painters. He lives and works in Bath and his website is oliverhurst.com.

Acknowledgements

HEROES by Anne Perry
From *Past Crimes*, edited by Martin Edwards (1998)

A CABINET OF CURIOSITIES by Christine Poulson
From *M.O.: Crimes of Practice*, edited by Martin Edwards (2008)

THE COST OF LIVING by Andrew Taylor
From *Perfectly Criminal*, edited by Martin Edwards (1996)

WHO KILLED ADONIS? by Amy Myers
From *Past Crimes*, edited by Martin Edwards (1998)

STRANGER IN PARADISE by Judith Cutler
From *Green for Danger*, edited by Martin Edwards (2003)

ORIGINAL SIN by Gillian Linscott
From *Whydunit*, edited by Martin Edwards (1997)

WAR RATIONS by Martin Edwards
From *Past Crimes*, edited by Martin Edwards (1998)

THE DEATH OF SPIDERS by Bernie Crosthwaite
From *Guilty Parties*, edited by Martin Edwards (2014)

HOME IS THE HUNTER by Catherine Aird
From *John Creasey's Crime Collection 1988*,
edited by Herbert Harris (1988)

DOCTOR THEATRE by Simon Brett
From *Original Sins*, edited by Martin Edwards (2010)

TOUR NEW ZEALAND IN FIVE EASY MURDERS
by Yvonne Eve Walus
From *I.D.: Crimes of Identity*, edited by Martin Edwards (2006)

FEDORA by John Harvey
From *Deadly Pleasures*, edited by Martin Edwards (2013)

Beyond & Within

THE FLAME TREE Beyond & Within short story collections bring together tales of myth and imagination by modern and contemporary writers, carefully selected by anthologists, and sometimes featuring short stories and fiction from a single author. Overall, the series presents a wide range of diverse and inclusive voices, often writing folkloric-inflected short fiction, but always with an emphasis on the supernatural, science fiction, the mysterious and the speculative. The books themselves are gorgeous, with foiled covers, printed edges and published only in hardcover editions, offering a lifetime of reading pleasure.

FLAME TREE FICTION

A wide range of new and classic fiction, from myth to modern stories, with tales from the distant past to the far future, including short story anthologies, Collector's Editions, Collectable Classics, Gothic Fantasy collections and Epic Tales of mythology and folklore.

•